BARE DEVOTION

A Bayou Bachelors Romance

Geri Krotow

LYRICAL PRESS
Kensington Publishing Corp.
www.kensingtonbooks.com

First Electronic Edition: September 2018
eISBN-13: 978-1-5161-0602-8
eISBN-10: 1-5161-0602-4

First Print Edition: September 2018
ISBN-13: 978-1-5161-0603-5
ISBN-10: 1-5161-0603-2

Printed in the United States of America

Sweet and sultry, hot and wild...that's desire, Louisiana-style. And there's no one better to explore it with than one of the Bayou Bachelors...

Returning to her flooded New Orleans home to face Henry Boudreaux, the man she jilted at the altar, is the hardest thing attorney Sonja Bosco has ever done—even before she discovers she's pregnant. Sonja backed out of the marriage for Henry's sake. He wants to be part of his father's law firm, and his parents will never approve of an interracial marriage. Better to bruise his heart than ruin his life.

Henry can't forgive Sonja, and doubts that he can trust her again. But learning that they're going to be parents means there's no avoiding each other. Springtime on the bayou is already steamy enough...now they're living in the same small space while their damaged house is repaired. And with each passing day they're getting a little more honest. A lot more real. And realizing that nothing—not even New Orleans at Mardi Gras— glows brighter than the desire they're trying to deny...

Also by Geri Krotow

Fully Dressed

Chapter 1

Sonja Bosco's grip on the leather-covered steering wheel lessened when she saw the empty driveway in front of the house that had been more than her home for the past three years. It had been her very heartbeat. Henry's car could be in the garage, of course, but she doubted it. According to what she'd ascertained from their shared receptionist, he was hard at work in the New Orleans office of Boudreaux Law. She'd gathered the courage to call into the main office in Baton Rouge, run by Henry's father, late last week. The senior Boudreaux knew she planned to report back to work later this morning. Three weeks and two days after she'd left NOLA, left St. Louis Cathedral, and more significantly, left her ex-almost-husband-to-be, Henry, on said altar.

Of all the degrees, positions, and dreams she'd aspired to, runaway bride had never made the list. The tug of remorse at her emotionally cataclysmic decision was strong, but her will to jump into her new routine, whatever that was going to look like, was stronger.

She parked her BMW in the driveway for what would be the last time. Her finances as a single woman demanded she sell the once cherished Beemer, and her status as Henry's ex meant she'd never again live in the house they'd built together. If only it didn't still feel like home. As much as she dreaded seeing the devastation the flood had done to it the last two weeks, maybe it would crack the code on the invisible signal that made her body home in on this place as if it were her last grasp for freedom. Hell, it wasn't just her body. Her soul had planted roots here, damn it all to hell.

The graveled drive felt so familiar under her sandaled feet she almost wept. Home. She'd needed to be here, by herself, licking her heart wounds these past few weeks, instead of holing up in a close elementary-school friend's backwater cabin. She hadn't had Wi-Fi and had refused to check her phone, save to let her parents and family know she was still breathing, and was safe from the flooding rains that pummeled so much of the bayou two weeks ago. The flooding had been so extensive she couldn't get back to the river house if she wanted to, not without a boat and the help of Henry or his brother Brandon.

She'd only gone out twice, each time to the tiny local grocery store.

Where the third pregnancy test she'd purchased gave her the same result as the previous two, before the wedding. She was pregnant, newly so. Not only was Henry Boudreaux her ex-groom and ex-fiancé, but he was also her baby daddy. She couldn't muster the tiniest of smiles, much less a giggle, at the humor of it. She, Sonja Bosco, didn't think she'd ever laugh again.

The heavy wooden front door opened with a single turn of her key. It stuck a bit in the frame, and she wondered if it might still be swollen from the devastating rains that soaked the area the week after the wedding. So much so that Poppy, her best friend and appointed honeymoon house sitter, had had to leave for higher, drier ground. And had promptly fallen in love with her rescuer, Henry's brother Brandon.

At least some people still believed in love.

Sonja sucked in a huge breath and faced the house she'd lived in with Henry for the past couple of years, where they'd planned their wedding.

"The un-wedding," she muttered to the empty house as she entered. It was worse than she'd thought it would be. The main floor had been flooded during the storm, and Poppy and Henry had done a quick storm prep by moving as much as possible to the second floor of the custom-built riverfront home.

Streaks of dried mud led the way from the living room to the French doors where the water had come in. Shadowed stains on the previously ivory cream walls indicated that the water had risen to at least eighteen inches, maybe even two feet, in the house.

Her and Henry's dream home had drowned. Not unlike their hopes for a future together. Certainly her tears that first week after the wedding that never happened were enough to drown her crushed dreams. She thought she'd cried out all the pain of her broken heart, but as she gazed at the storm's destruction, waves of anguish rushed up from her stomach and she turned around and ran back out of the house. The crepe myrtles had survived the storm, and she took shelter behind them as her morning sickness left her helpless until her stomach was emptied.

"Son of a bitch." She ran a shaky hand across her forehead. "Nothing personal, baby. You're sweet, don't worry. Mommy's just getting used to you is all." Sweet Jesus and iced lemonade, she sounded like her grandmother. Grandma Edwina had made her opinion of Sonja marrying a "white gentleman" clear. "I'll support whomever you choose, sweet girl, but you have to know that you're making your life harder than it needs to be."

Sonja had blown her maternal grandmother off, assigning the words to a generation that had marched on Selma. While Loving v. Virginia had been decided within two years of Selma, there was still such a long way to go, and Sonja's grandmother never let her forget it. Grandma was as protective of her as could be and didn't want to see Sonja risk the extra pain that an interracial marriage could bring.

Sonja had fallen for Henry as he had her—flat-out soul mate attraction. But the reaction from his parents was some kind of 1950s flashback. They thought the marriage was doomed before it started simply because Sonja was black. She'd been sad for Henry because she knew his relationship with his parents was going to suffer. Had suffered.

But had it been enough? She still wasn't sure that if he'd drawn a firmer line with his folks she'd never have run.

The doubt and guilt that had scratched at her conscience after each altercation with Henry's parents came screaming back, and she paused in her damaged house survey. Worry that she could be wrong; that it might be possible that somewhere underneath all of his wonderfulness Henry had at least the teeniest bit of bigoted asshole in him, like his folks. And guilt that she'd never mentioned any of the confrontations to him. They'd been almost non-events to her; racism wasn't anything that surprised her. And the Boudreauxs were so subtle, their passive-aggressive skills so finely tuned, that it would have been hard to explain her point of view without coming off as having a huge chip on her shoulder.

The best bigots were like that. Cunning.

She stood under the large arched threshold into the great room, and the memory of Henry standing next to her at this spot, over which they'd hung the mistletoe last year, immediately shifted her morose thoughts to sadness.

Her parents had been thrilled she'd finally shown an interest in something besides law and studying. And they adored Henry. Their disappointment at her decision to not follow through with her vows had been keen, but they'd get over it. Especially when they found out they were going to be grandparents. Her sisters and brother had always been on board with her marrying Henry and were still sending her texts to "Quick, beg him to take you back." They meant well, but their words were starting to wear.

The French doors opened up, and she breathed in the brackish breeze, allowed the strength of it to move across her face. Her hair was going to frizz to all get-out but what the hell? The wind helped her nausea. She had her hand on her nape, giving herself a massage as best she could, willing her stomach to settle. It wasn't easy, seeing how the deck was strewn with debris that Henry obviously hadn't taken the time to clear.

Or maybe he hadn't come back, either?

A definite thud stiffened her spine and made her grip the door handles. She was alone in the house, vulnerable. If it was an unwelcome visitor she could escape from the back deck, over to their neighbor's. As quietly as possible she turned around and looked into the living room, across to the open space's huge granite-topped counter, to the kitchen. No one. Nothing. Maybe the wind had forced the front door open. But she'd closed it tight, she was certain.

"This is a far cry from the cathedral." An unmistakable voice, the sexiest timbre on the planet, rocked her.

A startled gasp left her lips before she had a chance to even know she made the sound. She faced him, looked into the brilliant blue eyes whose look always felt like a caress. Right now it was more like a harsh slap of hail on her bare cheeks.

"I didn't see your car in the drive so I thought it'd be okay to come in." Her defensiveness surprised her. She'd practiced how she'd behave when she saw him again, and this was nothing like the detached air she'd hoped to project.

"Why wouldn't it be okay? It's your house, too." Tall, lean, and with the lethal stare he usually reserved for his toughest courtroom cases, Henry stared at her from the foyer. As imperious as ever but without his usual air of humor. The self-deprecation that had endeared him to her. He wore his best attorney mask without any sign of the warmth she'd gotten too used to. He was guarded, prepared for battle.

She drank in his presence anyway. Glugged it down as if he were a tall glass of iced ginger ale, soothing her belly, easing the tight restrictive cords she'd wrapped her heart back together with.

He stepped into the living area, and sunlight from the open French doors reached him. His eyes seemed brighter than she remembered, more aquamarine, though at closer inspection they had shadows hanging over them. Clouding them.

"It's impolite to stare, Sonja."

She licked her dry lips. "Sorry. You startled me."

His short laugh was surgically strategic as it knifed through her. "Oh, I believe you're the one with the element of surprise under your belt.

What's next, Sonja, are you going to tell me you ran off to Vegas to marry someone else?"

"You know I didn't."

"Do I? Let's go over the facts, shall we?"

She held up her hands. "No. No, Henry. I can't." She moved as if to walk past him but reconsidered. She didn't want to risk coming close enough to touch him. Her fingers tingled with his nearness, and she didn't trust herself to walk on by without reaching out to him. As much as her head knew they were done, that he wasn't her prince on a horse, not even her life's partner on a bayou dugout, her heart was not to be trusted.

"Can't what, Sonja? Tell me why you felt you had to wait until the last possible minute to run out on me? Tell me why you led me on so long, right up to the goddamned altar, mind you, before you took off? Thanks for helping me tell our guests, by the way." Henry's words were harsh as he relaxed into his stance in the middle of the room. He'd shoved his hands into the pockets of his jeans, and his open-collared long-sleeved shirt was rolled up to his forearms.

"Wait—aren't you working? Why aren't you in a suit?"

One side of his mouth lifted in challenge, and it was so much like the expression he gave her before he was about to go down on her that she wanted to weep with sorrow over her loss. She'd never feel the pressure of his most talented tongue on her again.

Buck up. You're the one who ran.

"You're not the only one who can change their mind, Sonja."

"What the hell is that supposed to mean?"

"You think you know everything about everyone. Even now, you're looking at me like I'm crazy, standing here and not measuring up to what, who, you think I should be." He pulled his hands out of his pockets and gestured at his attire. "Maybe I'm tired of all of the bullshit, Sonja. Not just you, not just the sham of a relationship we had, but of it all. I'm done playing the perfect corporate lawyer. I'm good enough at what I do. I'll wear suits in the courtroom, but why should I in the office?"

That stung. So he'd lumped her in with bullshit. He still didn't get it, and she had zero hope he ever would. This wasn't about her betrayal. This was about being able to trust him. Too painful to go there.

"You think loosening up your dress code will loosen you up? Take the stick out of your ass?"

His eyes narrowed, and she knew he wanted to tell her to fuck off. Before, when they'd been so in tune, he would have bent her over the sofa that usually was in the center of the living room, and they would have fucked themselves to the oblivion of the priceless chemistry they'd shared. And then laughed about it later, sprawled out on the same sofa.

"Maybe I'm not the one who needs to loosen up, Sonja." His drawl was pronounced, the way he knew she liked it.

Against her mind's best advisement, her body reacted in the only way it knew to. She crossed her arms across her chest, hoping he hadn't seen her nipple hard-ons. It had to be baby hormones. No way would she feel attracted to him like this, after all she'd done.

Would she?

"What's that supposed to mean?" She stood her ground as he took one, two, five steps toward her. They were no more than two feet apart. Too close, too soon.

"You were always so quick to place the role of the uptight legal beagle on me, sweetheart, but did it ever occur to you that you're the one with the rigidity issues?"

"No." It came out as a goddamned whisper even as she straightened her spine. As if he were turning her on as quickly and effectively as ever. As if she could forget the betrayal at finding out there was so much he'd never told her about himself and throw herself at him, beg him to make love to her.

He made a show of looking her up and down. His gaze lingered on her breasts, covered by her arms, before sweeping to her hips and back up to her face. "You're looking as hot and luscious as ever, Sonja. Who would know that underneath it all lies a woman who was able to leave her fiancé of two years at the altar?"

* * * *

Henry saw her intake of breath before he heard it—her chest rose in a decisive move of shock, and he waited for the satisfaction to curl through him.

Instead he couldn't take his gaze off her liquid brown eyes, eyes he'd drowned in every single time they'd made love. Had a conversation. Shared their lives for over three years.

"You have no moral high ground here." She looked around the wrecked bottom floor of their house. The house they'd built together, long before she ever agreed to marry him. "The entire time we were a couple, you told me that you'd had a few relationships before me. You neglected to mention your engagement to a college classmate, or how she'd never learned how to let go of you."

Christ.

"Can you let go of Deidre? She's nothing to me other than an ex at this point. Hell, she's my parents' friend, not mine."

"A friend who showed up at our wedding, ready to wreak havoc." Her expression faltered. "Look, I'm not blaming her. I feel awful for her, in truth. The fact that she still has feelings for you—no, don't argue this point, Henry. No ex goes to a wedding in such a sneaky way unless she wants to get back with the groom. But you didn't even give me a warning that you'd invited her in or tell me that she's a goddamn lunatic. How was I supposed to feel when I saw you and her in an embrace at the cathedral?"

"It wasn't an 'embrace' for fuck's sake. She came up to me, caught me off guard." He threw up his hands. "I knew I couldn't count on you to be reasonable about any of this."

"Reasonable? You do remember that I left you at the altar, right? What's so reasonable about that?"

"I don't need a reminder of what you did." He stared at her, unable to imagine anything sadder than the sight of the woman of his dreams standing in the middle of a room stained from the storm floods. In what had been their dream retreat from the world but now smelled like the dankest parts of the bayou. The stagnant parts—the places that didn't get any circulation.

"About that, Henry, I have to tell you something." A flash of her pearly front teeth as they tugged on her full, lush lower lip.

"Save it. The only talking we need to do is at the office." He turned to leave, or at least, he thought about it. But he couldn't take his eyes from hers. Sonja was the goddess he'd fallen for as she stood there in what he knew was one of her least favorite work outfits. She'd always complained that the two-piece skirt suit was too big in the waist. The golden silk jacket and skirt were set off by a creamy underblouse—more of a camisole. He knew because the last time she'd worn this suit he'd practically ripped it off her before they made love in her office. After hours, of course. They always did everything by the book. He was tired of following rules.

He mentally corrected his memory of their making love. They'd had sex. The love hadn't been mutual, couldn't have been. Someone who loved you didn't leave you with your goddamned heart pulsing in your fucking hand.

"Henry, I don't expect you to want to listen to me, or to be ready to believe me about anything, not now."

"Not ever."

"But there are still some things that you should know, things I have to tell you."

He stared at her and wondered how the sun always hit her rich mahogany skin just right. Sonja looked ten years younger than she was, and he suspected she'd always be beautiful like this. His dick started to respond, and not only to the memories that flooded his thoughts but to the here and now. He ripped his gaze off her. "I know all I need to." He walked over to the kitchen counter. How had their house been destroyed, had Sonja walked out on their wedding, his life blasted to hell, all within only three weeks?

"Henry." Her hand was on his forearm, and he thought his skin would blister from the heat. "I should have talked to you sooner." Her voice was raspy, the way it got after she cried. Or when she was wet and ready. His cock swelled, and he damned his erection, damned whatever it was that kept him attuned to this woman even after she'd made an absolute fool of him.

"Don't, Sonja." He wouldn't take her hand away, sucker that he was. He turned and looked into her eyes and saw sorrow, confusion, and a shadow of—regret?

She pulled her hand back and hugged herself. It was Sonja's go-to defensive posture. She never did it in the courtroom or law office, not while she was working. But with him, with either of their families, she'd assumed this posture countless times. When she doubted her gut instincts.

"I didn't expect to see you here." Her chin jutted the tiniest bit. Nothing he'd have noticed if they weren't standing so goddamned close. He turned away from her and took a few steps into the kitchen, unable to trust himself.

"I never expected you to bolt from our vows the way you did."

She had the decency to turn away then. "I don't expect you to understand."

"Try me." The words came out of a primal place, as involuntary as his sexual need for her. She'd dragged his heart over shattered glass, and it still beat loud in his ears with his want.

Her eyes widened, and she reached out for the island counter, her long elegant fingers splaying over the slab of granite they'd handpicked to match the tiled floor.

"Henry..."

"You know what really gets me, Sonja?" His anger simmered, but still it wasn't enough to dampen his desire. He took a step closer, and she swayed backward but didn't move her feet.

She shook her head. "No." A whisper. She still felt it, too.

He advanced another step, closing the distance he'd put between them. Of its own volition his index finger traced the line of her cheekbone, her soft skin dewy from the high humidity that blew in through the open French doors. "What keeps me up at night is how you were able to continue to live with me, sleep in the same bed as me, and never once mention that you had second thoughts about the wedding. About marrying me." His finger traced down to her mouth, and some part of his rational mind thundered at him to *stop, drop, and roll.* Get the hell out of the house, away from this woman who'd destroyed his belief in forever.

Sonja's lips parted, and he knew she was trying to keep her breathing steady. The same way he was trying to keep his hard-on from running the show.

"Theeeere you are, Henry!" A high-pitched Southern drawl pierced through the sensory curtain that always seemed to drape over them when they were together and made their sexual chemistry more than sex. A heavier curtain dropped down in Sonja's gaze, smothering the heat in her eyes and revealing only her hardened distrust of him. For what she thought she knew about him, and the woman who'd crashed their wedding. Deidre Jones walked into their shared home as if she owned the place. Could his life get any shittier?

He stepped back and looked at the woman who had hoped to strike the death knell to his marriage to Sonja. As much as he wanted to blame her, if he and Sonja had been better connected, communicating more, not even a narcissistic witch like Deidre would have made a blip on the screen of their future. "What the hell are you doing here, Deidre?"

The petite blonde gave him her full-wattage smile, the one he'd been stupid enough to fall for back in college. "I was in the neighborhood checking out my parents' villa and saw your car in the driveway." She pointedly looked between the two of them. "This isn't a bad time, is it?"

"It's a perfect time." Sonja picked up her bag and headed for the stairs. "I'll be upstairs putting together a few things."

Henry shoved his fingers through his hair. It was a sad replacement for what he wanted to do—shove his fist through the drywall that was going to have to be stripped back when the renovation started. How sad was he that he only felt it was okay to punch a hole in an already damaged wall? Sonja was right. He not only had a stick up his ass—it was up his whole damn life.

"Henry. Talk to me." Hell. He'd paused too long. The icy cold hand on his forearm wasn't Sonja's, and wasn't welcome. He shook free of her grasp.

"Again. What the hell are you doing here?"

Deidre blinked, her ridiculously long eyelashes reminding him of tarantula legs. "I told you, I was—"

"No, not what you said, Deidre. Why are you breaking the restraining order?"

Chapter 2

Henry glared at the woman who'd destroyed so much of his life during college and right after, and had returned to lay waste to his wedding to the one woman for him. The woman he needed to be upstairs with. "Why, Deidre?"

"That's years old, Henry. Isn't it expired by now? And you know yourself, your parents invited me to your wedding. I'm so glad I was there to help you through the rough patch." Her brow rose in an over-the-top, practiced way. If he hadn't caught her rehearsing her expressions in the mirror that one morning over a decade ago, he'd have never believed how deeply self-centered a person could be.

"You know I had it renewed last week. You need to leave. Now. And I'm reminding you to stay away from me. Come near me again and I'll report your restraint violation. We do not have a relationship."

"But your parents disagree. They were happy to see me." Deidre picked at some imaginary thread on her sundress, and he tried to have a flash of compassion for her. He wondered if it'd be easier if she were mentally ill and not the hard-boiled narcissist she was. Would he have been able to overlook her destructive manner?

"You tricked them into inviting you. For your sake I never told them what a lying, manipulative person you are. I regret that now."

Her head jerked up, and she stared at him.

"I didn't need them to invite me. I would have come to the ceremony no matter what. I knew that once you saw me again you'd realize that we—" She halted, readjusting her hunt. Classic Deidre. If she channeled her intelligence into something more fruitful than making every man's life who'd ever dumped her into a living hell, she'd be unstoppable.

"There are more natural ways to handle things, you know. Like what's between us, still." She said "things" as if she were talking about the weather and not her severely messed up moral compass. Fuck.

"There is nothing between us, Deidre, except a restraining order." He pulled out his phone, intent on calling the police. "Please leave, Deidre."

She picked up the designer bag she'd dropped on the kitchen counter, and he briefly wondered how she afforded it, when it had to be difficult for her to hold a job down. Not his problem anymore, and he'd proved once that all he did was enable her, prevent her from hitting the bottom of whatever the hell was wrong with her. Which his parents had unwittingly done by inviting her behind his, and Sonja's, back. Not that their motives were anything but selfish and destructive.

"I'll call you, Henry." She gave him a little wave. To an uninformed observer, Deidre looked like any other thirty-something single, dressed nice for work, if a little skinny. Her power of self-control about everything, including her diet, was as impressive as frightening.

"Please don't, Deidre. Goodbye." He closed the door behind her and threw the deadbolt. As soon as he saw her drive away he went and locked the back French doors. Deidre had been a master of unwelcome entry when they'd first broken up, and he doubted she'd lost that skill.

For the millionth time since the wedding day, he asked himself how his past had come calling in the cruelest manner at the exact moment he thought he was going to begin the happiest part of his life.

* * * *

Upstairs, Sonja allowed her fury to fuel her packing. Thankfully the upstairs didn't smell as mildewy as the main floor, and she'd stored her suitcases in her closet. She blindly grabbed whatever outfits looked like they'd be comfortable, eschewing her favorite skintight sheath dresses and higher heels. She found no reason to linger or wallow in her self-pity as long as Miss Let-Me-Fuck-Your-Jilted-Groom was in the house. With Henry.

"Son of a bitch!" Her hands shook, and she grasped the side of her largest piece of luggage, willing herself to not break down. Hadn't she shed enough tears? Crying over her stupidity that led her to believe Henry was in love with her and not using her to help him prove to himself he was different from the boy who'd people-pleased his parents was one thing. Sobbing over the vacuous perfect Southern belle who all but pulled kneepads out of her huge leather designer bag? No. Not happening.

The back of her neck burned, and she whirled around. Henry stood a couple of feet into the room, his hair uncharacteristically sticking up, which was difficult with the usual short crew he kept.

"Leave me be." She opened the nearest dresser drawer and grabbed handfuls of underwear.

"No. Not until you hear me out."

"Hear you out? I think I've seen all I need to."

"God damn it, Sonja. You're the one who left me. We already know your side of the story. Let me tell you mine."

She went into the master bathroom and began to clear the vanity of her cosmetics. Her fingers touched the edge of the bottle of her favorite perfume, and the perky designer shape seemed to mock the woman she was only two weeks ago.

"Say what you have to say. I'm listening, but I don't have time to stop packing, Henry."

He stood on the tiled bathroom floor, watching her as if he didn't know what to expect next. Good.

"I did not invite Deidre to the wedding. That was my parents' doing. With help from Deidre."

"Really? And you're telling me that such a well-bred Southern belle like her decided to show up without having received a formal invitation?"

Red crept up Henry's neck to his much longer hairline. "I, ah, I think my parents sent her a real invite, but she would have showed up anyway, from what she just told me."

Confused, Sonja paused. "You mean they used their invitation?"

"They asked me for a few extra invitations. I gave them five."

"And never mentioned it to me." Another chink in the armor she'd invisibly knit over her heart. She waved her hand under his gaze. "This isn't the issue. The issue remains what it was a month ago."

"Twenty-three days."

"Fine. Twenty-three days ago you hadn't told me that your former fiancée had not been just a bad breakup. That you had a restraining order against her, that she'd stalked you and the women you'd dated, and she may have had her sights on me!"

"But she didn't. I mean, yes she broke her restraining order, but that's not the issue, Sonja. The issue is that you and I aren't, haven't been in forever, communicating. Talking."

Sonja's gut twisted at that one. "The main reason we should never have considered marriage is that you never, ever were completely honest with me.

You've only told me what you had to in order to keep me pacified, Henry."
And she'd let him pacify her, an issue she was doing her best to dissect.

You weren't honest with him, either. She hated her conscience in this
moment.

He didn't answer and dropped his gaze after several seconds.

Sonja opened the linen closet and pulled out two towels. "Ugh!" Covered
in what looked like a black powder, the once pristine white cotton gave
off a telltale stench of post-storm mildew. She dropped the towels into
the master bath.

"Stop, Sonja. We're going to have to throw it all out, whatever we can't
clean. By the way? The homeowner's doesn't begin to cover most of the
damage."

"Do you think I honestly give a flying fuck about material damages?"
As if to agree with her, the baby chose that time to make her hormones
jump and her nausea swell.

"What?" Henry must have seen it in her face.

She felt hot and sweaty and had about five seconds to make it to the
toilet. Sonja slammed the door to the tiny commode room behind her and
let the dry heaves come. She'd already tossed her breakfast in the crepe
myrtle. And now Henry was witness to her "illness." *Shit.*

* * * *

Henry heard Sonja throwing up and guilt sucker-punched him. He'd
made her so upset that she was puking, for fuck's sake. Her stomach was
strong as an iron drum when it came to spicy Louisiana food, but get Sonja
emotionally riled up and it went to her gut.

He stared at the empty bathroom counter, save for her large cosmetic
bag that she'd stuffed to the gills with her beauty stuff. How had what he'd
thought was a rock-solid relationship blown to smithereens in one act of
poor judgment on his part?

Henry sank onto the floor, his back against the brass claw-foot tub.
Deidre had shown signs of stalking him again, or rather, stalking Sonja,
for the past six months. He'd meant to tell Sonja several different times,
but he didn't want to rock the smooth sailing they'd had since they'd moved
in together three years ago.

Even that was a lie. There'd been rough patches that he'd maneuvered
by going over-the-top in his adoration of Sonja. Told himself he was
distracting her with his charm.

All he'd been doing was avoiding his own discomfort at how gullible and blind he'd been to Deidre's manipulative actions. He destroyed Sonja's trust along with the incredible bond they'd shared from the moment they'd met. While his hopes of a future with her were gone—he'd never trust her again, either, not after the spectacular way she'd dumped him—he didn't want to leave things so acrimonious between them.

The door swung open, and Sonja didn't spare him a glance. At the sink, she threw cold water on her face.

"I'm sorry you're not feeling well."

Her eyes were bright and fierce as she glared at him in the mirror. "I feel fine."

"Liar."

She ignored him as she looked around the room for a clean towel. Of course there were none. "Hell."

"There's a roll of paper towels under the sink."

"They'll be moldy, too." She wiped her hands on her skirt and lifted up her makeup bag. "See you at the office."

He got to his feet, feeling awkward and unkempt next to her polished finesse. Even in what he knew she considered her worst-fitting suit, Sonja was the most beautiful woman he'd ever known.

"Wait—we aren't done here, Sonja."

The look she threw him was a potent combination of certainty, hate, and sadness. Definitely no regret.

"I'd say we are, Henry."

He watched her take her larger suitcase off the bed and pull it through the door and into the hallway. As the *thump thump thump* of her dragging it down the steps echoed in the hot, damp house, he couldn't ignore the weight that pummeled his chest. Desperate for a distraction, he walked back into the bathroom, pacing, opening and closing the vanity drawers. She'd taken all of her stuff. Every last bit.

Except for the bottle of perfume he gave her last Christmas. Her favorite scent. He couldn't stop himself from grabbing it and pulling off the cap, holding the sprayer to his nose. As he inhaled, memories flashed across his mind. Sheer torment. Sonja the day he met her in law school, Sonja taking on the most hostile client and winning, Sonja standing up to his racist parents. Sonja turning to him as the sun rose, her hands finding his cock as easily as her mouth. Sonja groaning with pleasure as he feasted on her pussy. Sonja laughing with him as they dragged a Christmas tree into the river house. This house, the house that represented their commitment to each other. Sonja in her wedding dress, bringing tears to his eyes.

Sonja telling him in the cathedral garden that they'd made a mistake, that marriage to him wasn't possible for her, not when he'd not been completely honest with her. She hadn't given him a fucking chance to explain.

There was nothing to explain. She'd been right—they'd made a mistake.

Henry lifted the fancy bottle as if it were a grenade and aimed for the large bathtub. Before he let go of it, his arm dropped and he hung his head. If he smashed the bottle, the entire house would smell like Sonja, even after the storm repair and cleanup. He'd never survive if he didn't start erasing every last memory.

He carefully placed the bottle in one of the matching hardwood bathroom cupboards and shut the door.

Chapter 3

An hour later, Sonja moved slow and easy down Charles Street, her pace matching the weight of the humidity that wrapped around her as only New Orleans in late spring knew how. Jasmine scented her path as the long vines climbed up the storefront buildings, and she caught a whiff of fresh ground coffee from her favorite café. A scent that had called to her like pollen to a bee only weeks earlier. Before different scents affected her stomach, before nausea tainted the edges of every morning. Every afternoon and evening, too, depending on how her hormones wanted to behave.

The local NOLA scenery soothed her as nothing else could after seeing Henry in their home two hours ago. Their house. Her former home.

And Deidre, that sorry excuse for a bitch. Sonja wanted to blame her for everything related to the failed wedding. It would be too easy to focus her sorrow and disappointment on a single person. But Deidre was a whole lot of the uglier side of Southern tradition and not a little bit narcissistic, wrapped up into a hot sticky praline. Sonja couldn't muster anything but disgust toward Deidre, but more at herself. No one else had forced her to run out on her groom. Sure, Deidre had shown up at their wedding ready to win Henry back, and it was as clear as a September sky over Lake Pontchartrain that in Deidre's universe Henry would drop everything and return to her. People like Deidre didn't see that they were borderline delusional—it was always all about them. The way Deidre had "popped in" to their—the river house. Stalking Henry, feeling it out to see what she needed to do to convince Henry it had been her all along. Pushing aside Sonja like overgrown Spanish moss. But Deidre probably didn't even know why she was so obsessed with Henry. If it wasn't Henry, it'd be someone else. Another sexy man that caught her eye.

Sonja wasn't a psychiatrist, but she felt in her gut that Deidre wasn't mentally ill, just batshit mean. Deidre was a catalyst to her decision to jilt Henry, but she hadn't been the reason. Her reason to back out of their wedding at the last minute was far deeper, and more basic.

Like Henry had said, he hadn't been totally upfront about how rough his relationship with Deidre was. And unbeknownst to him, she'd never revealed the burden she'd been unwilling to carry. The burden of making Henry completely break from his family and legal legacy for her. It wouldn't have even been his decision—his parents would have cut him off without a further word. Which made their appearance at the rehearsal dinner and wedding all the more damning. They'd come as a reminder to her, to make sure she knew what she was doing by knocking over the dominoes with her "I do."

"Hey, watch it!" The yell coincided with a harsh blare as a delivery truck roared around her, making her skirt flutter around her calves. She blinked and realized she'd stepped off the curb a few seconds before the green light.

Sonja had been doing a lot of this lately—drifting off into the last few months with Henry, replaying each conversation and interaction with his parents. It was wearing her out from the inside. She promised herself to focus on today. To let go of the past and put her energy toward her singular problem, or rather, surprise. She was going to be a mother. The fact that it was also the most miraculous thing to happen to her made it all the more complicated.

She'd have to tell Henry soon. He had a right to know that his ex-fiancée and runaway bride was pregnant. It'd be on her time, though. Especially after he hadn't allowed her to get a word in edgewise this morning, when she would have told him outright. She reminded herself that she no longer had any obligation to tell him anything until she was ready. Even that he was a baby daddy.

She pushed the office door open and stepped into the firm's lobby, still too early for clients, but Alesia, bless her, had her usual warm smile on the ready along with the pile of mail from the past three weeks that Sonya had been out of the office.

"Good morning, Sonja." Whoa. Alesia's usual chipper countenance had been replaced by a grim shadow of herself.

"Hi, Alesia." Sonja heaved her leather tote onto the tall counter and sifted through the envelopes. "How have you been?"

"Oh, same old same old." Alesia didn't meet her eyes. Hell. Better get it out there and squash the hot mess now.

"Look, I know that recent events have been unusual, but my breakup from Henry is purely personal. It won't affect my work here, or your office environment. I think you know me well enough to know I keep work professional."

"It's not you, Sonja, or the job." Alesia fidgeted with her skirt, part of a silky cream fit and flare dress with tiny rosebuds embroidered on a vine along the side and bodice. And then she raised her gaze from the stack of case files, and her liquid brown eyes swam with tears as she looked straight in Sonja's. "It's Henry. You look, um, fine. He's not been feeling himself since you, I mean, since, since—"

"Since I left him at the altar. Is that what you mean to say?" Calm, detached, the way she'd practiced. The way she'd wanted to be back at the house. Deidre wasn't the only one with her sights on Henry. And why shouldn't he have women falling at his feet? He was successful, kind, loving, and newly single.

She ignored the twist of regret. Ending their marriage before it began, while brutal, had been her best option.

"I'm not saying that, Sonja. It's just—"

"Exactly what you did, Sonja. You left me at the altar." Henry spoke from the other side of the entryway.

Sonja jerked, her stomach heaved, and she grabbed the high counter surrounding Alesia's desk. She lifted her chin and braced herself for the censure, the reproach, the curiosity she expected in Henry's expression. Son of a bayou bitch, it was as if she hadn't already faced him down a couple of hours ago.

When their eyes met he looked every bit the easygoing charmer who he'd become with her. Startled, she threw him her best glare. He hadn't reverted back to the tight-ass, born-with-a-silver-spoon-in-his-mouth lawyer he'd been when she'd joined the firm five years ago. Just as in their destroyed home, he gave off a different energy. The familiar sensual heat didn't radiate from his eyes. A twinge of sorrow hit her in the middle of her rib cage and caught her off guard. A reminder of how easy it had been to fall for Henry.

She'd been hired by his father almost four years ago. She'd watched his interest in her flicker on and off for three months before he'd read her mind, somehow seen her daydreams, and finally asked her out. And taken her to bed, the devout attention to detail he was known for in the courtroom turned on completely for her, to her, making her feel things and do things she'd never thought of. Or at least, never thought of doing sober, in broad daylight, like the time he'd taken one of his brother's boats out into the bayou and bent her over the wheelhouse rail, taking her with raw need and heat. It had been worth the mosquito bites.

She shook her head, needing the physical motion to release the memory. "Good morning." The two words were all that separated her from giving in to her desire to run or stay and stand her ground like the strong woman she'd thought she was. The woman who'd never have let Henry's parents talk to her the way they did, who'd have paid heed to the warning signs that a marriage to Henry Boudreaux was never going to work. The woman who would have seen the evidence in front of her that there was a major trust issue going on.

"Sonja." Henry graced her with one more scorching appraisal before turning to Alesia with a warm smile. "We'll need lunch catered for the McNeely account, main conference room. Sonja, Rick, and I will sit in, and there are six attending from their team."

Sonya's head buzzed with the drone of Henry and Alesia's conversation. She walked off to her office, unable to pretend that each time she had to deal with Henry was anything less than it was.

Cataclysmic.

* * * *

Henry had expected a huge surge of exultation at her shocked expression. It was what he'd intended to do. Shake her out of her professional composure, throw her off her damned too-sexy heels and let her know that she hadn't affected him at all. He didn't care if he'd made her throw up just hours ago. And he was grateful she'd fled their vows. The marriage had been a bad idea from the start. Living together had worked; why had they pushed it to the altar?

Why did you push it to the altar?

He stifled a groan.

"Do you want me to get the usual mix of wraps or something more local for lunch?" Alesia's attention was completely on him, and he'd barely heard her request.

He wanted to give in to his snide alter ego, the energy that had kept him moving forward through the hell that had become his life since Sonja left him a jilted groom only a little over three weeks ago.

"You decide. Your judgment is impeccable." He flashed Alesia the grin that had opened doors for him all across Southern Louisiana, throughout the New Orleans courts, even without his family name.

The grin that had initially drawn Sonja to him three and a half years ago, if what she'd told him was the truth. If she'd fallen for him at first sight, as she'd said. If her heart had really skipped a beat and she'd gotten the hiccups because her soul had "recognized" him. They'd been in this same office, Sonja sitting opposite his father as the senior Boudreaux interviewed her. She'd been sipping on a cola and showed zero signs of nervousness. And the way her eyes had sized him up had made him hard on the spot. Her expression had been priceless when that loud hiccup erupted from her mouth, her sexy as sin lips puffing, and all he'd been able to think about was how badly he needed to touch her, kiss her, have her.

She'd said it was love at first sight for her. That Henry was it. He let out a grunt of frustration. He'd never forgive himself for his own fucking stupidity. Nothing she'd said or done had been the truth, it turned out.

He closed the door to his office and crashed down hard on the leather sofa. And immediately bounced back up, unable to be in such close proximity to the very place he'd last made love to Sonja. They'd been working late to get ahead on their cases, knowing that they'd be in Tahiti for ten days after the wedding. Thinking about her in a teeny bikini, or better, nothing, had made him harder than the oak desk he leaned against, his hands wrapping around the edge. She'd let him go down on her as she lay across his quickly cleared desk, and with no one in the office, Sonja's cries had wrapped around him as they both came in a rush of lust. Combined with love, or so he'd thought.

A true love didn't abandon you at the altar, though.

His phone buzzed, and he gratefully grabbed for the distraction.

"Hey, Gus."

"Henry. You back at work?" His brother's long drawl was indicative of a happy man. Brandon "Gus" Boudreaux should be happy—he'd met the love of his life when Sonja's maid of honor had showed up for the pre-wedding festivities.

Poppy and Brandon had been all but inseparable ever since, and Henry believed his little brother when he told him he knew Poppy was "the one." Henry had thought Sonja was the one for him. Familiar pain squeezed just above his stomach.

"Bro, you still there?" Brandon sounded worried.

"Fuck. Yes, I'm here."

"A little early for you to be cussing, big brother. Let me guess, Sonja's back at work today. Am I right?"

"Yes." Through clenched teeth.

"Maybe it's a good day for you to take a breather. You've been working since what, last week?"

"Yeah. I can't take off—we have a big client meeting today."

"You, or you and Sonja?"

"Both of us."

A long whistle. "Sorry, Henry. That sucks moose cock."

He laughed despite his existential struggles. "Yeah. Yeah it does, man."

"Whatever you do, keep your chin up and don't let her see you suffer. Unless you want her back."

"Hell no. Never."

"Sounds a little too quick on the draw, Henry. You still haven't hashed out what happened at the wedding."

"There's nothing to hash out. And frankly, it started long before then." He walked around his desk and lowered himself into the chair, forcing his gaze out the window at the Spanish-moss-draped oak that sheltered the office from the hot Louisiana sun. "It's over. My only regret is that I didn't stop it sooner."

"Bullshit, brother." Brandon knew him too well, even with their several-year estrangement. Funny how the wedding-that-wasn't had helped bridge their pride. "How about you join me and Poppy for dinner?"

"Ah, thanks, Gus. I'm the worst kind of company right now. Can I take a rain check?"

"Sure. Always." He heard the sound of Brandon's breath, then a swish as he imagined his brother opening his sliding screen door and walking out onto his expansive deck that overlooked the water. "But don't think you have to call ahead or wait until you feel better. Come over whenever you want."

"Thanks, bro." He disconnected and stared at his cell phone. His estrangement from Brandon had been repaired by the same event that had broken his engagement and ended his marriage to the woman he knew he'd never get out of his blood. And as much as he appreciated his brother's concern, Brandon was seeing Poppy, Sonja's best friend. Henry didn't put it past either Poppy or Brandon to try to fix things by surprising him with Sonja being at dinner.

They meant well, but were clueless. His and Sonja's hurts ran deeper than a nice dinner and bottle of wine could mend.

* * * *

Sonja bit into the almond croissant with the hunger that had plagued her every day of the past few weeks. Like clockwork, her appetite returned late morning after the morning nausea passed. She knew the exact night she'd conceived the baby. Her body had felt "different" after the lovemaking session with Henry that had lasted the better part of a late winter night after they'd won a particularly challenging case. At first she hadn't been able to pinpoint it and blamed her exhaustion on prenuptial jitters. The week before the wedding, her breasts swelled, her nipples became sensitive to the shower spray, and she'd felt as though her period was about to start at any moment. But of course it hadn't. She'd known two days before the wedding for sure. Thank God she'd only shared it with Poppy. If Henry had known, she didn't think she'd have been able to walk away from marrying him as she had.

The memory of leaving her soul mate at the altar made the pastry feel heavy in her stomach, and she paused, closing her eyes and breathing in and out slowly to ward off a wave of nausea. Anytime she remembered their wedding day she felt sick all over again.

"Is it that good?"

Her eyes flew open at the sexy baritone that only a few weeks ago had coaxed an orgasm out of her as he spoke dirty words into her ear while he moved over her, inside her, again and again. They might not have been completely candid with each other about a lot of things, but their sex life had always been honest.

"It's delicious." She put the croissant down on a napkin, next to her stack of files. Henry's gaze dared her to look away, and she never backed down from anyone, so she stared back.

A quick flash of disgust shadowed his face before Henry looked away and sat in the seat opposite her, reaching over for his files. Usually they sat together, ready to work until whenever it took to get the day's items checked off. It wasn't going to get easy, ever, to know he thought so little of her. Knowing she deserved it for something he didn't even know about yet—the baby—made it worse.

"I imagine you need time to go over these." A deft verbal pitch to see how she'd react. Would she go high, admit she should have been back in the office last week, or go low and blame him for her staying away, or ignore it?

"Alesia sent me the files last week. I've read through them all."

He had to be playing her—Alesia told Henry everything. He'd know she'd had copies to analyze. Their round-trip tickets to Tahiti had gone unused, so it wasn't as if she'd been out of the country and unable to do any work.

"Any concerns?" He kept his face low, focused on the paperwork, but she saw the blood vessel just above his collar pulsing in rhythm to his heartbeat. Whenever Henry was agitated that was his tell.

"No, nothing to speak of." Her voice was low and throaty, and she wished she'd tendered her resignation. It would be so much easier, especially now when every damned hormone in her body was setting off emotions she didn't even know she was capable of. But a deft noncompete clause she'd signed when his father had hired her prevented her from going out on her own just yet. She couldn't afford it. And now the house needed to be renovated.

Brilliant blue eyes watched her with their usual alertness. "You sure about that, Sonja? You're acting like something's not sitting right with you."

"It's just this." She motioned very slightly between them, using her finger. "Awkward with a capital A, am I right? We didn't talk about it as much as we probably should have this morning." Of course, dearest Deidre's appearance had shut down any chance of the conversation they needed to have in private.

The curiosity in his eyes turned to frosted crystal. "Let's get it out on the table, then." He splayed both hands on the dark polished surface, and she wondered if he'd forgotten about the time they'd both arrived to work early, too early. They'd ended up here, naked, in under five minutes. Did he see her naked body as she'd knelt on all fours, waiting for him to take her? She shook her head, blinked.

"Sonja, you okay?"

"Fine. You were going to say?"

"Whatever we shared was wiped out when you decided to walk out on our relationship without the least bit of warning. You've never given me a chance to explain my side of things."

"Wait a min—"

"No, hold up." He shot down her attempt to interrupt him with a flick of his hand. "You made your choice. And you've decided to continue on at this firm. I'm guessing that's so that you can make your share of the money to fix the house, right?" He waited for her slight nod. "We both need to raise the funds to get the house rehabbed well enough to sell. Fine, I get it. But don't think for one minute that there is anything other than our working relationship at stake. We've always enjoyed that, correct? And I'm willing to work with you, until the day you decide to leave the firm. Because, let's face it, I'm not going anywhere. This is my family firm. You, you'll go out on your own or take a better offer elsewhere. That's okay. Until then I expect the best you have to offer, and for you to kindly refrain from referring to what we shared on a personal level. It's over."

Sonja stared at the man who'd hung the moon for her and only saw the stamp of Boudreaux on his expression. The same look his father had when she'd told him to take the money and referral he'd offered her to quit when she and Henry announced their engagement and shove them up his tight white racist ass. He'd never fire her, not as a black woman in his otherwise very white, very male firm. And regardless of his racist views, Sonja brought in a lot of business for their firm that they'd otherwise never catch. She'd expected Henry's father to give her a hard time, but not so much Henry.

She'd been a fool.

"Our professional relationship never had anything to do with our personal life. Why should it now?"

Henry didn't respond but instead glared at her. He may as well have thrown a machete at her for how his silent gesture pained her.

The door clicked open, and Alesia entered with trays of lunch food, followed by two clients and Rick, the firm's other NOLA attorney.

As she and Henry stood to greet them she eyed her almost-husband. Her ex-fiancé. The man who'd broken her heart.

Henry was tall and professional-looking, whether dressed in a classic suit as he was now or in cargo shorts and a T-shirt. He'd been born to inherit his father's firm, a lawyer's mind part of his gene pool. And until their wedding weekend, she hadn't seen that he'd also inherited the insatiable need to make everything appear perfect. Hence the pristine wedding they'd almost gone through with. Henry wasn't a people-pleaser though, especially not to his parents. He'd bucked their sensibilities and desires by choosing to marry her, a black woman from a bayou family. Henry had never seen her as anything other than the woman he'd decided to marry. She believed that.

What Henry had refused to see, however, was that his father was never going to leave the firm to Henry as long as Sonja was his wife. The firm was going to be dissolved and all of his father's money locked up in trust funds for future grandchildren, be it theirs or his siblings'. Sonja didn't care about the financials for her, but she cared for Henry. He deserved more, and his constant state of denial with his parents drove her nuts. Henry's younger brother, Gus, had formed his own life with his shipbuilding business in New Orleans, and Henry's sister, Jena, was very much her own person.

Henry's younger sister was a social worker who thrived on her job in New Orleans, but she was also in the U.S. Navy reserves and often traveled overseas. Jena had missed the un-wedding because she was somewhere in South America doing who knew what kind of operations for the government. She hadn't gone to law school; neither had Henry's younger brother, Brandon, always "Gus" to Henry.

It wasn't about the money, which was significant, but about family legacy. Henry was the man to change it, to turn the law firm into a contemporary, relevant part of the community, serving diverse clients and causes. He saw that corporate law didn't have to mean serving the same good ol' boys his father had.

But Henry would never have the chance to improve upon his family legacy if she were around...unless he'd taken her up on her suggestion that they start his own family firm. She remembered offering her opinion after work last Christmastime. He'd looked at her like she had horns growing out of her head, so she'd dropped it. Thought Henry would come around to seeing he needed to start his own legacy. She'd been wrong. Henry was too loyal to the Boudreaux legacy. His father might be a jerk, but one of his great-grandfathers had worked to rebuild a free South after the Civil War. Henry wanted that to be his legacy.

The younger siblings had gotten the hell away from the family dynasty. But not Henry. Henry needed to be part of his father's legacy in a way the other two didn't. Because Sonja saw this, saw the need in the man she loved so desperately, she'd had no choice but to back out of their marriage. She'd do anything for Henry's happiness, and Henry would never be happy without knowing he'd made a difference in what his father had begun.

He'd never forgive her for leaving him the way she did, and that was all right. Sonja didn't want Henry's forgiveness. She'd wanted his love, understanding, and trust, but her expectations had been too much.

Henry didn't have it to give. And just as well—she hadn't been completely honest with him. All of the discussions she'd had with his parents, no matter how acrimonious, should have been relayed to him.

And as she watched him, the one man she'd ever pinned all her hopes on, she had to face the cold hard truth. She was as unworthy of trust as Henry.

Chapter 4

Sonja was relieved beyond measure when the business meeting with the McNeelys wrapped up early. She needed a break and ducked out of the office to meet her best friend Poppy Kaminsky for a quick cuppa.

The promise of Poppy's soothing presence made her pick up her pace, eager for the solace only a best friend can give. Poppy wasn't in the café yet, so Sonja gave her order at the counter. When Sonja turned to find a table, Poppy walked in the door and offered her signature full-wattage smile.

Sonja waved. "Hi, boo."

"Hey, girlfriend." Poppy enveloped her in a hug, and Sonja soaked up every last drop of affection from the woman who'd been with her through thick and thin. Poppy took a step back and gave Sonja a once-over.

"Geez, Sonja, you look good, really good. Even though I know you're feeling like hell." Poppy's wonder was evident in her open expression, the way she looked Sonja up and down like she was some kind of suffering fool.

Which she was.

"I'm okay. I'll save us a table while you get your order."

They sat at the tiny table, and Sonja waited for Poppy to ask the obvious.

"So you haven't told him about the baby yet?" Poppy didn't disappoint as she eyed Sonja over the frothiest cappuccino Sonja had ever seen.

"I couldn't this morning. I tried to, at the house. I stopped in to take a look at it, and Henry showed up. And then so did Deidre." She filled Poppy in on the Deidre scene, and the more awful exchange she and Henry had in the master bathroom. Poppy took it all in, compassion evident in her large eyes. Sonja couldn't stand the feeling of being pitied and squirmed in her seat. "You know, Poppy, if that foam was any higher you'd fall in it." Sonja preferred to keep their conversation on the light side, but nothing was ever that simple with her college roommate and soul sister. Poppy saw through Sonja's bullshit and was never afraid to call her on it.

"Stop deflecting." Poppy's eyes were sharp. "The baby. You should have told him by now. How do you know that crazy bitch isn't going to try to move in on him? Or do something else to scare you?"

"You mean like leave a squirrel boiling on my stove?"

Poppy's eyes widened in recognition. "Yes. It's not funny, Sonja. You said yourself you think something's not right with her. Take it from me, there's a lot more going on there. I should know—I went pretty crazy myself when I found out my ex was cheating on me. She could be a real psycho, though. Look what she did showing up in front of you like that at the wedding."

"You did your share of over-the-top tantrums in front of your ex's family, too." Sonja didn't want to hurt Poppy, but it'd been all over social media. Poppy had quite the reputation as a wronged woman out for revenge before she'd found her happiness in New Orleans.

Poppy put her chin on her hand. "I did. And I'm telling you, if I hadn't had your wedding—I mean, you know—to focus on and escape to, who knows when I would have stopped going after Will and that pathetic excuse for an assistant I had?"

"You were wronged."

Poppy shook her head. "That's my point. Deidre was wronged, too, even if it was a long time ago. And she has more than Henry as an ex, right? She's got a lot of bitter to spew. Henry and you are her most convenient target right now."

"It's hard to reconcile the sweet Southern belle I met that day and just saw at the house with the woman who made his life a living hell. And I don't think she's actually crazy, just incredibly self-absorbed and used to getting her way."

Poppy nodded. "Exactly. That describes me a few months ago, too." Poppy stirred the dusting of cocoa into her coffee, making it look more like café au lait. "Henry's one tough dude, if he put up with all of that in college and even Brandon never knew about it."

"He and Brandon were estranged back then, remember? I know it looks to you like they're the best of brothers, friends, but it's only been since the we—since the rehearsal dinner. What, three, four weeks?"

"Almost four." Poppy's smile was back. The daze of new love.

"Feels like a lifetime ago." Sonja sipped her seltzer water. It was all she could manage this afternoon.

"And you still haven't told him you're having his baby." Poppy's face was open, nonjudgmental.

"No. There hasn't been a right time. And now with the house flooding, the fallout being more than I imagined it would be, it's harder than ever to nail down the right time to talk to him. I tried this morning, like I said, but it was a no-go." She sighed. "It's making me wonder if I shouldn't pick up and go." Not that her bank account could support it.

"You're kidding, right? You already took off from your wedding and Henry. How did that help anything, really? You have to tell him, Sonja. Henry's not a monster. No matter how much you try to make him out to be one."

"I'm not trying to make him anything. It's all on me, I know that."

"Your trust issues." Sometimes Poppy's frankness wasn't refreshing. It was sobering, almost painfully so.

"Yes. My trust issues." Sonja tore her cocktail napkin into tiny bits as she spoke. "What was I thinking, marrying that man, any man? You've known me the longest, Poppy. I was happy living with him. Why the hell did I agree to tie the knot?"

"There's something else you're not telling me. Does it have to do with his parents?" Par for the course, Poppy wasn't going to let her veer off course again.

"No. Yes. Yes, they don't help matters. But I can't blame their racist view of the world on my decision to leave Henry." As she mouthed the words, her stomach curdled but not from morning sickness. From regret, sorrow, the grief she'd yet to process through.

"I really thought you two had worked through all that. But if you haven't told him about how awful they've been to you, Henry wouldn't see anything to be concerned about."

The Boudreauxs had left New Orleans proper after Katrina and made the family firm headquarters in Baton Rouge. Henry's father had opened a satellite office in New Orleans that he assigned to Henry right after Henry passed the bar. It enabled the legacy of the law firm to continue, and to in fact expand their client base. But Henry's father didn't have to sully his hands with working through a post-Katrina New Orleans, or the racism it unveiled in all its depravity to the world.

"It's more complicated than that. It's about his entire future, the firm's future. And let's face it, if we were meant to be I would have been able to tell him about it all right away. Who did I think I was, protecting him? His mother?"

"You still care about him." Poppy's soft words sent her heart hammering.

"Of course I do. I always will care about his welfare. But we're not ever going to be a couple. We're through." She blinked furiously, trying to keep the tears from falling. Oh boy, she did have a lot of grief to still work through.

"Even with the baby surprise?"

"Don't throw that at me. We both know I don't need a man to be a good parent."

"I'm not saying that. You'll be the absolute best mother. Which is why I know you'll want the baby's father involved. Especially when the father is Henry. Henry, Poppy. Not some dude you hooked up with in a one-night stand, or a guy who'd been abusing you that you had to leave. *Henry.*" Poppy's steady gaze at once nailed Sonja to the spot, making her see how foolish her actions were, while also conveying the depth of respect Poppy had for her ex.

"You lost your objectivity when you fell for Brandon."

"Maybe. A little. But do you know what's really happening with me, Sonja? I've realized that in order to make the most of my life, I had to shed everything I knew before. Not because I was a bitch in my previous life, which we both know I was." They shared a laugh, which Sonja treasured. Even in the midst of her personal crisis, Poppy still made her laugh with little effort.

"What did you shed, besides your career in New York?" Sonja was loath to bring up what she knew had hurt Poppy deeply. Not only did her fiancé cheat on her, but because of Poppy's over-the-top temper tantrum at The Plaza Hotel, the entire social media world had been privy to her unprofessional behavior. It had cost Poppy the contract of her dreams, and the promise of financial freedom, when a major chain department store canceled its design contract with her last minute.

"I let go of the overly heavy expectations I put on myself. I expected to keep going in the same business forever. Even though I knew I wanted to reach out to the world in a more local community way, I had no idea how to implement it or make it happen. By falling on my butt, I landed here in New Orleans at the perfect time. The boutique downtown that I work in was looking for extra help, and it gave me an office and apartment where I had space to think and figure out my next steps." Poppy had given Sonja the apartment key as soon as she committed to move in with Brandon. Sonja was grateful for the place to call home since the river house was gutted.

"I have to figure out my next steps now, I suppose. Not just with me, or my job, but the baby. How am I going to manage the hours I work and raise a kid? It's one thing to say I can do it, hell, we have a lot of friends doing it. But putting it in motion..."

"Which is why you need to tell Henry. You're not in this solo, even if you don't want to marry him."

Poppy had her there. But with sharing parenting came the reality of having to see Henry regularly, as he helped raise his child, which he would. Henry did nothing in half-measures. She snorted, thinking about how he'd insisted on a full-scale society wedding ceremony. She'd gotten her way with the more casual entertaining during the days leading up to the wedding, but Henry would accept nothing less than being married in front of the entire world in the cathedral downtown.

"What's so funny?"

"I'm thinking about how far from myself I went to attempt a marriage with Henry." Poppy stayed silent, so she went on. "I never wanted all the fancy stuff. I'm getting rid of my car, going for something more economical, environmental. Why didn't I do that right away?"

"There's no sin in enjoying nice things. You'd worked and studied so hard for so long. Stop beating yourself up." Poppy had been her strongest supporter when she'd decided to apply to law school their senior year in college.

"If I don't look at myself, then I have to look at Henry, and I don't know why he didn't trust me enough to tell me the full story on Deidre."

"Ask him."

"That's my point. I shouldn't have to ask him."

Poppy snorted. "Did you think that just because you found the right guy for you that everything else about it would be easy?"

Sonja blinked. Had she?

"You lived together for almost three years, Sonja. You knew him, you *know* him." Poppy was in her wise sage mode, which Sonja usually found humorous as Poppy had wild curly blond hair, big amber eyes that were offset by her porcelain skin, making her look a little like a Celtic witch. Today it only made Sonja want to curl up under the covers. There was too much to process.

"I knew Henry well, yes. But he did change, in some ways. I don't know, it's like the minute we moved into the big house it all went to shit. That's about the time we started the wedding planning, too." The disappearance of the long talks they'd have on the small porch of the cottage they'd lived in as their house was built the first time. It was on the property they'd bought for the river house, and they'd converted it into a functioning guesthouse. How had they gone from that intimacy to her jilting him? She was awash with emotions too heavy to number. Nothing she wanted to talk to Poppy or anyone about, not yet, maybe not ever. "I've got to get back to the office." She fished around in her designer bag for change.

"Have you decided what you're going to do for a place to live?" Poppy tilted her head. "I mean, if it was up to me you could have the downtown apartment as long as you need it, but Bianca has already rented it out again."

"As she should have." Although Sonja desperately wished she'd been able to secure the efficiency, she truly couldn't afford it. She was lucky Poppy had been able to let her stay there, gratis.

"It's got to be hard, being so close to him after all of this. Are the sparks still there?" Poppy slipped in the kind of quiet, unassuming yet jarring, thought provocation she'd been good at since they'd met as freshman in college.

Sonja placed four quarters on the table and sighed. "Yes."

* * * *

Henry helped himself to his second bourbon after work. He stood at the tiny kitchen counter in the cottage they'd lived in for six months while the house was built. The riverfront property was hauntingly quiet since their breakup. That was about to change when the contractors came in to do the flood repair and restoration. The guesthouse had become his home again, as it was untouched by the flood. At night though, he still found himself wandering around through the ravaged house, facing the memories of what he and Sonja had shared. Wondering how he fucked up so royally.

He carried his drink with him as he walked across the property to the main house, through to the expansive back deck. As he took the wooden steps down to the short pier, he recalled how, only a few weeks ago, his brother had pulled up in one of his eclectic boats and offered the entire wedding party a ride into NOLA to celebrate the upcoming nuptials.

The bite of the liquor hit his tongue, and he savored the burn as he swallowed his drug of choice. Bourbon had been his nectar and he its lovelorn bee as he nursed his aching heart. He grunted out a bitter laugh at the moving water, the current evident in the small eddies that formed around the bank and large tree trunks that floated along as easily as a fiberglass kayak.

How stupid he'd been, to think he'd be lucky in love. To fall for Sonja's act. He'd believed her, thought she'd really fallen in love with him, too. But then she'd changed, right before his eyes. All of the wedding planning replayed much uglier in his memory as he walked himself through each stage of their relationship.

He'd fucked up, yes, forcing Sonja's hand on the wedding. He saw that now. She'd wanted something much more casual, laid-back. Something her family would be comfortable with instead of the over-the-top event he wanted to announce how much he loved her. By the time Deidre showed up as an "extra" guest invited by his parents, it was too late.

Even his family didn't know about the crazy ex in his back pocket. They knew Deidre and knew they'd been engaged, briefly. But they didn't know how batshit crazy she was. Some of it through no fault of her own—Deidre was a spoiled rich girl from way back. Her parents had appeased her every whim, and when she'd met him, she assumed he would, too. When he told her they were done, she'd gone insane with jealousy, rage. She sharpened her stalking skills over the next couple of years, ending in him seeking a restraining order against her.

He'd told Sonja about his short engagement in the early days of their relationship, because he didn't want Sonja to think he was ever holding anything back from her. But he'd held back the crazy stalking parts. The dark memories of feeling he'd never be able to have a normal life again. It'd been a source of pride for him to not tell his parents the full Deidre story—he'd needed to handle it on his own. And part of him had been ashamed that he hadn't seen her coming a country mile away. He'd been a kid back then, comparatively, but there was nothing he'd do differently, looking at it from ten years out. The restraining order had been a step toward his maturity and a way to set a healthy boundary.

Regret gnawed at him. Maybe he should have told Sonja all of it. Every last ugly bit. But shouldn't the woman who loved you accept you completely, no matter what you told her? Or didn't tell her? And while he was certainly guilty of not sharing the entire Deidre past with her, how was it that an ex ended up axing their big day?

There was something else, something she wasn't telling him. He thought maybe his parents had said something to her, made her think twice. But even if they had, it underscored the sad state of their bond if she didn't come to him with her concerns.

It wasn't just the wedding, or the day, or the fact that he'd kept some of his past from Sonja. He'd not fought harder to keep the initial connection they shared alive. He swirled the bourbon in his glass. Working for relationships wasn't his strong suit—he'd proven that with his parents, hadn't he? Instead of fighting them like Brandon and Jena had, he'd ignored what needed to be done. A tug of recrimination forced him from his pity party.

His parents—had he been too willing to overlook their worst character defects because he'd been so desperate to throw the huge society wedding he felt Sonja deserved?

Christ, Sonja was the love of his life. If she wasn't, this wouldn't be so hard. But he could never, ever let her see it. The last thing he ever wanted from the woman who'd jilted him at the altar was pity. Compassion was pushing it, too. And if he didn't have much else, he did still have some fucking pride left.

It'd taken being jilted for him to realize what he'd always feared. He wasn't worthy of Sonja, never had been. The fact that he'd started to believe he was, to the point he'd been slayed by her wedding escape, made him question his sanity.

He wanted nothing from Sonja but for her to go away and let the good memories somehow remain intact, unsoiled by the ugly anger, resentment, and bitterness his runaway bride had left in her wake.

God damn his conscience.

Chapter 5

The next day Henry stayed in the office all afternoon, refusing to leave except for coffee and bathroom breaks. It was one thing to have to work with Sonja on the McNeely case but he wasn't a sadist. Each instance of seeing her in person that he spared himself was worth it. Seeing her again had affected him in more ways than he'd expected. He'd assumed it'd be difficult, that the rage and frustration at her last-minute betrayal would flare, big time. And it had. What he hadn't counted on was their connection.

It was still there. Frayed like a steel cable that's on its last two threads of dozens, sparks arcing about as the strain placed on it waxes and wanes. But the cord between them wasn't completely severed, not yet.

And he couldn't for the life of him figure out why.

A text illuminated his phone, and he felt the cold dread surround his insides. Deidre.

She's still working for you how stupid do you think I am? You need to cut her off completely or I'm going to share some photos.

Fuck. This was the last thing he needed. Of course, Deidre didn't have incriminating photos of him, or of them together in college, but she had a long streak of nasty shenanigans that assured him his worry was justified. She'd make something up. And he shouldn't give a flying shit about Sonja being hurt, but it was more about making sure Deidre got the hell out of his life again.

"Hey, Henry." Rick, their newest attorney, stood in the doorway, his expression neutral. "Got a minute? I'm having a hard time with this part of the McNeely case." Rick was fresh out of law school and, while smarter than anyone else, often needed more expert guidance around more complex cases.

"Can I come to your office in about five minutes? I've got to make a call."

*   *   *   *

An hour later he found Sonja in her office, sipping a can of ginger ale with a straw. The ordinary sight of a woman enjoying a soda was in direct contrast to the fact that it was the woman he'd lost, the woman he'd somehow stopped sharing everything with the minute they began planning the wedding. Ironic that now, after they'd lost everything between them including their house, he was being forced to tell her what might have saved them this pain in the first place. At least some of it.

"You're drinking a soda?"

"Starting over on many fronts."

He liked talking to her about something ordinary. Anything but admitting his volatile ex had been a stupid secret he'd kept from her. "You never drink soda. You gave it up when we moved in together."

"I did. And I wanted one today, so what?" She made a show of shuffling a pile of file folders. "We've spent a lot of time on the McNeely case but I need to go over the Randall account with you, too. I don't think they're going to be able to use a mediator. Too much at stake." She spoke in her usual cool manner, no hint of how emotionally charged the Randall divorce was. Would going through their breakup, while not a divorce but equally significant, shake her off her professional pedestal?

He looked at her, really looked at her. The way her skin had a luminousness to it. Her white sleeveless blouse was snug across her breasts. Nothing unusual, as Sonja had the most beautiful, full breasts. But the top button was about to pop. Shit, he could see the pearl bead that was sewn into the center of her bra.

And she'd left her favorite, body-tight dresses hanging in their closet. As if she didn't need them. Two days ago, when she'd thrown up in the bathroom right next to him.

Holy. Fucking. Shit. Cold sweat beaded on his forehead, and he felt a trickle of it down his neck. He didn't know if he was going to throw up or pass out. Maybe he should take a knee. He sank into the chair in front of her desk instead.

"You're pregnant." He didn't mean to say it so angrily. Didn't mean to say it at all.

Sonja's hand jerked, hitting her files. They flew across her slick desk and knocked over her can of soda. Ginger ale spilled over and down the front of the desk, dripping onto the plush carpet. Sonja jumped up, grabbed a few tissues from the box on the credenza behind her desk and started blotting on her desk, righting the aluminum can. She was leaning over, showing her deeper-than-usual cleavage to advantage, but his gaze didn't stay there. He looked lower, to her midsection. Sonja was all curves but always had a flat stomach. She worked hard to keep it, she said, but he knew for a fact that even when her workload precluded her cherished gym time, her abs remained flat.

Not slightly rounded, pushing against her linen skirt.

How had he missed it?

"Answer me, Sonja." Anger simmered low in his gut, rising into a rolling boil. "Are you pregnant?"

Sonja sat back from trying to mop up the spill without getting too close to him. Her lips parted as she let out a soft sigh, her eyes watery and full of sorrow.

"I planned to tell you on our honeymoon."

"On our—you knew before the wedding?" He pieced things together. The way she'd seemed to lose her energy for the wedding festivities. She was still incredibly happy, or so he'd believed, but not with the usual enthusiasm. "You didn't even sip your beer at the rehearsal dinner." They'd been at the old hometown diner, where beer suited better than wine or cocktails alongside fully dressed po' boys and crawfish étouffée.

He sank into the seat in front of the desk. "So you are? I'm right? You're going to have our child?"

She nodded, slowly. "Yes. I'm pregnant."

"When, when did we, ah..." His ears buzzed.

"Here." A pop of a can, and Sonja shoved a second can of ginger ale into his hands. "Have a sip. I know, it's a shock, isn't it?" It was the most open she'd been with him since she'd fled the wedding.

"We always used protection." They were both adamant that their family wouldn't happen until they could afford it. Until they were sure what they wanted to do career-wise. They still hadn't hammered out whether they'd both continue with the family firm, or if Sonja would break out on her own, doing more pro bono than Boudreaux Law.

"Until we didn't. The time we thought it was impossible for me to get pregnant, so soon after my period." Her soft words, spoken without a hint of regret, reminded him of the day they'd found themselves hot for each other while setting up their new patio furniture in preparation for the upcoming wedding weekend. They'd made love on their deck atop the two-person chaise longue, in view of the river as the sun set. Without a condom.

"But you're on the pill."

"Was. Obviously." She blushed. "It's not one hundred percent, as we both knew. We took a chance, and it happened."

His gaze sought hers, and when their eyes met it was as if they were back there, behind the house, with nothing but joy in front of them. Sonja's eyes reflected the rush of lust that swamped him, making him painfully hard. Her lips parted, and he saw her pink tongue flick out, her signal that she was ready.

Henry was on his feet and around her desk without thought.

"Sonja." He didn't touch her, but she didn't back away, either.

"No, Henry." Her voice was quiet, a soft moan with no conviction of keeping him away. He reached out and lifted her chin.

"I'm not going to, God, Sonja." The words were rough against his dry throat.

She looked at him, her hand on his wrist. But she wasn't trying to take his hand off her face as she stood stock-still in front of him. He felt the shakiness of her exhale, saw the bare vulnerability in her eyes.

"Henry, this isn't enough reason for us to try to go back in time."

She didn't want him anymore, no matter how he was trying to read into her every move, her quaking, her hesitant manner around him. It wasn't from a need she was trying to repress. It was her emotions from the past few weeks and the baby hormones—he'd had enough friends have kids and had heard all about how women turn into heaps of feelings when they get pregnant.

"Trust me. Going back to anything we had is the last thing I want."

* * * *

Henry's words sliced through the temporary sense of shared joy. His eyes had reflected the surprise of finding out he was going to be a father, followed by his obvious pleasure at the thought, Clearly, he'd quickly tamped back any happiness with his current feelings toward her.

"I heard you the first time, Henry. We're through."

He stepped away then, resumed his seat in front of her desk. To her credit Sonja didn't prevaricate or let one single tear well from his brutal honesty. She sat back down in her chair, too, taking a long sip of the ginger ale. How had a common soda become such an elixir?

"I, I never want you to think I'm asking you for anything. Not just with the baby, but...anything." She broke the silence.

"Our attraction's always been there. It's not going to disappear because our commitment to one another has. And I'm sorry if I crowded you. It's my shock, I think."

"No, it won't disappear, you're right." She watched him. He looked surprised, yes, but also a little, no, make that a lot, annoyed. "You haven't said anything about the baby."

"I need some time to process it."

"That's it? You're not going to ask why I've decided to have it? How we're going to raise him or her when we're not together?"

"I don't need to ask those questions, because I know the answers. You're in your early thirties, the usual age that women get serious baby fever, if not sooner. You've got your law degree and license; you can support a child on your own. You may have needed me to help you get pregnant, but you don't need me to help you raise a kid. So why wouldn't you have the baby?"

She tried not to laugh at his recitation of facts. So Henry. "Wow. I have to say I'm surprised. I thought you'd be more shocked, since we were both set on not having kids for a few more years."

"Maybe that was a dumb plan. Sometimes impromptu works best." Impromptu and Henry were not acquainted. Or hadn't been, up to almost three weeks ago.

"So you're okay with me having the baby? Even though we've broken up?" She forced her breathing, told herself his response didn't matter.

"Why wouldn't I be? I'm going to be a dad."

* * * *

Henry would be damned if he let Sonja see him sweat, witness his desire to be in total denial of what they were facing. The need he had for a clean break, a new start, was already being postponed for as long as it took their house to be renovated and sold. As long as Sonja kept working at his father's firm.

But now, now they were bound together forever—by a child. Holy shit.

"I wasn't sure how you'd take it. I knew I needed to tell you, of course." She fiddled with her keyboard, her body language shouting for him to get up and leave her office. Sonja's smug lawyer expression, something he'd treasured when it unnerved courtroom opponents, made him see red.

"Hold on, Sonja. You've already decided to keep the baby. If you hadn't, I trust that you'd have at least told me before you did anything. That said, the bottom line is that you'd have the final say." And he meant it. Did he want a child? Yes. Right now? It wouldn't have been his first choice. But the thought of his baby growing inside her filled him with something he hadn't felt in too long. Hope.

Against all odds, warmth spread through him that he'd thought Sonja's running wedding heels had crushed out forever. He was going to be a father.

"As much as I'd prefer that we both move on, I recognize that we're going to have to come up with a contingency plan of sorts. A way we'll both be able to raise the child with minimal involvement with one another."

"That sounds like the Henry I know. Knew." She offered him a faint smile, and he wished he could rip back the past six, seven months and bare his soul to her. Make her do the same. Just be together, no fancy river house, no wedding to plan, no interference from his parents or Deidre or anything else. But it was too late.

"You don't know me anymore, Sonja. Or maybe I should say that I have no idea who you are any longer."

"Well, that makes it clear. I didn't want you to think that the baby was my way, or a way, of making us be with each other. More than work, I mean." She looked flustered, but his well of compassion for her discomfort was dry. She'd known she was pregnant before the wedding and still ran. He thought he was a contemporary man but for the life of him didn't understand why the baby didn't make her walk up that aisle, even if he hadn't been enough.

"Don't worry about that. We're not. But we're going to have to hash this all out, at some point. Fair?"

She slowly nodded. "Fair." Sonja looked around her desk, at her computer screen. "You know, it's been a long day, and we have an early start tomorrow. I think I'm going to pack it in." She shoved the stack of files into a coral leather tote, dropped in her phone and charger. She looked at him as if she'd expected he'd be gone. "Is there something else you want, Henry?"

"Not at the moment." He got up and left her office, needing space before he blurted out what was racing through his head. Sonja didn't think he'd sit back and watch her have his kid and not help? Not be a full father to the baby?

He clenched his shaking fists, and by the time he reached his office and logged onto his computer, his anger had yielded to determination. He might have been a lousy fiancé, but he was going to be an incredible father. The best. And Sonja was going to have to get over her obvious revulsion of him and deal with it.

First, he needed to convince her why she had to let him fully participate in the baby's life.

Chapter 6

Sonja eased herself out of the tepid bath, grateful it was Saturday morning and she'd been able to sleep in and enjoy the one nice feature in the tiny apartment Poppy had rented and was letting her stay in temporarily. Until the lease ran out next week. Sonja had to find a place to live, but money was tight. She shook her head in the small bathroom. How had she gone from feeling financially sound to being on a shoestring with the drop of a hat? More like a drop of a wedding and the flood. The flood was unpreventable, no one could have seen it hitting when it did. But the wedding... She'd gone along with Henry's big plans, not wanting to disappoint him and now had no emergency funds to draw on.

Thank God for Poppy's offer. At least Sonja had a few nights on her own before she faced either moving back in with her grandmother or finding something she could pay for with her credit card. Neither were options she wanted to look at.

Poppy only used the apartment as a NOLA pied-à-terre, since Brandon had insisted Poppy move in with him. A tug of envy that had nothing to do with her pregnancy made Sonja pause as she toweled off.

She didn't get it. She and Henry had been so careful, so circumspect about their relationship, as hot as it was. They'd taken their time, lived together for a good while before agreeing to become engaged. There was no reason on paper that it shouldn't have worked. That she shouldn't have walked up that aisle instead of running away from it.

Except for the trust issue. And it wasn't the fact that Henry hadn't told her all there was to tell about Deidre, to include the court order he'd filed against her. Sonja had to face the fact that she hadn't earned his trust, either. By never telling him what complete passive-aggressive jerks his parents had been to her, she'd deprived him of the chance to make up his own mind about how they'd proceed. The emotionally abusive ex-girlfriend was a detractor, more stress on the relationship they'd stopped nurturing. They'd done better when they dated, and the early days after they'd moved in together. The tiny cottage had been a true refuge from their complicated work schedules, and they'd been able to focus on what mattered.

How was it that she was looking back on their first year together as if it was the good old days? What was she, eighty? Definitely not eighty. The body reflected in the bathroom mirror was young and full of curves—especially her belly where she was certain she could see a slight bulge, even if the doctor and the books said it was too soon for the baby to show.

Shame flushed heat on her face as she remembered how quickly she'd turned into a throbbing heap of want for Henry yesterday. First at the river house and then in the office, her attraction to him had felt like a neon sign. It had to be the pregnancy hormones.

Shrugging into her favorite soft peach cotton tea, she tugged at the hem and knew it was time to start getting a few larger pieces of clothing. Because her waist was usually so small, relative to her curves, she'd outgrown her basic wardrobe almost immediately. The same clothes that didn't fit when she had her period absolutely didn't fit now, and wouldn't for months after the baby was born.

Henry had been wrong about nine months to go, but she hadn't corrected him. As if telling him that she was already two months pregnant was more than she could bear for him to know.

The doorbell rang, and she quickly patted her tight curls, promising herself she'd condition them later. The doorbell was outside the side door, down a level, and she heard heavy steps ascend the wrought iron stairwell. She wasn't expecting anyone, but maybe the pregnancy and childbirth books she'd ordered had arrived.

Sonja opened the door before the footsteps stopped, figuring the screen door was enough protection if the person turned out to be trouble, which she didn't expect. Her breath hitched at who it was.

"Sonja, hey." Deidre stepped up the last step to the small landing. "I'm so glad you're home! I wanted to have a chance to talk to you alone, after we didn't have any time to talk at Henry's place." *Henry's place?* Right. The river house.

Frissons of warning sparked on her nape, and Sonja held her ground while keeping the screen door shut. It'd be too easy to take her frustration with her life out on Deidre. Not that she had any love lost for the woman who was way too emotionally invested in Henry's life.

God, it hurt to realize that she was one of Henry's exes, too.

"I can't imagine what you and I have to talk about, Deidre." She kept her voice neutral, grateful for all the times she'd counseled not-so-stable clients.

Deidre giggled. "Why, we have Henry to talk about, silly!"

Sonja wasn't silly, and she wasn't going to talk about anyone with Deidre. But she didn't want to stir up Deidre's crazy part, either.

"I'm sorry, but Henry and I are no longer together. You'll have to address your concerns to him."

"But I can't, Sonja." Deidre spoke to her as if they'd known one another for years. Which in a sick, twisted way they had. She'd always been a part of Henry that he'd never shown to Sonja. "I don't want him to worry about me. I'll admit, I did go off the rails back when we were engaged and we had to end it. It tore me up that I had to break it off with Henry. The man was so sad. But it was for the best. And it looks like that's happened to him again. You do understand that you and Henry were never meant to be, right?" Deidre looked at her, her head tilted at an annoying enough angle that it reminded Sonja of a Chihuahua bobblehead. Without the cute.

"Fill me in on that, Deidre?"

The other woman's face fell for a split second, offering Sonja an unguarded glimpse of a spoiled brat. "It would be easier to have this conversation sitting down." She looked past Sonja and into the living room, her obvious fish for an invitation downright creepy. Sonja's compassion only went so far.

"I'm sorry but I'm on my way out." A lie.

"Why don't I come back when you're available?"

"Honestly, Deidre? As I've already said, I don't see that we have anything to say to one another."

Deidre's perfectly made-up face screwed into a scowl. "You'll regret this, trust me." In an abrupt move, she turned and stalked down the stairs, her tiny frame taut with unexpressed anger.

Sonja watched her through the screen door for a minute before she walked out onto the wrought iron balcony to see better. She made a mental note of the vehicle Deidre got into, looked at the plates before the car disappeared down the old bricked street. Attorney attention to detail was something she never let go. She wasn't worried about Deidre—the woman wasn't a sociopath from what she'd pieced together. Just a spoiled single child who'd never grown up. And never gotten over Henry.

As soon as she was sure Deidre had driven off, she went back inside, shutting and locking her door. She tapped into her phone, saving Deidre's license plate, make, and model. Her hands shook as she did so, and this time she willingly admitted the strong reaction was due to her pregnancy. And not the pregnancy hormones per se but the fact that she was pregnant, was carrying a tiny human being who counted on her to keep both of them safe. It was one thing for Deidre to pull a stunt like this on her, as she saw Sonja as the woman who'd broken Henry's heart. And now, it was clear she saw Sonja as the woman who had been between her and Henry. Unbeknownst to Deidre, she'd inadvertently threatened Sonja's unborn child. Sonja wasn't able to shake the wave of protective sensations that made her hands shake. Since figuring out that her period wasn't late due to stress but that she was indeed pregnant, her emotions had been all over the place, but these feelings of primal protectiveness had blossomed as each day, each week, passed. And while her head knew that Deidre posed no threat and was gone, for now, Sonja was frozen with the strength of her feelings.

This was full-on maternal rage. Without giving herself time to think or convince herself why she shouldn't do it, she acted on instinct.

She called her baby daddy.

* * * *

"She's a pain in the ass, Sonja. You don't ever have to open the door to her again, and we're going to file a restraining order against her, for you." Henry sat on the small lavender love seat, dwarfing the apartment with his lean height. He'd come right over, and so far hadn't slammed her with one iota of his anger from the wedding.

"I don't know about a restraining order, yet. You've already got one against her, and she's still come back. Wouldn't a letter of warning be enough? And while you're at it, how about telling me what you should have years ago?" Before they'd planned a wedding and she'd had to accept how fucking stupid she'd been. "Because it's not about just you and me anymore. This is about keeping our baby safe."

Henry's face paled. As it actually grew whiter than it normally was, she couldn't help it. She reached out and placed her hand on his forearm. She knew what it was like to figure out that someone else depended on you—a helpless little being. Their baby.

His expression grew more pinched, and she sensed he was fighting for words. She swallowed and refused to budge. No matter how much touching him scorched her, or made her realize how much she'd given up.

She'd turned in all her chips when she'd fled her wedding.

"I'm freaked out, Sonja. You're carrying my child, and I'm not sure how to act anymore. All I want to do is, is..." He ran his fingers through his hair.

"Protect him or her? The baby?"

His eyes grew wide before he put his game face back on. "Yes."

She leaned back, needing to break the physical contact before she forgot what their new truth was. Two adults who were going to be raising a child together. Working together for the time being, until they were each on sound financial footing. But not as a couple.

"I get it." She let out a shaky laugh. "When Deidre was here I wanted to throttle her. She wasn't doing anything unexpected for what I know of her, but she was on my turf, on the baby's turf."

"I mean it, Sonja. Don't open the door to her again."

"Have you ever tried to talk it out with her? Just face her down with the facts? I had a couple of boyfriends who didn't get a clue until I confronted them."

"And that worked?" His doubt echoed around the room.

"For the most part. One of the guys couldn't be shut down to leave me alone until I completely blocked him." He'd been one of her brother's teammates. She'd relied fully on her sibling to talk sense into him.

"You're talking about the football player, right?"

"Yes." Anger stole in. "I told you about my exes."

"Sue me—I didn't give you the total deal on Deidre. I thought she was done messing around with me. And frankly, I think she will be, again. This is a diversion for her. I found out through a classmate that she's just been through a bad divorce from her second husband."

"She clearly wants you to be her third."

"We haven't been involved in over a decade. There's nothing there for her to hang onto." He set his theory out as if it were one of his cases.

"You were more than 'involved.' You were engaged to her. In love with her, too, right?" He'd never said that, but she knew him. Had known him. Henry would never commit to a woman he didn't love. Commitment wasn't his problem—it was in fully revealing himself where Henry shut down.

"Of course I thought I was in love with her—I was twenty fucking years old." As if he read her mind and wanted to keep his wall up, he stood and walked around to the back of the sofa, where he paced in the tiny space between the sitting area and kitchen table. "You're right. I should have told you sooner, but it wasn't a huge secret. We met in college, in psychology class. How's that for irony? The dating came easy. She was the perfect girlfriend." He looked at her, his blue eyes uneasy. "The sex between us was the best I'd had until then. Nothing like you and—" He stopped himself, stared out the window. "Before Deidre, it was catch-as-catch-can, you know, college. She was big on us spending every spare minute together. It should have suffocated me, looking back." He walked to the window that overlooked the colonial New Orleans street. "Some things are perfect on paper. We were both from the same area, both looking forward to more school—me law and her med school. It was clear that we weren't going to make it for the long haul, and I never should have proposed to her. I was trying to please everyone back then."

Sonja knew he was talking about his parents, too, but didn't press him. The guilt that had gnawed at her since she'd fled the cathedral would have to wait.

"She's obviously successful." She knew that Deidre worked in a private pediatric practice in town, but that was about it. A large part of her wanted to keep digging, but all Deidre had done, besides showing up on her doorstep uninvited, was help to light the fuse that got Sonja running from a wedding that she knew was for the wrong motives.

Marrying someone you love had to be for the choice of commitment, not to fulfill either partner's wedding fantasies or expectations. She'd done all of the above up until twenty minutes before their scheduled vows.

"That's just it. She's got a great career, she's a good person, except for this inability to accept it when things don't go her way." Henry appeared truly puzzled. "It's as if a switch flipped in her again when my folks invited her to the wedding."

"Because you hadn't heard from her in a long while?"

"I've run into her here and there, and even saw that she was engaged a year back. But that must have not ended well, and she's back in her stalking mode."

"I wouldn't call her a stalker as much as a nuisance, but you'd know better than me on that one."

"That's the piece that still stings the most. I should have seen it coming. We dated for a year, were engaged for eight months before I put it all together senior year."

"It's clear she won over your parents."

"My parents don't know shit. To this day they have no clue how bad it got with her. How close I came to..." He stopped. His back was to her as he remained at the window, hands on the window frame. He turned toward her, and the anguish on his face sent shocks of concern through her midsection.

"She started by needing to know where I was at all times. I chalked it up to jealousy. It wasn't uncommon in our crowd, with other couples.

We were young and immature. But then she'd show up wherever I was, in classes and then where I worked the year between college and law school."

"You worked at your father's office when he moved it to Baton Rouge, I thought?"

"I interned there, on and off, but never took a penny from him for that. I worked two part-time jobs to save enough so that my law school years would be a little easier without having to ask my parents for a handout."

Surprise radiated from her head to her toes. In all their time together Henry had never mentioned this. "You've never told me anything about that time." Why hadn't she noticed?

"We haven't talked as much about our pasts as most couples."

"Wow, that's the first real thing you've said to me since...before." She didn't want to bring up the jilting scene. If it was raw for her it had to be oozing pain for Henry.

"By the time I met you I was free of Deidre and hoped to keep it that way. I was psyched about a new start." He let out a short laugh. "I'd planned to have my share of women, date around for the next ten years."

"And then you met me, what, five years later?"

Something flared in his eyes, but he quickly tamped it down. "We met and I have no regrets, save for the last year or so."

"It wasn't just when we started planning the wedding, Henry. We never bothered to do the housework on our relationship that most people do."

"Do you think it's because we saw one another every day, all day at work?" His words reminded her that what had been thrilling when they'd been a couple was now excruciating. She dreaded each time she'd see him in the office, wanting to simply work and ignore the rest of the world.

She stood up. "I need something to drink. I can offer you coffee or tea, ginger ale or water. I don't have anything stronger since I obviously won't be indulging anytime soon." He'd never drunk much more than a cocktail or beer once or twice a week, so she knew he wasn't looking for alcohol on a Saturday morning. But the circumstances were grim enough that she wouldn't have been surprised if he'd asked for something stronger.

"I'll have a glass of water, thanks."

She walked the half dozen steps to the kitchen counter and pulled a glass from the single cupboard. His footsteps reverberated through the wooden floorboard, and she tensed before turning around.

He was right next to her, filling her senses with his scent, his concern, his sheer masculinity. Goddammit.

"Henry, I can't, I can't go through this every time we're together. The hating stuff."

"I'm doing the best I can, Sonja." The ragged edge of his voice reminded her that he'd been wronged. This wasn't all about her.

"I can't say I'm sorry for what I did, either. Am I sorry I waited so long to see we weren't going to make it? That I left you in front of our family and friends like that? That I disappointed our families and missed out on a great bash with our dearest friends? Yeah, I'm sorry for all of that. But not for the leaving part. I had no business in that church with you."

"Maybe you were the brave one, for both of us." His words stunned her but not as much as his fingers, which he lifted to her cheek.

Sonja wanted to turn her face into his hand, kiss his palm, nudge him into a caress.

As if nothing had passed between them.

Chapter 7

Sonja's eyes were bright, her lips moist, and she emphasized the latter by licking her lower lip. The brief peek of her pink tongue made his hand shake as much as his dick hard. It'd always been like this with them, between them. The insta-lust as he'd jokingly referred to it. Except he had no recourse for it now.

Henry allowed himself to lift his hand and touch her cheek for a split second, allowed himself the soft feel of her skin before he dropped his arm and took a step backward. A sharp pain wrenched his back as he banged into the retro refrigerator, its handle kidney-height. "Christ. Could this place be any smaller?"

"It suits me." She handed him the water, and he reveled in the way her slim fingertips touched his. Not that he'd tell her.

"It's not good enough, Sonja. Our—the river house has to be rebuilt and won't be available for at least three months, minimum. But you have to live in another spot that's safer for you." He walked back to the tiny sofa, crouching so that a beam wouldn't hit his head.

"This is very safe."

"Not after dark, on weekends. Not when Deidre knows where you live. And how long can you rent this, anyway?"

"The fact that she knew where I live was a little unsettling, I have to admit. The only way she'd know I'm here is by following me." Sonja's chin jutted, and he hid a smile. No woman was stronger than she, and he almost felt sorry for Deidre. Sonja must have given Deidre her classic look from hell. He'd been on the receiving end of it enough times to know how uncomfortable it was.

"Trust me, if she followed you here, she's been keeping an eye on you for a while now. Like you observed, she's not dangerous but annoying. No boundaries. Typical Deidre." He gulped his water. He'd have to talk to Deidre, get Sonja off her radar. "But you're not answering my question about the rent here. How are you going to afford it?"

"Deidre wants you." Sonja kept ignoring the apartment question. "As far as she's concerned, you're single again. She saw it firsthand at the wedding." She paused. "I mean, the un-wedding."

"That's what you're thinking of it as?" He looked at her, noting how she grimaced, caught. He grinned. "It fits, doesn't it? The un-wedding?"

"It's as if it were doomed from the start." Her dour expression stilled him.

"What was doomed, Sonja?"

Her eyes filled with tears. "The wedding. Us."

Something tightened in his chest, as if he were bracing against her verbal spear.

"I thought we had a great thing going." He couldn't keep his anger at her out of his voice, didn't even try.

"When it was all fun and great sex, sure we did. When we were winning cases left and right, building your father's firm into what it is today, yeah, that was incredible." She put her ginger ale down on a tiny coaster. "But we never looked at the long haul."

"I'd say buying a house together was a long-term commitment."

"The house was maybe the smartest thing we did."

Of course, now they had to rebuild, then sell. His gut hurt at the thought of letting the river house go.

"The house." Not being together. Not her choosing him.

"Henry. Face the facts. You and I are too high risk in the long run. You want to maintain the status quo in law, with your family. I want to push it to almost all pro bono cases."

"That's a cop-out, Sonja. There's more you're not telling me."

She stood up. "Maybe. But I can't deal with all of this right now. I'm tired, and I need to rest. I'm sorry I called you—I overreacted about Deidre."

"No, I'm glad you did." He stood, not wanting to leave but wanting to be a burden to her even less. And he hated how quickly his anger at her for jilting him dissipated in her presence. Nothing he'd been able to count on was steady anymore, as if his life, his family, his relationship with Sonja had all been built on bayou swamp ground.

"Why do you think Deidre really came back, Henry?"

"I don't know. She sure as hell didn't know the wedding was going to happen, not until she got the invitation my parents sent. I'm not on social media like you are, and you aren't in the same circles as she'd be. That must have been its own little thrill for her, to get that invitation." He couldn't keep the bitterness out of his tone. Fuck it. If Sonja wanted to know it all, here it was. "There's something else you don't know—you need to know."

Sonja's liquid brown eyes were steady, her body totally receptive to him. He hated knowing that in one more breath, one sentence, this would be the last time she was ever so receptive to him.

"While we were engaged, it was the end of senior year, Deidre got pregnant. We were both surprised, or at least I thought she was—now I think it was all part of her plan to lock me in—but decided we'd deal with it. Start our family early. She lost the baby very early on. She miscarried."

"And that's why you didn't leave her sooner. You felt guilty."

"Yes. I would have loved and raised any child I had, at least I hope I would have. Who knows? I was an immature jerk then."

"Give yourself a break. You were in college."

"I know that, but it's never erased my guilt." He paused. He didn't have to tell her the rest but owed it to her. "I still feel it at times. When you and I were together and things were going really well, I'd remember how relieved I'd felt when I broke up with Deidre, and I wondered if I deserved to be happy."

"Why on earth would you feel guilty? Miscarriages happen. Breakups are part of life." She placed one hand on his back, between his shoulders, and her free hand over her lower belly as if to ward off what had happened to his previous child. It was typical of Sonja to multitask her compassion, both for him and her child. He marveled at how protective a mother she already was.

"My guilt wasn't over the miscarriage, Sonja. It was over my relief when she miscarried that I didn't have to stay with her anymore. I didn't owe her anything but the truth at that point."

"And she didn't want the truth from you." Sonja's hand went still on his back. "That would be harsh, being dumped after losing a baby."

"I didn't do it immediately. And I tried to make a go of it again, hoped that a fresh start of sorts would make a difference."

"But it didn't for Deidre." No censure in Sonja's words, just an honest declaration.

"No. I thought we were past it, though, when she got married the first time, and then the second. I heard about it through the alumni news and grapevine, basically. I never reached out to her again—I'm happy she moved on and frankly didn't want to ever risk stirring up the pot again."

"Understandable."

"But it seems that this was the wrong time for my parents to decide to invite her to the wedding, and it's triggered her. Along with her recent divorce."

"That's the thing I don't understand, Henry. You didn't tell me you were giving your folks those extra invitations, no biggie. We were so slammed with work and wedding stuff, it was the least of my problems. But didn't you ask your parents who they were going to invite?"

"It didn't occur to me. Like I said, I only gave them a few. It wouldn't have made a difference in the head count, for catering purposes. Besides, the invites all had the RSVP cards." He looked at her, not wanting to be a jerk but Sonja had been the exclusive handler of all RSVPs. It was one way they'd kept the planning more streamlined.

"We did a good job dividing up the tasks, didn't we?" She looked wistful, as if maybe she hadn't minded the wedding planning as much as he'd assumed.

"We make a good team. In the courtroom and out." The words left his lips before he took the time to think. Fortunately Sonja appeared distracted by her phone, scrolling the screen.

* * * *

Sonja listened to Henry with her lawyer self, noting how what transpired a decade ago was relevant to Deidre's behavior now. Her heart felt every shred of misery, anguish, fear, and regret that Henry had kept to himself. Emotions he hadn't trusted her with when they were together, she reminded herself.

She withdrew her hand from his back where she'd been rubbing, giving him her support. "That's in your past, Henry. And it sounds like Deidre might be reasonable, once she faces the truth." Although the truth was up to Henry now, not Sonja. Exhaustion washed over her. "If you can arrange a sit-down with her—"

"That's fucking not going to happen."

"Well, that's your choice. Look, I've got to—"

"I'm not leaving until we establish where you are going to live once this place is rented out again."

She stared at him. "'We?' And how do you know about this place renting out again? And it doesn't matter—I can move in with my grandmother."

He laughed. "As bad as it might be between us, I know you don't want to go back to living with your grandma. You two are too much alike."

She glowered at him, unable to speak.

"Gus told me—Poppy told him."

"There's only one way in here—that door. I'm safe." For the next six days, anyway.

"And there's only one bedroom." He looked at the love seat. "I can't sleep on this."

"I don't need a guard, Henry."

"Did you have a chance to look at the guesthouse when you went back to see the flood damage?"

"No. I'd only been there a few minutes when you showed up."

"It's intact. The flood line didn't go as far as the cottage. It's where I've been staying."

"Oh. I thought you were at Brandon's." His brother had a guesthouse, too, a much bigger and more modern one. "Poppy never said either way, which I took as a privacy thing."

"We're both strapped for cash right now. None of our investments should be touched, and our liquid assets were all in the wedding, honeymoon, and now the remaining funds are going to go to the renovation. You're pregnant with a child we'll both raise. We need time to save money so that we can each live in a decent place for the baby. With the private bedroom and sleeper sofa, we can both fit in the cottage. It'll be tight, but it's doable." As he spoke she saw the tiny, cramped house they'd already survived six months in when the main house was constructed. What had been romantic and very doable only two years ago would be hell at the moment.

Not for the reasons she'd give Henry if pressed—too much together time after their breakup, too hard to see one another after the pain they'd tossed at one another like live grenades. No, what made living with Henry in the cottage so difficult was the memories. Memories of their cherished time there already and of the future memories that would never happen.

"Do you really think the cottage will work for us? Now?" She already knew what he'd say but needed time to think. There was no way she was going to give up what little freedom she had, even if it meant going to live with Grandma. Although Grandma hadn't rushed to tell her she was welcome back there, either. She'd need a bigger place after the baby came, too. There was still time. If only the homeowner's had covered the entire rebuild!

Time was growing short.

"We have to work together whether we want to or not, Sonja. The house has to be rebuilt so that we can sell it and cash out, if that's what we decide. I know you're strapped for cash flow, as am I, since we poured so much into the wedding and decorating the house for the garden party." He said it so matter-of-factly. Clearly he'd not been as deeply distressed as she by their breakup. Or he was just being a guy.

"You've wasted no time figuring it all out."

He had the nerve to appear as if her words hurt him before he stood up and walked back into the kitchen, as far from her as possible. "Forgive me if I assumed you wanted what I do—to liquidate any of our shared assets."

Ouch.

"So the house... I thought the insurance company would come in, hire contractors, and they'd repair it?"

"Not quite. First, what we're covered for isn't black-and-white. There's flood insurance, sure, but that can't overlap the homeowner's, which won't pay for natural disasters. There's a bright spot, though. As you know, while you and I were in law school, my brother was building boats and had his shipbuilding facility constructed from the ground up. He has a network of contractors and contacts who can get the house back in shape sooner than the average predicted time. I've already met with them. They've come in lower per square foot than most estimates in our neighborhood, too."

"You've already had estimates?"

"I couldn't reach you for two fucking weeks, Sonja. What did you expect me to do?"

* * * *

Her eyes widened, and he regretted losing his cool, but it was that or cave and tell her the truth. That he'd had to get busy with something or he'd lose his mind. That his heart couldn't handle losing her, and yet he wasn't going to try to force her hand in anything. They'd always been a shared-power couple—complete equals.

"I guess I thought you'd be as upset as I was that our dreams had shattered." Soft but sure, Sonja wasn't holding back her truth even now when she was more vulnerable than ever. Whether she knew it or not.

"My emotions are beside the point. What's important right now is that you're safe, the baby's safe, and that you both stay safe. Living with your grandmother won't cut it."

"I'll find another place."

"The cottage is perfect, Sonja. There's plenty of room for both of us, and you'll have the bedroom to yourself for complete privacy."

"What, wait, what do you mean 'the both of us?' You can stay at Brandon's now, right?"

"I could, but it's getting cramped with Poppy there all the time. They're like two goddamned lovebirds." His comment elicited a curve on her lips, and he felt as though he'd climbed Mount Everest. It was the first time he'd sparked her humor since she'd come back.

"That wouldn't be the best thing to have to be exposed to, after what we—you've been through." Her contrite admission floored him.

He planned to remind her that he'd been the one wronged, that she'd jilted him. Unlike the way he'd felt those first hellish three days after she'd run, however, he had a new awareness that he'd had a role to play in their failed wedding, too. Since before they'd moved in together.

* * * *

"I don't get it. You're acting like you're the one who was jilted." Poppy's amber eyes nailed her to her wrought iron bistro chair for two full heartbeats before her expression softened. "I'm not judging here, Sonja. But as close as we are, I don't know where your head's at right now."

"Yeah, well, having mind-blowing sex day in and day out doesn't leave you a lot of time to worry about me." Sonja couldn't keep the note of envy out of her voice. "I'm happy for you and Brandon, boo. You know I am."

"You miss sex and someone to cuddle with though, right?"

"Hmmm." Sonja shoved her half-eaten plate of pancakes away and sipped on the ice water that had replaced her morning coffee. "I haven't been a very good friend to you lately. You haven't even given me all of the details on how you and Brandon finally got together. Besides the storm."

"There'll be time enough to talk about me and Brandon. You haven't answered my question."

"It's complicated."

"Of course it is. I've never known you to make a simple decision."

Sonja laughed. "You do know me well." She didn't point out that it was because they shared a common bond of having suffered from low self-esteem because of childhood family chaos. Sonja's was her father's stepping out on her mother, and Poppy's was from an abusive boyfriend her mother had dated when her parents suffered a brief but brutal break in their marriage. Sonja and Poppy had discovered each other's trauma secrets after they'd become fast friends freshman year in college. Their personal histories were so understood between them they were unspoken.

"So?"

"So. Henry was, is, the most fascinating man I've ever met. That hasn't changed." If anything, she had a new appreciation for him after he'd revealed his history with Deidre. "It would be too easy to blame it all on his parents and their racism. Believe me, I thought about it. But how many parents aren't the least bit bigoted? My mom and stepdad were surprised about Henry and me, for sure, but never had a problem with the interracial deal. But my grandmother? Shit, she sounded like a bigot of the highest order when I told her I wanted to marry Henry. Grandma, the one who did marches all over the South in the sixties."

"And then there's the fact that *you* didn't want to marry him."

"True. I was happy living together and would have let that go on for a lot longer. I've never been one to need formal tradition or any of its frills. Why would I when my biological dad, a preacher for God's sake, stepped out on my mother?"

"That's complete bullshit, Sonja. You're an attorney—you thrive on legal and justice and all that. And you totally know that each situation and relationship is individual. Your mom and dad were different people, in a different place when they had their speed bump."

"Speed bump?" Sonja blinked. Poppy was right. What had seemed total devastation all those years ago was now but a rough spot.

"Uh huh." Poppy stared at her with those big eyes.

Sonja couldn't help it, she laughed.

"You are something, Poppy. What Henry and I had was beyond just and fair. It was wonderful. And then he decided we deserved a big fancy wedding, and I believed him. And he told me that he'd had a fiancée at one point, they'd had an ugly breakup where she refused to accept it was over. Years ago, in college. And of course, he seriously dated another girl, you know, Kelly. You met her at the dock party." The reminder of the weekend made her stop, swallow.

"Why are you so hung up on Henry's dating history? I get the Deidre stuff, but he asked *you* to marry him."

"Yes, but I feel he should have told me the whole picture about her. He told me that he'd been engaged to her but he never mentioned that she had caused him so much trouble after their breakup. She stalked him for over a year after he called off that engagement." She bit her lip. "His parents invited her to our wedding. I do believe him on that—he had no idea she was going to show up. When I saw her coming in, while I was getting ready, I almost left then. It was when you were buttoning up my dress and we were watching the guests arrive through the side church window. I saw him come out of the church, and they embraced one another. From where I was, it looked like a full-on kiss." She realized now that Deidre had staged the whole thing, and the woman's connection to Henry had clearly been one-sided. But in the moment, with her emotions already stretched so thin, it had been all she needed to bolt.

"You never said a thing, Sonja. What were you going to do, swallow it for the rest of your life like you do with your uglier emotions?"

"Does that surprise you, boo?" She'd always called Poppy the Cajun endearment. Only Poppy could see through her so easily. And Henry.

"No. You were wound capital-T tight that day. The whole few days leading up to it. And you hadn't talked to me on the phone much for the month before. I chalked it up to my own problems, being caught up in them." Poppy's wry grin underscored the hell she'd been through with her ex.

They shared a quick laugh. "Yeah, you had your social media war going on."

"That's in my past." The dreamy look was back on Poppy's face. "If I'd only known then what I've found out with Brandon."

"Okay, enough lovebird stuff. Some of us are back out in the wilds."

"You're not lost, Sonja. You're just trying to find your way back."

"Back to what?"

Poppy shook her head and looked pointedly at her half-empty cappuccino. It was a classic move her best friend used when she refused to add her opinion to anything. Clearly, Poppy believed it was Sonja's business to figure out. Where she was going, where her life was headed.

She had no freaking clue.

Chapter 8

"You don't want to hear it, Sonja, but like I told you two years ago, there's nothing but trouble marrying a man from such a fussy family." Grandma Edwina sniffed as she snipped mint for the iced tea brewing in a huge jar on the front porch. They stood on Grandma's expansive backyard lawn, at the edge of one of her many flower beds. She'd placed huge terra-cotta pots of herbs all over the beds, to include the one sprouting tall stalks of spearmint.

"The same could be said of you with Pappy. He was nothing according to your family, and you were going to college. A Catholic school, to boot." Their family was steeped in Creole, but somewhere along the line a Bosco had converted from Catholicism to Baptist.

Grandma laughed in that sideways grin that Sonja loved. "My family was more angry with me at the time. There I was, the daughter of a preacher, going to a Catholic college! But I was determined to go to school. That didn't change how much I loved my Daniel, though." Her smile grew wistful for a brief moment before she pointed her garden shears at Sonja. "But we were from the same place, we had the same idea of what family meant. And your granddaddy was Baptist, too. From what you've told me and what we've seen, Henry grew up in a very repressed home."

Sonja sighed. "He did. And he's turned out to be a wonderful man." At least she'd thought he had.

"If he's so wonderful why did you leave him waiting on you at the altar in the downtown church of all places? What I really wonder is why did you even bother to plan that big fussy wedding?" Grandma's opinion was etched in the lines on her face. She thought Sonja had made her own problems.

"The first reason is that he hadn't been completely honest with me." As she said it, she knew it wasn't true. He'd been trying to protect her. And now there was more to protect, more to consider forging a better friendship going forward. Their baby. She wasn't ready to tell Grandma about the baby. Not yet. She hadn't told her mother or father. "The second is that I wanted to make him happy, too. He was so excited at the thought of our wedding being big and grand, a real New Orleans event. I got carried away with it."

"Sounds like it's more than a conversation can solve." Grandma walked up the steps of her huge wraparound porch, and Sonja followed, her hope for a similar house on the water shattered since the storm. Since before the rains, if she were honest. Since she'd stopped talking to Henry. "And for the record, there are a lot of other ways to celebrate a wedding in New Orleans." As if Grandma were reaching inside her soul and plucking her heartstrings, Sonja realized that Henry might have agreed to a smaller, more intimate affair. Like he'd agreed to having the rehearsal dinner in the bayou back road restaurant. But she'd never asked him if they could give up the cathedral wedding. It hadn't occurred to her at the time.

"Grandma, did you ever have a time when you couldn't explain it all to Pappy? When you weren't sure you knew what you wanted?"

Grandma sipped the tea, a sprig of mint floating on top. "I'm not sure I know what you're getting at, Sonja."

"I want to be able to trust Henry, Grandma, but he didn't tell me everything about his past. I don't know if I can ever trust him again." Or herself. Was she willing to open up to him, share all her thoughts, tell him what his parents had said to her?

"So it's not about his parents, or anything they said to you at the rehearsal dinner? Or about that ex-girlfriend who looked a little off-kilter?"

"No. I mean, maybe a little. They, they said some things to me that made it clear they'd disown him if I went through with the marriage. I never told him, and besides, it's not the real reason I ran. It's easy to blame it on all of that, but it's not the truth. Henry isn't his parents. And his ex is a selfish bitch, but she didn't end our wedding. I did." Because she didn't trust Henry, but what about trusting herself?

"My whole point about the culture, race, and religion issues is only that I'm trying point out that you're taking a tough road here, even in the twenty-first century. I'm not against you marrying Henry. I want you to be happy, and you seemed very happy with him leading up to the day you started getting measured for a wedding gown." Sonja's breath hitched. Holy crap, Grandma didn't miss a thing. "If you think you have trust issues, maybe it's time to take a look into your past to see why you don't trust when you should."

"You mean Daddy and all the church business?"

"Uh huh." Grandma Edwina was Sonja's rock and had been all through her tumultuous high school years when her father had an affair with one of the church members while her mother was working hard to raise Sonja and her sister. Her mother had stepped out, too, bringing home a man who'd attempted to molest Sonja. She and her brother had fought him off and gotten him out of their house. Her parents had forgiven one another, and to her father's credit he'd been a model husband ever since, but Sonja had never forgiven him for hurting her mother. Or for the heartache that it had brought into the house.

Edwina Bosco had been a high school teacher and principal for over forty years. In her retirement she was more active than someone decades younger. She was everything Sonja aspired to.

"How did you manage working and having kids, Grandma?" Regret immediately hit her gut. Grandma would know.

Sharp pecan-hued eyes on her. Grandma had the grace to not look at her stomach. "You do what you have to. I had help from my sisters and your grandpappy's family."

"Mmm." Sonja sipped her tea, careful to dilute it with tons of ice cubes. The baby didn't need caffeine. She started to giggle.

"Want to let me in on it, child?"

"You knew the day of the wedding, didn't you?"

"No." Grandma didn't pretend to not know what Sonja was talking about. "I knew at the rehearsal dinner, when your hush puppies came."

Sonja kept laughing. "I thought it was wedding nerves." She'd known she was pregnant by then but didn't believe morning sickness could start so early along.

"I knew it was more. You were too happy about marrying Henry up until then. Or weren't you, honey?"

"I was happy with Henry, and I wish I could still be. But he's got to learn he can trust me completely, and I don't think it's possible he'll do it in time."

"You mean by when the baby comes?"

"No. I mean by when my heart can't take it anymore. It's too hard and hurts too much. I want, I need the baby to start life in a peaceful way. Not with the uncertainty of whether their mom and dad are going to stay together."

"So that's it, you've decided?"

"That Henry and I are through? Yes. As far as anything permanent between us. Romantically."

"Sonja, you and Henry will always be connected with that child. There won't be a day he doesn't come into your thoughts, not while you're raising a son or daughter you conceived together." Grandma grew quiet.

"What, Grandma?"

"Don't throw Henry away just yet. It's a miracle if he's even talking to you, after you left him like that."

"But he lied to me." By omission. Just as she had done with her pregnancy. And his parents' threats.

"Lied or was trying to protect you the best way he knew how?"

* * * *

Grandma's words still rang in Sonja's mind as she stared at Henry, her heart pounding from the exertion of unloading her belongings into the guesthouse.

"You didn't pare down anything, did you?" His tone was calmer than the words felt as they hung between them in the small cottage. And the unspoken, undeniable sexual tension that seemed to ooze out of every crevice in the humble dwelling.

It's just the memories of before. She sucked in a breath and willed her body to stop humming around Henry.

Her belongings were piled into the middle of the guest cottage's small sitting area, atop the pullout sofa bed that Henry insisted would be his for the duration. She'd already brought in the few kitchen utensils and placed them in the single cupboard. Somehow they had to find room for her clothes.

"How did an entire family live in this space?" Sonja looked over the tiny room, seeing past the contemporary finishing they'd added at considerable cost to the two-century-old bricks that made the foundational walls of the guesthouse. "The original deed had the first family in this house as nine." Husband, wife, seven kids. She shook her head.

"People do what they have to do, Sonja." His annoyed tone rankled her.

She was getting tired of wondering if every single damn emotion was real or a by-product of her pregnancy hormones. At this point it didn't matter as she swore the walls were closing in on them.

"This is crazy. We're going to be on top of one another."

"You used to beg for that." Said as he'd always done, with quick wit. But no sparks of humor in his eyes, no playful slap on her ass. Another reminder of what she'd thrown away. Correction. What they'd both lost.

"You never complained." She froze, stunned at how quickly she'd been willing to fall back into their banter. "I don't want to do this." She motioned between them. "Those days are over. I don't expect you to ever forgive me for jilting you, but you're going to have to come up with another way to get under my skin. Sexual flirting is out."

He stared at her in open-mouthed shock. "Who are you? And in case you've forgotten, not every time we flirted led to the bedroom."

"Apparently we each have parts of ourselves we haven't shared." She wasn't in the mood to discuss how she'd been the more subtle one in their sex life. She never had a problem being the aggressor or initiating, but as much as she was an extrovert in her daily life, Sonja was quiet and reverent in her sex life. It was deep for her. Henry knew that. He was more shy in public but an absolute animal in bed. A very capable, expert animal at that. The too familiar pool of heat landed between her legs, and she leaned against the tiny kitchen counter, trying to will her horniness away. The flare of awareness in Henry's eyes only pissed her off more.

"Knock it off, Henry. You want to do this, protect the baby and work on the house reconstruct together? Fine. I've agreed to it. I'm here, goddammit. But you've got to agree to some ground rules or I'm out."

"You're not out until we have the house finished and an agreement on how we're raising our kid." Grim, determined, unyielding. Reminding him of why she was here obviously slaked his desire, because his playful mood vanished.

She wasn't sure how she felt about this side of him. Although the honesty in his response was...refreshing.

"What?" He noticed her change in mood, too.

"I'm sorry, Henry. If we'd figured out we weren't talking enough, communicating effectively, even a couple months before the wedding, we wouldn't be in this predicament. We would have gotten our security deposits back."

"There's no way to know what we would have done."

"We're two of the smartest people I know, and we're not the first couple to break up and raise a baby together."

"Maybe you're right. It's been a lot to take in, finding out you're pregnant after you called it quits, and now Deidre's shenanigans." His voice was calmer, and she was relieved to see some of the tension ease out of his face, his shoulders. As if they were still connected and his pain was hers, too. It made her all the more reluctant to admit she had a lot more to share with him than he expected.

"It'll work out, Henry."

* * * *

Henry didn't agree that it would all work out, but it seemed they'd declared a kind of truce for now. He groaned as he watched the most infuriating woman in the world unpack her possessions. "Where do you think all of those clothes are going?"

She shot him a grin, and he wanted to call foul. Keeping her smiles to herself had to be part of the ground rules. Worse, his dick instantly got hard from her un-flirting. "I have a rollaway rack in my car. Let me go get it."

"Give me your keys, and I'll get it." Anything to get out of here before she saw that she still turned him on. At least in the office they had work as a buffer. He'd just listened to her talk about ground rules and here he was, hard as a dog on a leash. He fought to maintain control of his emotions and not for the first time wondered who the hell was pregnant. He vacillated between total rage and vulnerability with one look from her.

Fuck. Next thing he'd be stuffing the freezer with half gallons of Blue Bunny ice cream.

He walked to the main house's gravel driveway where he located the clothing rod and yanked it out of her trunk, along with two more bags of clothing she'd yet to bring in. Typical Sonja. It took the hounds of hell to convince her to do something she didn't want to, but once she made up her mind she was all in. The grunt that emerged from his midsection was more like a laugh but damned if he'd let her hear it.

As he walked along the short twisting path back to the guesthouse, the irony of their situation blindsided him. Here they were, moving in together. What had been such a great time, a wonderful memory of their early years together, only made the anguish sharper. The realization that he'd never convince her to come back to him, to trust him, to live with him for any reason but pure pragmatism, made him fucking sad.

"Just put that stuff on my bed, and I'll make us some lunch." She was at the refrigerator, stocking it. He couldn't tear his gaze off the domestic gesture.

"When did you have time to get groceries?"

"I didn't. This is what's left over from Poppy's apartment."

"There's enough there to feed a starving alligator."

She always had too much food on hand. While it had annoyed him to see how much ended up in the garbage, now he found it comforting. As if the woman who'd jilted him, who was determined to start her life over without him, still had a piece of the woman he'd fallen in love with.

"I'll let you know when it's ready." Sonja-speak for "fuck off."

Henry placed her bags in the single bedroom, trying to ignore the memories that lambasted him. He and Sonja house hunting, looking for land to build the river house in the height of the rainy season. They'd found this old house and broke into it, staying out here through a torrential thunderstorm one evening. Not that they'd seen much of the storm. They'd been too busy driving each other crazy.

Fuck. Would he ever hear her come again? And would he ever stop obsessing over it?

"Lunch is ready." Her voice reached him, and he walked out into an empty kitchen where she'd left him a nice-sized roasted turkey sandwich on a bakery roll.

He peered through the tiny window over the sink and saw her sitting on one of the two rocking chairs on the porch. It offered a view of the river, but unlike the majestic up-close panorama from the main house, this was a slice of water as seen through a forest of bayou gums. The trees surrounding the cottage were its main attraction, keeping it cooler in the summer.

Sonja rocked and ate as she looked out through the tree trunks. She probably wanted to be alone. But he didn't.

"The view's expanded lots since the storm." He sat in the hardwood chair next to hers, placed his bottle of water on the table between them, careful not to touch her glass of ginger tea. "You living on ginger?"

"Pretty much." She didn't look at him as she ate, slowly rocking with one bare foot, the toes painted siren red. The other foot curled under her frothy white skirt.

"Thanks for lunch. I'll make sure I do the next grocery run." He felt awkward talking to her, as if they'd just met instead of lived together and known one another's bodies as well as their own. Better.

At her continued silence, he ate. His sandwich had two bites left when she finally spoke. "I fully understand that this isn't easy for you, either."

"We made a mess of it, didn't we?" He chomped on a chip. "For two people who had it so together."

Her silence enveloped them like the bayou humidity, and he wanted to kick himself. "Too soon?"

Deep brown eyes on him, a glint of knowing. And then she laughed, which loosened up the place in his chest that he'd only allowed one measly laugh to escape from just minutes earlier. The sound of their laughter fell like firework sparks around them, and he wished they didn't have to go back inside and remember that they weren't a couple any longer. He wanted to say something, anything to make it all right.

He felt his heart pound and knew the vein on the side of his neck was throbbing. She used to like to lick it right before he came. As if she'd done that, his logic ceased.

All of his blood seemed to be pumping through his pounding heart, straight to his groin, making his erection impossible to ignore.

She didn't respond as he set his plate down on the deck and took hers, putting it on the side table. He kneeled in front of her, grasped her hands and pulled her forward in her rocking chair.

"Henry, um, we're outside..."

He saw the same need that refused to let up inside him. That refused to let go even after she'd dumped him at the altar.

"You still want me."

Her soft moan was her only response, and all he needed. Henry crushed his lips onto hers.

* * * *

As if it had landed back home, Sonja's body reacted in perfect sync with Henry's. She opened her mouth to accept his tongue, hot and greedy, and put her arms around his neck, pressing up against his chest with her breasts. Her humongous, swollen, tender breasts. But instead of hurting like they did in the shower or if she tried to sleep on her stomach, they swelled at the contact, and her nipples hardened with unabashed desire.

"Sonja." His voice vibrated in her ear, the way he knew she liked it, and his tongue whirled around once, twice before his lips trailed to her lobe and he gave her a love nip.

"We shouldn't—"

"I don't want to fucking talk, Sonja."

Neither did she. Exes had farewell fucks all the time, didn't they?

Henry didn't give her the option as he sank to his knees and pushed her skirt up and over her hips. The rocking chair moved back, forward, adding to the tension tightening deep in her center. His breath was hot as he forcefully blew through her panties, the heat against her pussy only adding to her need. Sonja leaned back in the chair and held on to its arms as the promise of an orgasm with Henry stopped her from doing anything else. She ignored the guilt, the voice that told her she didn't deserve this after leaving him the way she did. It was always like this between them. Unstoppable.

* * * *

"You're so wet." Henry took his time with Sonja. He knew she wanted him or she would have said no, would have pushed him away. He'd never had to work hard to convince her. Their physical chemistry had always trumped any conflicts they'd had.

He refused to entertain his guilt over never telling her everything about Deidre, or his misgivings about forcing her hand with the big wedding. Not now. They both needed this too much.

He pulled her panties down to her ankles, seeing only her very essence— Sonja in all her glory. Her sheer beauty mesmerized him. Pregnancy enlarged more than breasts, as every glistening part of Sonja was more stunning than ever. He slid his hands up to her ass and pulled her most intimate self to his mouth.

It was so good. Always had been, but this was different. As if knowing how close he'd come to never ever doing this to Sonja again made it all the more intense. His erection pressed against his jeans, needing release as his tongue licked and savored her taste. Sonja's moan followed immediately by her quiet stillness told him how fucking close she was. And he had to send her, had to push her over her edge. Unable to stop, unwilling to ask himself why, he shoved two fingers into her slick heat as his tongue circled her clit. He was rewarded as her muscles tightened around his fingers, followed by spasms that signaled her release. He bit on her soft creamy thighs, kissed her wetness as she quietly moaned her pleasure.

"Henry." Her voice was drugged from the orgasm, and as he looked up at her, she had her head tilted back against the back of the rocker, her face flushed and eyes bright, looking at him.

He allowed himself one last inhale of pure Sonja before he stood. His erection was almost painful, but he'd get over it. He leaned to smooth her skirt back down, but she grabbed his hands.

"Henry?"

He was afraid of what he'd see in her eyes.

"It was for you, Sonja."

"Oh, no. If we're going to do this, learn to work together again, it has to be both ways."

* * * *

She smiled as she first unzipped his jeans and pushed them off his hips, along with his knit boxers. His erection was more than she remembered and yet everything she knew. Acting on pure need, she got on her knees and took him in her mouth. He leaned against the pillar that supported the house, and she used every skill she had to give Henry the most incredible blowjob of his life. It was always like this when she was with him. He got her turned on, she came, she lost all sense of where she was and any time that passed.

"Sonja." His gasp was more of a plea as his hands wrapped around her head, and she opened her mouth, her throat to take as much of him as physically possible. But Henry didn't want it, or at least he wanted something else. He cupped her face, urged her to her feet. "I have to be inside you."

She stood and for a moment wondered if it would get awkward, being naked in the middle of the day on the cottage porch. Before her thoughts encroached, Henry's hands were on her waist, pulling her to him, lifting her. She wrapped her arms around his neck and let gravity do the rest.

His cock filled her with exquisite friction. She panted and moaned as he expertly entered her again and again, leaning her against the cottage wall.

"I don't want to hurt you, baby."

"Then don't." She wriggled out of his arms and leaned over the porch railing, his hiss confirmation that he liked seeing her ass up high and her center ready for him.

He filled her again, and she clung to the railing, pushing back against his thrusts until the tightness in her center sprang loose into an explosive orgasm. Henry cried out, and within seconds his long form curled over her, his chest against her back, his hands over hers on the wood beam.

Chapter 9

They stood like that for a long while, coming back down to earth. Down from where they'd always found release and relief. Sonja clung to the connection as fiercely as she told herself it was temporary. After-breakup sex was common, wasn't it?

But this felt like so much more.

"Hell, Sonja, I hope I didn't hurt you." Henry lifted off of her back, and she shook her skirt down, amazed that they'd had such incredible sex with their clothes still on.

"That was—unexpected." She kept her face forward, away from him. She was certain that her regret and need for him was stamped all over it.

"Sonja."

The warmth of his hand on her forearm seared, and she pulled away, his expression sending an alarm through her. "What?"

"Look." He pointed down the drive, and her stomach clenched. Deidre's car was leaving the main drive, heading out of the neighborhood.

"You don't think she saw us, do you?"

"Doubtful. We would have heard her."

"No way in hell would we have."

Henry grunted. "Maybe not. But chances are she doesn't know about the cottage."

He was right; the cottage was off from the main house and surrounded by trees on all sides. Unless someone knew about the original property, they'd never know there was another dwelling other than the large river house.

"I'm going to make this right." Blue steel in his eyes. "She can't keep showing up."

"You can't fix everything, Henry. Just like I can't take back running from the church. But we can work together to keep us all safe." She looked back down the drive, half afraid that Deidre's car would come barreling down the drive. "We probably should have gone inside, with our concerns about Deidre showing up."

Henry's grim profile was a stark contrast to the muted greens of the spring vegetation that surrounded the guesthouse. "No. We, us, that was special."

She met his gaze and saw the raw emotion, laced with concern.

"You think she'll be back."

"Unfortunately, yes."

"You were so fastidious about the security system when we built the house. It was because of Deidre, wasn't it?" She'd assumed it was because of his father's reputation as one of the most successful attorneys in Louisiana. She'd thought that by namesake Henry had to protect his property, assumed to be more than it was by most. Few knew what she did—that Henry had forgone his father's offers of financial support ever since he'd finished undergrad. Like her, Henry still wasn't a full partner in the firm. And never would be if she'd married him.

You have to tell him.

"I wasn't detailed enough. There needs to be a system here too, in the guesthouse." He didn't deny why he'd had the state-of-the-art system installed in their dream house. The house that was in shambles from a flood, and that they'd sell as soon as it was ready to be listed.

"That should be easy enough, to connect it to the main house." She hoped he didn't hear the sadness in her voice. She'd tell him about his parents, just as he'd told her about Deidre. But it wouldn't change anything. As cataclysmic as their lovemaking had been, nothing would patch the rift they'd both allowed to form between them.

"Once we get power back, it'll be an easy enough job." His voice sounded distracted. The low hum of the generator that was keeping the guesthouse powered filled her ears, reminded her of storms past.

"You'd think it was Katrina all over again, with the power still out from the floods."

"We knew we'd picked an outlying area when we built." Henry nodded toward the generator. "It's annoying but it works. And it was worth every penny."

"That's why you stayed here. Not just to avoid the Brandon-Poppy love scene, but for the house. You wanted to keep it safe." Respect for him welled.

"Yes."

"Did you really think Deidre would come here, after the flooding?"

"She showed up the other day when we were here, didn't she?" He looked away. "And it felt like the right thing to do. It's all we, all I have. I invested my life savings in this property. We both have. And now, it's our baby's future."

"We don't have anything in there worth much, save for the TV." And a few old computers.

"No, but I don't want to have to deal with squatters, either." It was always a possibility when people lost homes after big storms, they'd both grown up seeing it. "That's why I didn't want to wait on the insurance company to recommend contractors. I went to the adjuster with Brandon's recommendations, and they were more than happy to let me get started, once they had the estimates in hand. This way the insurance company had their assessment finished weeks ahead of where we'd be if I hadn't."

"Thank you for taking care of this, Henry." She'd never asked him to handle it, he simply had. She'd acted like a spoiled child in many ways, no matter how right she'd felt about following her instinct and not saying her vows. While she'd nursed her misery in first her friend's cabin and then Poppy's apartment, he'd done the hard work.

"How much is this going to cost us?" She already knew it was going to be catastrophic, financially. The river had devastated their home. House. It was their shared property now, nothing more. But she needed facts.

"Insurance will handle all of the basics, but if we want to prevent this from happening again, we need to fork over some money for more generators and sump pumps. A larger retaining wall. And the neighborhood association is talking about hiring engineers to put in a dam upstream. That will take longer to happen, and involves the parish and state, not to mention the Corps of Engineers."

She shook her head. "I never thought we'd have a problem with heavy flooding this far from the city."

"You know it's not about that—it's about the river. As long as we're anywhere near the Mississippi we're at risk. It's why my folks moved to Baton Rouge after Katrina."

"Your folks moved because they're fucking racists."

"That, too." His eyes sparked with conviction. "What did they say to you, the night of the rehearsal?"

"Nothing that makes any difference now." She pushed back from the railing. "But you deserve to know it all. They're subtle, your folks. They made some of their usual 'doing it for Henry's sake' comments, made it clear it wasn't for me. And of course they were over-the-top friendly to

Deidre." She thought about that moment when it hit her they cared more for a long-lost ex of Henry's than their future daughter-in-law. "It sucked, but it wasn't what made me run. I made me run, Henry."

"So you say."

She shrugged, noting how tight her shoulders were. Made sense as the tension between them never lessened, she never let her guard down since the wedding. Save for the other day in the office, when their desire had flared. And just now. "They mentioned they'd invited some additional friends and hoped I wouldn't mind. They'd been close to your friends before you and I were together, so I didn't think anything of it."

"Why didn't you tell me that night?" He faced her with his hands at his sides, his blue eyes reflecting his frustration.

"Oh no, you don't get to play the outraged victim, Henry. I didn't tell you because I lov—didn't want anything to mar our perfect day."

He slowly shook his head, his lips twisted in disgust. "You're telling me that as of after the rehearsal dinner, you were still planning to walk down that aisle? That you hadn't planned your escape for quite some time?"

"Yes." It stung that he thought she'd planned to ruin their big day that far in advance. "I'm not justifying my actions to you. What I said is the truth—I was going to marry you until I saw Deidre. Your parents brought her into the garden next to the bridal dressing room and introduced us." At his incredulous growl she held up her hand. "No. I expected your parents to play dirty pool, especially when they decided to show up at the wedding. They weren't ever going to have anything to celebrate with me as a daughter-in-law. And that wasn't when I decided to leave, anyway. It was when I looked out the window of the dressing room and saw you and her embracing."

"You owed me the decency of talking to me first, before you bolted."

"Um, no. I was owed the full backstory on Deidre before having to deal with her face-to-face, alone, on the day I was going to commit the rest of my life to you."

"You met her with my parents at the rehearsal dinner."

"I don't know about you, but that night, the whole week leading up to what was going to be our big day, is a blur to me. I barely remember her there, because I was so focused on our wedding vows." She hadn't been feeling great, either, coming to terms with the baby growing in her belly.

"And that you weren't ready to make them." Said for the first time without the ugly rancor he'd been wearing like a favorite T-shirt.

She let out a long, slow breath. "No. No, I wasn't. And Henry, I know it's a day late and a dollar short, but I am sorry. I know I have to own up to my stuff."

He wasn't interested in her deep thoughts. "What did Deidre say to you? On our wedding day?" His earnest need to know made it too hard to correct him. It hadn't been a wedding day, after all.

"Not a whole lot. Enough." She waved her hand in front of her, batting at an imaginary mosquito. "It's not the point. Shit, Henry, it could have been a zombie or serial killer for all I care. It wasn't about anything at that point but you and me. The lack of communication that led to me being blindsided by Deidre's presence and crazy behavior on our wedding day. We're lucky she didn't come unglued and do more than embrace you or come talk to me in the garden behind the cathedral." She had a clear memory of that moment. Sitting on the cold stone bench, staring at her bouquet, trying to allow the fragrance to soothe her. And then Deidre suddenly there, talking to her as if they'd known one another their entire lives. That woman had balls, Sonja gave her that.

"I don't have control over what Deidre does, Sonja."

Her insides quaked, and her hands shook. She couldn't remember the last time she'd been so angry. Whether at herself or Henry or their miserable situation, she wasn't sure and didn't care.

"You had control over what you shared with me about your life from the moment we met, Henry. You had control over telling me that your parents had asked for extra invitations. You had control over trusting them—the parents who disowned you for the first eighteen months of our relationship—with said invitations." She poked him in the chest, hard. And winced as her finger bent painfully backward. "God damn you for being so strong and immovable, Henry! For playing the fucking clueless wonder boy. Do you really expect me to believe that you, the top of his law school class, never anticipated your parents' motives? Or that you never worried that Deidre might pop back up and try to cause trouble for you? You've already admitted that."

"No more than I ever expected that you'd have decided on the spur of the moment to leave me hanging at the altar like you did."

They glared at one another, their emotions and basic friendship at an impasse.

"Uh, folks?" A cleared throat.

Sonja broke eye contact with Henry and looked at the man who'd appeared in front of the guesthouse porch. Clad in a long-sleeved work shirt and jeans, he was probably one of the contractors she'd noticed taking measurements earlier.

"Hey." Henry was the first to recover his voice.

"We've got a problem with the entry off the patio."

"Okay." Henry was playing it cool.

"You're going to want to come see this."

* * * *

"You stay out here." He didn't want Sonja going in and out of the mildew-damp house, not while she was pregnant. It had nothing to do with not wanting her to have to see the house so damaged. She already had, and had shown no emotion about it. Except for puking her guts out, but that was probably more the pregnancy and the shock of seeing one another for the first time after their epic wedding fail.

"Like hell." Her voice was low as she stomped alongside him, both of them following the contractor. "I called and asked my doctor. I'm fine and so is the baby as long as I don't stay inside very long. I won't touch anything."

"Whatever." He sped up, closing in on the workman, needing to be anywhere but in stride with her. It was too familiar, too easy, too damn painful.

Once in the house, he was impressed with the half dozen or so laborers in various modes of tearing down the damaged drywall and lifting up the water-swollen hardwood planks.

"Over here."

They followed the contractor to the double doors, the river breeze floating through the opening and making the inside of the house bearable without the usual air conditioning.

The contractor pointed at the doorjamb, moving his hand up to the locking mechanism. It had been torn out of the wood.

"What the hell?" Sonja was next to him, her heat palpable.

"I was here last night and didn't notice it." He wouldn't have, though, because he'd been too distracted. Too sad.

"Looks fresh to me—maybe this morning, before we got here. You need to take a look around and see if anything's missing. Might want to get that big screen TV out of here, too."

"The house normally has a full security system engaged." Henry rubbed his nape. "I can have a generator brought in to fire it back up, but it was working fine on its batteries as of last night."

"The swelling of the doors and windows messed up any contacts, and nothing's going to work right until the house is completely refinished." The contractor looked from Henry to Sonja. "You two up for being in that small cottage for the next three months?"

Three months.

"We'll do whatever we need to." Sonja's confident tone was as refreshing as an ocean swim in December. Yet inexplicable relief eased the ache in his chest. "So you're thinking twelve weeks for everything? In my experience that means at least sixteen."

The contractor chuckled, obviously taken in by Sonja's natural charm. Henry admired that about her—being more of an introvert, easy conversation wasn't his best skill.

"It's always good to plan for the longest stint, but I pride myself on finishing on time, if not early. We've got so much going and will for the next six months, the more jobs my team can close, the better for this year's bottom line."

"I trust your judgment." Henry nodded. "You can reach either of us at the numbers I gave you with my business card. And of course, like you did today, feel free to come over to the guesthouse."

"I admit I felt a little odd going up to your cottage. It's tough enough that your privacy is so limited for the next several months."

"No worries. Knock on our door at any time." It wasn't as if he and Sonja were going to be in the sack like they would have been only weeks earlier. He caught himself up short. The contractor could have walked up to them in the middle of what he could only think of as relief sex. Something they'd had to do, to clear the air.

"Here's a list of what you'll need to pick out. It's all there, from paint to backsplash tiles to flooring." The contractor handed Henry a large folder.

"Why would we need new backsplash?" Sonja took the folders from Henry, peering at the lists of supplies.

"I know your kitchen looks intact, but we're going to have to rip out more than you'd expect, thanks to the mold. If we don't, great, but this way you'll know what you want, and we can order it as we go along." He named a local construction supply store where he had an account. "If you can get that information as soon as possible, it'd help me out."

As they walked back to the cottage, separately but together, Sonja was silent, and he wondered where her thoughts had strayed. The hardest part was that it wasn't any of his business, not anymore.

It was going to be a long hot spring in the bayou.

"You think Deidre broke into the house last night?" Her tone was non-accusatory.

"I don't know. Yes. Probably." He didn't want to deal with it.

"With the power off there was no way to stop her or warn us." She referred to the alarm system.

"No. I can talk to the contractors about running a line from the generator to it." They only had one generator, and he'd had to wheel it out to the guest cottage.

"Maybe it's time to install a permanent generator as we rebuild the main house." She said nothing about being worried that Deidre was stalking them.

He stopped a few feet from the guesthouse. "You sure you're not afraid of Deidre doing anything crazy?" He didn't want her stressed, didn't want the baby getting the effects of her worry.

Her eyes were clear. "I expect that she's up to no good, Henry. I'm not obtuse. And while criminal law isn't my area, or yours, it's pretty certain she's after at least one of us. You know her far better than I do. What do you think?"

"I don't want to believe she'd ever do anything to harm you, but she's shown back up and is causing trouble after all these years. I can't rule it out."

"You've been reporting her recent stunts to the police, right?"

Henry's guilt made his throat tight. "There's nothing to report. Except for today, if she did come up on the property." He could call in trespassing then. "The restraining order expired years ago, and I renewed it right after the wedding. Frankly, I thought the less I did to engage her, the better. Which is why I didn't renew the order when it first expired. Until now, it's worked well, ignoring her. She hasn't been in my life for the better part of a decade."

"Until she got the wedding invitation."

He clenched his teeth. "Yes."

Sonja looked past his shoulder, in full concentration mode. "So we play it safe. Get the cottage rigged for security, get power to the house's security system. And at the first sign of trouble, we report it."

"You know as well as I do that as long as she's obsessed with you or me or us, she's not going to let anything stop her."

"I do know that. But I have faith. Maybe we're supposed to help her get back into treatment."

"Unlike you, I don't buy the Divine Timing bullshit. Not with something like this. We have to keep ourselves safe, first and foremost." The thought of anything happening to her paralyzed him.

"And we are." They'd reached the cottage. "When are we going to pick out the tiles?"

* * * *

"I can't take you out to look for paint samples without feeding you first." Henry pulled up to the dive diner they'd had their rehearsal dinner at. "Is this too soon?"

"Not for me." She was all for making new, fresh memories everywhere they could. The sooner she accepted their new partnership of sorts, otherwise known as parenthood, the sooner her heart might heal.

Liar.

"I wasn't sure if you'd be up for food this early."

"I'm okay today." And she was, a nice change from the last few weeks. Maybe the morning sickness was finally fading. It was about time for it to.

The smell of the diner—powdered biscuits and gravy, grease, and coffee—challenged her stomach a bit, but as soon as she was in a booth and sipping cold water she felt better.

"Looks different from when we were in here before." Henry took in the orderly tables and booths.

"They shoved all those tables together for us." Did he really want to talk about the rehearsal dinner?

"You know, you acted a lot different after my folks showed up. Neither of us expected them to, and I thought it was the surprise of it. Was there something more?"

She met his eyes and couldn't pretend any longer.

"They were going to completely disown you, Henry."

"What? That's crazy. They were there."

"I know. But they were going to make sure you'd never get one dime of the family's money. The law firm—your father would let you work there, like he has been, but he'd never make you a partner."

"Sure that isn't your resentment toward them talking? Not that you don't have a right to be resentful. They're racist idiots."

"This was about you, Henry. If I had married you, you'd have lost it all."

"And that's why you ran?"

She bit her lower lip. "I thought so, at the time. Along with the Deidre drama. But now—"

"Hey, folks, how y'all doin'?" Louise, the longest-working waitress at the diner and the woman who'd made the rehearsal dinner run so smoothly, smiled at them. "How was the honeymoon?"

"Ah—"

"Well—"

"That good, huh?" She poured coffee into Henry's mug. Her smile slipped when Sonja covered her mug.

"None for me, thanks."

"Actually, Louise, we didn't go on a honeymoon. We didn't get married." Henry spoke quietly.

Louise looked from Henry to Sonja and back again, her incredulity comical. "No shit? And you're still here, together?"

"As friends." Sonja spoke up.

"Okay." She shook her head. "As long as you're both healthy and happy, that's all I care about. What'll you have?"

They both ordered their favorites and sat back after Louise walked away.

"That was awkward."

Henry shrugged. "People will figure it out when they see we have a kid we're raising together. We're not the first couple to call it off while still being parents."

"You surprise me. Only a few days ago you'd never have considered remaining friends, no matter what."

"People can change, Sonja."

He didn't ask her anything more about his parents, and she didn't volunteer her experiences, either. For now, establishing their new status quo seemed more important.

* * * *

A cacophony of voices, lumber saws, and forklifts hit Henry as he and Sonja walked into the home construction supply store. He loved this place and had enjoyed time here when they'd picked out the various colors and materials for the river house. When it had been their dream home.

"I can't stand this color." Sonja held up a beige paint chip.

"Isn't that what the entire stairwell is painted?"

"No, the entrance and hallway are terra-cotta cream."

"Which is dark beige, like that sample you're holding."

"You think this is beige?" She shook her head. "This is why I'm going to pick out all of the colors this time."

"We didn't do too badly the first time around. Why not keep everything the same?" He didn't see the need to get excited about the shade of the walls.

"Keeping things the same doesn't work—if we're going to sell the house for what it's worth, we have to make sure we have the latest color schemes. I knew I should have asked Poppy for help with this." She worried her bottom lip with her teeth, and the tall industrial shelving, loud noises, and even the little sparrows that flitted in the top rafters, chirping to one another, faded into white noise. It was just him and Sonja.

"Poppy's obviously talented, but don't you think—" He stopped. "I think we should put the house back together. You and me." Oh shit, he was pushing too far.

Sonja slid the offensive paint chip back into its spot, amongst a gazillion other shades of off-white. Her fingers played with the edges of the chips, strumming them like a deck of cards. Finally her eyes met his, and instead of irritation or the shut-down expression she'd worn too much lately, he saw agreement.

"Okay, Henry. We'll do this together." She nodded. "We seem to get in trouble with distractions, don't we? Like the house, the wedding. We did our best work together before all that."

He didn't know if she was referring to their legal work or their failed relationship.

"What do you think of yellow?" He grabbed the first chip that caught his eye that didn't make him think "boring."

"I think a pale butter is nice, for the kitchen." She plucked a chip and held it next to his.

"Mine looks like a canary next to yours."

She laughed. "This is a change. Normally I'm all out there, and you're the subtle one. The quiet, let's-keep-it-all-even nice guy."

Henry smiled, but her observation was too astute for him to appreciate the humor. He was tired of being the goddamned nice guy.

* * * *

Sonja's hesitation over working with Henry on the finer details of the renovation eased away as they wandered the long aisles of the home improvement store. As much as Henry detested her labeling him a nice guy, it was the God's honest truth. Henry was as nice as they came. It was what had drawn her to him—his constancy, his belief that everything worked for good.

"I'm glad we can use our granite." She ran her hand on a smooth rose quartz countertop in the kitchen display.

"That's the good thing about rock—not a whole lot can damage it." He raised his gaze to the tall cabinets. "I never thought about putting in glass doors."

"We didn't think about anything. We checked the boxes, picked whatever the builders suggested." While easy, it had given them a house that looked similar to so many other homes.

"It'd be nice to make it more custom this time." His wistful tone tugged at her heart.

"Yeah, well, that costs more money, and we're trying to flip the house, right? We want to keep it neutral for the best chance of a quick sale." Was that her voice, sounding so professional and emotionless about the home they'd planned to raise a family in?

Henry didn't answer her as he walked out of the remodeling example and down a shelving aisle. She had to trot to catch up to him.

"Henry."

He stopped but still wouldn't look at her, his fascination with closet shelf fasteners so contrived she had to bite back a laugh.

At his continued silence, she dug deep for her truth. "Look, I was being a little too hasty back there. We didn't, I didn't, put enough focus on us, on the house, the first time through. If you want to customize parts of it, I'm okay with that. As long as we can afford it, in the overall budget."

Had his face always been like the granite counters, impassive, solid, revealing nothing of his thoughts?

"We robbed ourselves of the fun parts."

She took a step closer. "Define 'fun.'" For her, they'd always had fun. In the bedroom and out, in the courtroom and out. And weren't adults supposed to take things more seriously, anyway?

His eyes were as blue as the flame on their gourmet gas stove. "The little details. We're really good at the big stuff, Sonja. The big careers. The big house. The incredible sex." He ran his fingers through his hair, leaving the trademark conservative style rumpled and more...more like the Henry she was getting to know. The Henry she'd missed in the goal-driven life she'd lived for the past year.

"We were busy—"

"Wait—hear me out. We didn't take the time to hash out the little details of our everyday life. I can only speak for myself, but I was only worried about the next case and meeting the projected dates for the house, and then the wedding planning."

Sonja saw Henry's obvious distress at what boiled down to their immaturity, and at the same time mentally scanned their financial picture. Neither of them could make it on their own, not until the house was done. And anything extra in the renovation was off the bottom line she needed to be able to make a clean break and start over.

But there would never be a clean break with Henry.

"Sonja, what is it? The morning sickness?" Just like that, his concern for her was forefront.

"No, not at all. Tell you what, Henry. You're right. Let's make the house better than it ever was. It's an investment—we'll get top dollar for a house that doesn't look like every other McMansion." And they'd have to work together on something that wasn't work, wasn't a wedding.

He flashed her the trademark Boudreaux grin, and it was as if they'd crossed another obstacle, post-un-wedding.

"That's the Sonja I know."

They spent the next hour wandering the store, taking photos with Sonja's phone, figuring out the costs to make their house more their own. Sonja ignored the heavy corner of her heart that insisted she stop this immediately—the house was going to sell and what difference would it make, anyway?

For once, Sonja just let herself go.

Chapter 10

Henry did what he should have done at least a year ago. He hadn't given his parents any warning that he was coming; they were always best confronted without any opportunity to plan their attack.

He pulled up to the front of the house, the circular drive covered in gumdrops that had fallen from the trees that lined the asphalt. The tall silhouette of his father at the front door didn't surprise him—Dad liked to wander the house with his coffee cup on Sunday mornings, sitting wherever the mood and weather permitted.

Henry reminded himself that his sole purpose for the hour drive to Baton Rouge was to confront his parents and find out exactly what the hell they'd said to Sonja.

"Son."

"Dad." They nodded at one another, wary predators sizing up their prey.

"What are you doing here?"

"Nice to see you too, Dad." He stepped up to the top of the marble porch. "Where's Mom?"

"I'm here." She walked through the open front door, her hair and makeup impeccable even at nine o'clock on a Sunday morning. But her eyes held a new weight he hadn't noticed in the weeks after the wedding. "Hi honey." She stood on tiptoe and kissed his cheek. He gave her a brief hug.

"Look, you two—this isn't a casual visit. We need to talk."

His parents exchanged glances, but it wasn't the usual we-know-best-just-ask-us kind of communication. His parents looked...weary.

"We've been hoping we'd have a chance to hash things out, Henry. Come on in."

With a combination of stunned surprise and suspicion that his father was in the midst of some cover-his-ass stunt, Henry followed his parents into their fortress of a home.

* * * *

They sat around the high café table on the back deck. Henry had poured himself a cup of coffee, needing the bite of his mother's custom blend.

"We've wanted to reach out to you sooner, son." Hudson's voice had a note of trepidation in it that Henry was unfamiliar with.

"Yet you didn't."

"We knew you needed time to heal." Gloria offered him a tremulous smile. Not her usual smug mother-knows-best look.

"What the hell is going on with you two?" He'd come to get the dirt from them he knew existed—they'd said more to Sonja than she'd told him. But they were acting incredibly odd.

Hudson looked him directly in the eye. "It's our fault Sonja didn't marry you."

He had to keep it together, play his cards close.

"Why do you say that?"

A sniffle. A goddamned sniffle from his mother. "We, we only ever wanted what's best for you and your brother and sister. Sometimes that means we did stupid things."

"What your mother's trying to say is that I told Sonja we'd disown you if you two married."

Holy shit. His parents were actually apologizing. Henry had never been a huge fan of cartoons but at the moment fully appreciated the vision of the top of his head blowing off.

"Why the hell did you do that?"

"It's not that your father, that we, would really ever disown you." His mother blew her nose. "But we've already blown it with Brandon, and now Jena is halfway around the world a lot of the time." His mother's red-rimmed eyes showed a rare vulnerability. "It's hard to not see that you kids don't want anything to do with us."

"Jesus, Mom, you're going to play the victim in this?" His imagination was spinning with the visual of his parents telling Sonja she was going to ruin his career and life, basically. They'd said that to Sonja. Fuck.

"Your mother is upset. We both are. I've made a huge mistake, Henry. There's a lot about me you'll never change. I'm a dyed-in-the-wool Southern man from a long line of attorneys."

"Yeah, well, you didn't keep the entire legacy of fighting for social justice for all, did you?"

"Your mother and I haven't worked on knowing what's important to you kids. And we've irreparably damaged your happiness."

"You're telling me that you've seen the light, that you're no longer racists?" This was rich.

"We never thought we were. But I see now that my actions, professionally and personally, need to match what I thought was my good intentions."

"What about staying out of my business?"

"About that, Henry. It's never going to make up for my behavior, but I want you to take the firm where you want it to go. It's yours. I'm going to retire and close the Baton Rouge office within the year."

Henry wanted to tell his father to go to hell, to point out that he wasn't really changing if he thought he'd buy his way out of the hurt he'd caused Sonja.

"We'd like a chance to talk to Sonja, too." Gloria was looking better, probably because Henry hadn't totally lost his cool.

"That's not necessary." He wasn't about to tell them that he and Sonja were sharing the cottage again, or the biggest revelation—that they were going to be grandparents.

His parents needed to stew in their own sick past for a while. He was keeping the treasure of a future child to himself.

* * * *

With Henry out of the cottage it seemed too pathetic to stay there, so Sunday morning Sonja went to see Grandma Edwina for breakfast and then decided to do some mindless shopping. Just for fun.

She enjoyed meandering through a favorite craft store, not needing a hobby with her caseload and pregnancy but needing a distraction for when she was in the cottage with Henry. Grandma had taught her to bake and whip up a good roux, but cooking in the tiny kitchen wasn't fun. Crafting wasn't her normal gig, but maybe something new would help keep her from freaking out over her life at the moment.

The thought of going back to the cottage with the rest of Sunday stretched out before her was too much. She'd gone to church with Grandma and had a huge helping of sausage grits before driving around, looking for any distraction. Her appetite's return had surprised her, but Grandma always had a way of making her calm down.

"I didn't peg you as a crafter."

The hair on her forearms stood up straight.

"Deidre."

"Hey, Sonja." The petite woman didn't meet her eyes, shifting from foot to foot, her flip-flops sparkling with huge rhinestones. "Why aren't you back home with Henry?"

Deidre's knowing smile made Sonja grit her teeth. She should have filed a restraining order already, just like Henry told her to do. At least then she could call 9-1-1 and walk away. Instead she had to face Deidre and not allow Deidre to see her fear, her anxiety.

"I'm not with Henry. You were at the wedding, you saw that it never happened."

"You were visiting him yesterday." She'd seen Sonja's car, thought Sonja was in the house with Henry. But Deidre thought it was a visit, not a move-in. Sonja wondered if the woman knew they'd seen her, or suspected she'd been the one to attempt the break-in at the river house.

"We have a house to rebuild and sell. You saw the flood damage for yourself."

"That doesn't mean you have to be around Henry all the time. You're really cruel, aren't you, Sonja? First you treat him like dirt, leave him at the altar, crush his dreams. Now you're playing him like a fool." Deidre's expression was downright chipper while her voice was almost monotone and very, very sinister.

Sonja felt in her dress's skirt pocket for her phone, which she pulled out and pointedly tapped on while Deidre continued her tirade. Forget what she'd said to Henry about Deidre being more annoying than dangerous. This woman was out for blood.

"Oh, so now you're going to call the police? Have me arrested?" Deidre's peals of harsh laughter grated on Sonja's composure like metal on slate.

"Why would I do that, Deidre? I have nothing against you. It's a free country. You can go wherever you need to." De-escalation was key to handling Deidre's cagey behavior. Just like she did with clients whose emotions got the better of them.

Deidre's face went blank as though a switch had flipped. "No one likes me. They all think I'm bad. That I'll hurt them. I've only ever loved Henry. No one can love him like I do."

"I'm sure you're right." Sonja murmured as she texted Henry, letting him know exactly where she was and that Deidre had shown up.

"Stop that!" Quick as lightning, Deidre's pale, thin hand flicked out and slapped the phone out of Sonja's palm. The solid thwack of the movement foretold the definitive crunch when it hit the concrete floor.

Sonja saw red and leaned over Deidre. "Who do you think you are? You need to stop this right now. You have no business talking to me or following me. If you don't stop, you're going to be arrested. I promise. Do you think you'll be able to be a doctor when you're in jail?" Pure rage fueled her words, her pulse throbbing in her ears.

"Ma'am, step away."

Sonja looked up and saw the security guard.

"She followed me here and is on record for stalking my, my—" What was Henry? He wasn't her fiancé any longer, would never be her husband. Sonja stood motionless, staring at the security guard, unable to make sense of the tug of war in her heart.

"Ma'am. Step. Away. Now." The strong voice broke through the cloud of her anger.

She immediately held her hands up and backed away.

"You've got this all wrong." She pointed at Deidre. "She's the one who's the problem." As she spoke, Deidre crouched in a cowering position.

The guard's raised brow indicated what she thought. Holy hell, she thought Sonja was the aggressor.

"Please don't hurt me. I didn't mean to drop your phone." Deidre whimpered, her dramatic performance as much impressive as it was chilling. Son of a *bitch*.

Stay cool.

"Look, we can clear this up." She had to dig for her attorney professionalism.

"Take your phone and leave the store." The guard looked at her as if she were a criminal.

Sonja fought against her instinct to put the uniformed woman in her place, to explain the entire situation. That would be the biggest mistake.

Sonja did what she knew how to do best. She left without looking back.

* * * *

"Where are you now?" Henry's voice came over the BMW's hands-free system, and she fought the usual response she had to it. As if her DNA was wired especially for him and attuned to the timbre of his voice as no other.

"On the bridge, heading hom—back. To the cottage."

"You should have called 9-1-1 instead of texting me from the craft store."

"Have you heard anything I've said? There wasn't any time. Deidre was strung out. And that wasn't the scariest part." She still couldn't shake how quickly the woman had switched from threatening her so viciously to playing the victim. And the security guard bought it, of course.

"Let me guess. The security guard assumed you were the perpetrator of the altercation?"

The short laugh left her throat with force. "Spoken like the white boy lawyer you are, Boudreaux. As a matter of fact, yes, the guard was white, and female. Was there a racist vibe? Maybe, but that wasn't the bottom line. The security guard assumed I was to blame because of how well Deidre played the part of the wronged party." But now that Henry brought it up, yes, the whole situation was rife with ugliness from racism to possible psychosis. She expelled a long breath, compelling her mind to stay present in the conversation with Henry.

"Are you okay to drive? Maybe you need to pull over."

"Where? Into Lake Pontchartrain?"

He profusely swore, and it echoed through the car.

"You wanted me to call you and have you come get me, but that would have only thrown oil on her crazy, Henry." She looked out at the sparkling water on either side of the miles-long bridge. "You're right—I can't file a restraining order soon enough."

"It won't stop her." Frustration saturated his reply. "I told you that after the wedding I filed a new one. It's like gas on fire with her right now."

"You never told your parents about her obsessive behavior. That I don't get." He hadn't told her, years later, that was one thing. But his parents had been there in his life at that time.

"I was a college kid, and you know Hudson and Gloria. If I told them, they'd have been on the phone with her folks, the dean, the authorities, God knows who else. It would have been a bigger mess than it was."

"You had nothing to hide, though. It's not your fault that the girl you thought you'd marry turned out to be an obsessive bitch."

"My parents have their reasons for a lot of things. As a matter of fact, that's where I'm coming back from. I talked to them, Sonja. They're going through their own changes."

"You mean like some kind of epiphany?" Of course they'd be all apologetic now, they'd gotten what they wanted. Their son wasn't going to marry her.

Silence.

"Henry?"

"I'm here. And I don't want to have this conversation like this. Get home safe." He disconnected.

Henry never cut her off like this. He was always the epitome of a Southern gentleman. Until she'd jilted him. It was as if some layer of gentility had peeled off when she'd left the cathedral. And it wasn't just Henry who'd begun to reveal a different side of himself. Her insides were raw, too.

* * * *

Sonja parked the car in the main drive and walked through the overgrown path to the cottage, where Henry immediately enveloped her in a hug.

"I'm so glad you're okay." She allowed him to embrace her, allowed the security of being in his arms to soak in. Just a little bit couldn't hurt, could it?

"Me, too." She pulled back and looked up at him. Into those impossibly blue eyes. Would their baby have them, too? "Henry, maybe I'm being a wimp about this. Deidre is a doctor with a full life—she's just screwing with us. She wouldn't really hurt either one of us, would she?"

"Don't know." He caressed her cheek. "And I don't want to talk about her. She's another distraction. We have to keep the focus on us. So tell me, do you really feel okay right now?"

She nodded. "I do. Just run-of-the-mill, vanilla pregnancy hormone stuff. I was scared in the store, of course, but not for long." She'd been more angry than anything.

His eyes narrowed. "Is that what happened with us, Sonja? Did it get too humdrum, too vanilla?" His voice coaxed as his fingers made her skin tingle where he touched her.

A tight curl of lust coiled low in her belly and shot a jolt of sizzling awareness between her legs.

"It was never about that." Her breathy reply bared her need for him.

Henry traced her cheek with his finger, as tantalizing as if he'd pressed himself up against her, spread her legs and ground his pelvis to hers. She bit her lower lip to stifle the moan that started deep inside, in the place that only Henry could reach. She heard his harsh intake of breath, and he lowered his half-lidded gaze to where her teeth sunk into her flesh. He moved with the grace of a predator, his thumb pad tugging at her lower lip as he closed the space separating them.

"We can't, Henry." Her voice didn't even sound halfway convinced of what she needed to protect her heart.

"Oh, but we can, Sonja. Don't you think it's okay for two consenting adults to get some pleasure in the midst of incredible pain?"

Her mind fumbled over all the reasons she'd fled her own wedding. But the ruins of their relationship weren't enough to smother the desire that raged inside her.

"This time it's your turn." She placed her hand on his chest, hissing when she felt his heartbeat. "You took care of me yesterday."

"God." He groaned and captured her lips.

Sonja met him, standing on her tiptoes to make the connection as intimate as possible. She took the lead, licking and sucking at his mouth until he opened it fully and allowed her tongue in, greeting it with his. He sucked on her tongue and scraped it with his teeth. She buckled against him, needing his rock-hard support as much as she yearned to have his cock in her mouth. Pushing two hands against his chest, she broke the connection. His dislike of her move was evident in his half-growl, half-moan of protest.

"Don't worry. It's going to get real good for you, really fast." She unbuckled his belt and unzipped his pants, watching his face as she grasped his hard, hot length. Her hand shook with need, and how much she'd missed him hit full force. "Do you want this?"

"Sonja—"

"No talking." She didn't want to think about keeping it all-sex, didn't want to worry about not letting the wrong words of endearment slip. Sonja wanted to give Henry his turn at the chemistry they'd always shared. Sinking to her knees, she tugged his pants down along with his underwear, ignoring the sharp pang that flexed when she saw he was wearing the same knit boxers she'd given him last Christmas. Shut out the memory of him modeling his new gift, right before he fucked her senseless on the living room sofa.

She relished the taste of him as she took him fully in her mouth, cupping his balls with her hands. His hands held her head, and his fingers gripped her scalp in the way he always did when she got him this excited. But this was different. It wasn't a natural roll-off-the-bed into lovemaking feeling. Instead, confidence empowered her every lick and suck. She wasn't doing this because she was under Henry's spell, or because she had no idea of what he was holding back from her. Instead, she knew there were layers to Henry she'd never explored, and instead of dismay or disappointment she was thrilled by the prospect.

"Oh, fuuuuck, Sonja, that's so good." He groaned, and she smiled against him. Never had she enjoyed giving head to anyone the way she did Henry.

She found herself anticipating his usual moves—Henry rarely let her finish him, but pushed her away right before he thought he was going to come and insisted on fucking as the way to reach his orgasm. So she was as surprised as he sounded when his cock stiffened and then pulsed in time to his grunts of total abandon. She savored every last taste of him, reluctantly pulling away only after she was certain he was completely spent.

Silence shrouded them as she pulled his pants up, zipped them, and stood in front of him. No touching, just Henry and her standing in the cottage's tiny living room, their breath mingling in the stillness. His eyes were glowing with satisfaction, and her fingers itched to touch his face, wrap her arms around his neck and tell him she'd made a huge mistake.

Then the image of Deidre pretending to be afraid of her in the craft shop shattered Sonja's illusion. This was still the man who'd kept some mighty secrets from her.

"That was incredible." He made no move to touch her. Definitely not the man she'd fallen in love with, who'd taken every opportunity to caress her and let her know she was his queen.

She nodded, unable to keep a grin from cracking the serious demeanor she struggled to maintain. "I'd say we're even, counselor." She'd meant it in jest, a reference to how he'd made her come with his mouth the other day. The way they used to tease one another.

"Even?" The glow she'd detected in his irises extinguished as quickly as if she'd flipped a switch. "I didn't know that physical intimacies between us had become tit-for-tat."

Nothing was how it used to be.

Chapter 11

A huge pile of folders landed with a smack in the middle of Sonja's desk.

"There you go." Henry's face was the picture of satisfaction. It couldn't be from yesterday's blowjob, surely. Although she still had to admit it had been one of her best.

"What's this?"

"The paperwork we need to sign to go nonprofit."

"What?" What was with his "we?" "Henry, yesterday was, was a release. I'm sorry if you took it to mean I wanted to go into business with you. I know you can't think it's a good idea."

Henry held up a hand, dismissing any talk of yesterday's sex from the office. "You wanted, we wanted, to do pro bono work. My father was never going to support that. Except now, he is. I've sent a note to my sister to see if she wants to join us." Henry and Brandon's sister was in South America on a Navy exercise that was part of her time in the reserves. She was a certified, licensed social worker in her regular day job.

"What makes you think she'll want to work with us?"

"She doesn't have to, but at the very least she has clients that need help. My guess is that this is the start of the new Boudreaux Law interests."

"What about this firm's current clients?"

Henry shrugged. "Dunno." He had the controlled look about him that always indicated he wasn't giving her the full story.

"I told you that I'm going to keep working here until I find another place and until I get my current cases wrapped up. I want, I need, to go out on my own, Henry. This isn't the kind of law I want to practice forever."

Henry shoved his hands in his dress pants pockets and stared at her. "What about the baby, Sonja? How will you find a new job, a nanny, and put in the hours you're going to need to make partner somewhere else?"

"Hell, I don't expect I'd ever make partner here even if I loved it. And having a baby is no reason to stay in the same job longer than I intended."

"We've agreed to live in the cottage while the house gets rebuilt. If we can live that close together after breaking up, we can work together. We're a great team."

"We are a very good *legal* team." She still hadn't gotten over that she'd ended up in the cottage again, though. Never in her life had she been so aware of her financial situation, which was pretty grim. "We're broken up, we don't have a future together, but neither of us has been good about definite boundaries at the cottage."

"Maybe we're drawing up new boundaries?" His lids had dropped halfway across his eyes, and he shot her his surefire cocky grin, the one that let her know that he could read her mind. But he couldn't. Not totally.

She ignored the answering heat in her face and forged ahead. "I'm not sure what you're referring to, counselor, but we've got to lay down some ground rules and stick to them."

"Let's stay that discussion until we're home, tonight."

"Not home, Henry. The cottage. We're bunking together. Period." She couldn't think of it as home anymore.

"Fine, whatever. I'll agree that the office is not an appropriate place to indulge our needs. We're past that, right?"

"Hmmm." She didn't have another answer. From the gleam in his eye she could tell he was baiting her, looking to see if she'd say anything about all of the hot, uninhibited sex they'd shared after hours, behind their closed office doors. That had been in the early stages of their relationship, before they'd made a serious commitment. Before they'd both let said commitment go to hell.

"Let's go back to the nonprofit. You're not planning to leave the city, are you? And is it so awful to work with me, even when we're no longer together?"

He stood there, posing a very sane, deliberate question, and all Sonja saw was how handsome he was, how so many other women would want him and would have him. He was no longer hers. Regret was destined to be her constant companion.

"Working with you has never been awful." It was the personal relationship part. The trust part. Which she was starting to see was her problem, not his. She hadn't trusted a man fully since her father had stepped out on her mother.

He studied her, not talking, and she refused to allow herself to drop her gaze. He gave a quick nod. "Fine, then. Read over the contracts, and we can talk about it at dinner tonight."

Henry turned and left her office as if he'd handed her the answer to a difficult court case and not the very situation she had to avoid at all costs. If she even began to look at the possibility of launching the nonprofit with Henry, she'd be embroiled in working with him for at least the next several years. It made sense that it should be okay to work together, lots of couples did after a marriage dissolved. And they hadn't gotten as far as the altar.

Close enough, though. The heartache was no less.

* * * *

Henry's stomach sank at the amount of black mildew that covered the drywall piled on a tarp in the middle of the huge great room.

"Wait—when did you do this?" He looked at Judd, the lead contractor. They both wore facemasks as protection from what could be a lethal problem.

"We had to make sure it hadn't spread, once we found it above the baseboards. And as you can see, it has." Judd motioned around the large space that encompassed their living room, kitchen, and dining room. "The good news is that we've contained it to this area. Nothing upstairs, which we've cordoned off while we do damage control here."

Holy hell. "How much time will this add on?"

"At least four more weeks. We have to rewire the entire downstairs, too. There's no way to make sure the mildew's not in every nook and cranny otherwise."

"Thank God for insurance." And for contractors like Judd and his team. If he hadn't asked Brandon for the contacts, he and Sonja might still be waiting on repairs. The mildew would have reached upstairs if it hadn't been caught now.

"Yeah, well, insurance won't pay for everything, as you know."

"We'll cover whatever's left over." Of course, he needed to talk to Sonja first.

"What's going on?" Her voice cut through him, even in the unfamiliar construction atmosphere. Not the usual laid-back serenity of their previous life on the river.

"We have to re-do the entire first floor." He turned to answer her and saw her blink at him. The facemask—*shit.*

"You have to leave. Now."

"Excuse me—" She was in full tigress mode.

"Sonja. Black mold."

"Oh. Oh!" Her expression shifted as comprehension dawned. "Sorry!" She turned; he followed.

Once in the driveway, he tore off the paper mask. "Sorry about that, but the baby, Sonja. It can't be good for you to breathe in any of that stuff."

"No, you're right." She looked weary. "I wasn't thinking. It's quite a shock to see the house torn up like that. It's worse than right after the flood, which I didn't think was possible."

"I know."

"Thanks for talking to the contractors. Do you need anything from me?"

"No." He should tell her he'd meet her in the cottage, but he didn't want their conversation to end. Once there she'd either hole up in the bedroom or sit on the porch where he didn't bother her. She'd said she needed space, and he'd held up his end of the bargain, since this past weekend. So far.

"What?" She was always able to sense his mood.

"I just—wondered if you had a chance to go over the forms for the nonprofit?"

Her shoulders sagged. She didn't want to work with him. He braced for her words.

"It's not a good idea to think about it until we get something else cleared up."

"What's that?"

"Deidre's pressing assault charges against me for what happened at the hobby and craft store." She spoke like the accomplished attorney she was, but he saw the weariness, the annoyance.

"You're fucking kidding me."

"I wish I were." Her voice was tired but not without the thread of strength that was signature Sonja. "I really wish I'd known your whole history with her before the wedding."

He studied her. And only saw the amazing, beautiful woman that she was. That he had never deserved. As though the fact she'd coldly jilted him never happened. "I should have told you more before."

"We both should have said a lot of things over the past few years." She shifted her weight in her skirt, showing the length of her legs.

"Let's talk now. But not here."

"Fine. I'll go back to the house and change. There's some chicken in the refrigerator I was thinking of roasting."

"Wait—why don't we go out?"

She stared at him, and he held his ground, his chest threatening to burst from the breath he held, afraid to move a muscle lest he frighten her away.

Her eyes narrowed. "Out? Where?"

He named her favorite bayou dive joint. At her silence, he forged ahead. "If that's too greasy, especially now, we can go somewhere better downtown."

"The last thing I want to do is go back downtown. Let's head for The Route Hoot. I'm still going to change."

He watched her walk away, and it hit him with the force of a Louisiana hot sauce that he never wanted to feel like this again. The horrible despair that she was walking away from him, from any chance of a life together. He knew that raising their child would be a partnership of sorts, but it wasn't enough. He wanted Sonja back.

And it was the fucking worst time to figure that out.

* * * *

Nestled into a worn leather booth in the far corner of The Route Hoot's main dining room, Sonja reveled in being able to enjoy her meal without an ounce of nausea.

"You look like you haven't eaten in a year."

"Mmm. It's so nice at night, when my stomach is calm. I can have my favorites, within reason."

"You worry too much about nutrition." He thought of how fussy she'd become about making sure she ate enough vegetables. "You eat well overall. If some extra grits or a po' boy hit the spot, it can't be that bad for the baby."

She grinned through her enthusiastic chewing. "I'm not worried about the baby as much as I am me—I'm eating well for him or her, of course. But the baby doesn't need a momma with cholesterol clogging her arteries."

"Stop. You're in great shape. Have you found out if you can go to the gym?"

She nodded. "I have my second visit to the doctor, in two weeks, but they gave me an information packet at the first visit, which was really quick—enough to verify I'm pregnant. I'm good to work out at whatever I was doing before. Nothing different, though. No new crazy boot camp classes."

"That makes sense." He missed their Saturday morning rides through the bayou roads. It had been a mainstay of their shared life until, until the wedding planning took over. He groaned.

"What?"

"I'm just realizing how much the wedding took from our regular life together."

"Three weeks after it was canceled and you're just figuring that out?" She sipped her decaf iced tea.

"I'm an idiot, what can I say?"

"Not an idiot. Just a guy." She didn't meet his eyes, and he knew she had more to add, and for once, he was grateful she didn't share them all. "I'm going to get rid of my Beemer. It's too costly at this point."

He shook his head. "No. I have the clunker—you keep the BMW. It's not just you you're driving around anymore."

"True, but there are far less expensive cars that are probably just as safe, or safer."

"Maybe, but hold off."

He surprised her. "It's not really your decision. The car." Obviously the baby's welfare rested on both of them.

Henry ignored the comment, his expression fierce. "About Deidre—I didn't tell you everything because I wanted to protect you."

"Protect me from what? This is the part I don't understand, Henry. You know as much as I do that knowledge is power. Had I known how ill she is, maybe I wouldn't have lost my cool at the wedding."

"Bullshit. You weren't going down that aisle no matter what. We both know that now. And for the record—" He studied her.

"What?"

"I'm sorry you had to be the strong one. The one to wave the bullshit flag. It wasn't fair of me—if I'd opened my eyes to reality, we would have postponed the wedding, or not even thought about marriage yet."

"Wow. I don't know about you but I never thought we'd be having this discussion. But I don't want to dwell on what we should have done—we'll end up 'shoulding' all over ourselves." A fun phrase Grandma Edwina had taught her. "Can we agree that neither of us should have been willing to commit at that point? Not until we had hashed out several things."

"Fair enough." He sipped his water. "I've never gotten over the fact that I never saw Deidre's obsessive behavior coming."

"Are you kidding?" She saw that he wasn't. "Henry, that's one of your character flaws, you know. You think you're God."

"I never looked at it that way."

"Think about it. You're always taking responsibility for things that are way beyond your control."

"Maybe." He clearly didn't like playing therapist.

* * * *

"What did you do after you broke up with her?" Sonja was in full counselor mode, and while he didn't blame her for wanting to know every last detail, he didn't think he'd ever know what really made a woman like Deidre tick.

"That's just it. I didn't do anything. We both agreed it wasn't working. I actually thought she was relieved we'd called it off. And then she got squirrelly."

"Poppy pointed something out to me that I hadn't thought of—Deidre's acting a lot like Poppy did, after her ex dumped her and got her assistant pregnant. As a woman, I get it. If you'd dumped me for someone else, and then I found out that person was going to have your baby, I'd be crazy pissed off."

He watched her lips form the words, saw how her eyes lit up with her passion.

"I'd never cheat on you, Sonja." He knew she knew this, but it felt good saying it to her. She deserved to know what she meant to him, even if there was little chance of a future together other than being parents. Had he ever expressed just how much she meant to him? Other than his sincere declarations of love, had he taken the time to tell her he'd be lost without her?

He *was* lost without her.

"I know you wouldn't. That's what makes it so hard to forgive myself for hurting you the way I did. You're one of the good guys." Softly spoken, her entrée long forgotten. Sadness mingled with the compassion in her expression.

"I did my share of hurting, too." Even if by omission. "What are your thoughts on Deidre's charges against you?"

Sonja blew out a breath and crossed her arms. Over her luscious breasts, fuller than ever with the pregnancy, which he fought to keep his eyes off. He inwardly groaned. What the hell was wrong with him? She was under stress from his selfish ex, because of him, and yet his dick still did the talking anytime she was near.

"Emotionally, as a pregnant woman? I'm beyond incensed. Practically? As soon as the judge sees the security footage from the store, it'll be clear that I did nothing to hurt her. She went from being a demon to a suffering saint the minute the guard showed up. If I'm lucky, the judge will suggest that Deidre get some help. That should wake her up to the fact that her behavior is over-the-top. In all reality, though, the judge will probably just dismiss it."

"And if you get Judge Perkins?" They had a longstanding silent feud with one of New Orleans' most infamous judicial players. Marla Perkins had ruled against almost every custody case they'd brought before her court.

"Then I'm screwed." She laughed, and the soft rolling tinkle made him smile for the first time in what felt like a lifetime.

Regret sucker-punched him. His refusal to share everything about his life with Sonja had taken these moments away for good.

"She can't rule against the facts."

"She could, and will if she wants to, but let's face it—Perkins is a fair judge. No matter how she feels about you or me and our cases, she's going to do what's right." What Sonja left unsaid, the bitter spur in their heel, was that the Boudreaux Law offices represented the most financially solvent population of New Orleans and southeastern Louisiana. People who could afford the best and relied on them to make the custody and divorce terms as palatable as possible, even when their client was blatantly against favor. Immorality didn't equal illegality. Which was why Sonja had lobbied him and his father for a nonprofit arm to the firm, or at least the ability to take on more pro bono cases. Sonja wanted to do what she called the "real" work. Lifting people without advantages up.

"She'll make you sweat when you walk in there. I'm going with you, by the way."

Sonja shook her head. "I'm not letting it get that far. I'm filing a motion to dismiss."

Guilt made his shoulders tighten painfully. He rolled his head, stretched his neck. "I'm so sorry you've been caught up in this, Sonja."

She put down her utensils and leaned over the diner table. "You still don't get it, do you? This isn't your fault. It's not all about you, what you did or didn't do. It was never your place to not tell me. You're not God, for Christ's sake!"

* * * *

Sonja watched Henry's eyes widen, his Adam's apple bob as he swallowed. "What the hell, Sonja?"

"You played God by thinking all of this is your fault or doing. That's something we do in our teens, maybe twenties. Don't you think it's time to grow the fuck up?"

He sat back, stared at her. "Wow. I never saw this side of you before."

"Deal with it." She dug back into her meal, suddenly hungry again. She'd never liked her ability to rage but damn, it was empowering.

"I'm not complaining. It's refreshing. You're human, like the rest of us."

"I never knew you doubted my humanity."

"Sometimes it was hard to believe how perfect you were. You handled my parents as if you were a saint. I never saw you get angry at them until the wedding."

"There's no reason to put any energy toward the kind of behavior they've demonstrated. But when it came to you, to hurting you, I, I saw it differently." There. She'd bared her heart to him. He'd been her heart, her everything. And a big part of her wished he still was. But not the way they'd been living, showing only their best to one another.

"I appreciate that." His somber tone reflected sincerity.

The sudden intimacy in the very populated, raucous diner left her searching for an out. She couldn't do intimate with Henry or she'd get her heart broken again.

"As for Deidre and her antics at the craft store—I know I didn't commit a crime. But Judge Perkins is only human. There's always a risk she or another judge will get sucked in by Deidre's sweet smile."

Henry shook his head so quickly she thought he'd strain his neck. "Not likely."

"So you've been keeping tabs on her all these years." Another stab to her heart, another confidence he'd not shared, not that she was counting anymore.

"Wouldn't you want to know where the person who'd done their best to ruin your life for several years was, if they'd ever escalated beyond obsessive into criminal behavior?"

"I don't know." She honestly didn't. "But I'd have told you."

"God damn it, Sonja, give me an inch here."

"I want to."

"No, you don't." His mouth was in that grim line that indicated he'd already made up his mind.

Anger flared deep in her belly but she forced it down, needing him to see her side.

"How would you feel if on our wedding day an old flame of mine had shown up, a man who you later found out had stalked me and made a mess of my life?"

"Don't you think I've asked myself that every fucking day since?" The raw emotion in his response sent her lineup of accusations tumbling into the compassion that erupted the second she saw the pain on his face. He ran his fingers through his hair, and her own itched to smooth it back down, to soothe his obvious distress. To kiss it all away, make him feel better.

This was what had doomed their relationship before. Her need to please, instead of doing what she was now. Digging in.

"We're talking more today than we did in three years."

"At least that's one thing." His mouth was a straight line.

"I'm going to need you to sign a statement about your relationship with Deidre, for the motion to dismiss. I know Judge Perkins won't use most, if any, of it in her decision, but I want to be thorough."

"There's an option we haven't talked about." Henry stared at her. "You could criminally counter-sue instead." His observation made her insides tense.

"No. That's energy in the wrong direction. Let's see how this goes. I did nothing to hurt her, and wouldn't placing legal strictures against her only add fuel to the fire? The last thing I need is Deidre coming after me again. Don't you agree?"

Henry was silent for a long while. "Deidre is a lot of things, but she's not stupid, and I don't believe she's truly crazy, as in mentally ill. She's a spoiled rich girl who's always had her way."

"Except with you."

"Except with me."

The depth of his suffering, no matter how much she thought was self-inflicted, was laid out bare and vulnerable between them. His sense of guilt was part of every line on his face. For once she had no words, no opinion, no way to reach him and smooth the lines between his brows. And it tore at her more than leaving him alone in the cathedral had.

Chapter 12

The following Friday Sonja left work a little early and escaped to the cottage porch. Henry was still at the office, and it had been tense between them since they'd talked about Deidre last weekend. By silent agreement, they'd tabled their discussion about the firm going nonprofit. They weren't mean to one another, or even rude. Just coolly polite. Something they'd never been before.

She reached for the sweating glass of iced mint tea at the same time as her phone erupted in a cacophony of dings. It'd been another long day at the office, and all she'd worked on was the firm's regular caseload. It was going to get crazy busy when she filed the motion to dismiss Deidre's case against her. And she knew she'd feel all the more anxious once her appearance before Judge Perkins was scheduled. She shoved back her anxiety and looked at her screen.

Most of the texts were from Poppy. But not the usual "hey, miss you" or "call me" texts. These SMS messages came with links to social media and online news sources. Poor Poppy. It looked like someone was online stalking her again. She'd already gone through so much when her ex-fiancé dumped her for her college intern, whom he'd gotten pregnant while still engaged to Poppy. Some of Poppy's antics had been detailed in social media ad infinitum. Maybe some of the old stuff had resurfaced. Without looking at the texts, which were bound to be over-the-top dramatic, Sonja called Poppy, who picked up immediately.

"Hey, boo. What's up?"

"Sonja, I'm so sorry. This woman is crazy with a capital C, isn't she?"

"I didn't read your texts so you have to fill me in. Is this about Will's new wife, as in your former assistant? I thought you worked out the lawsuit over your logo and brand when you went to New York."

"Sonja, you didn't look at one single link I sent you. Look at the freaking links. Where are you, by the way?" Poppy's voice wasn't dramatic or self-involved. It was steady as the Mississippi in July.

"I'm on my porch, small as it is, enjoying some peace and quiet before Henry comes home."

"Answer me one thing, Sonja. Did you attack Henry's ex?"

"What? No! She slapped my phone out of my hand and pretended I'd hurt her when the security guard walked over. Wait—I already told you this. Is this what your texts are about?"

"Yes. But now the whole world knows about it. It's hit the local online news and social media picked it up. They've connected the dots to your wedding, and well, the way you *didn't* go through with the wedding. Maybe you should wait for Henry to get there before you look at all of what I sent you. But you need to be prepared."

Sonja was already clicking through, having placed Poppy on speaker. Photos of Deidre, a reporter's microphone in the frame, as she spoke to an off-camera interviewer. Grainy freeze-frames of the security footage, showing Sonja's tall form bending over the tiny Deidre. "This is ridiculous. And oh my God are you kidding me—she did a press interview?"

"Yes." Poppy's regret laced her words. "Don't worry so much about the TV spot. That's only local, and that reporter is pure trash, an affront to good journalists everywhere. She's been sniffing around Boats by Gus, trying to get the dirt on how Brandon's CFO took off with fifteen million."

"That sounds like a normal reporter to me."

"No, no, it's how she's doing it. She never once approached him or anyone associated with the company in a straightforward manner. She's always pretending to be someone looking for a job, or last week she drove a lunch truck into the parking lot under the guise of bringing downtown food to the shipyards. It's all about sensationalism with her. What you need to worry about, as far as I see it, is the damage to the law firm, long-term. Because the people around here have long memories if you haven't already figured that out."

"Hello? As in, I'm the one who grew up here, spring break visitor."

Poppy laughed, and Sonja sopped it up, needing the shared connection. Sonja had convinced Poppy to come home with her for their spring break senior year, instead of going to a popular beach destination like Daytona. She'd introduced Poppy to her church, and they'd gone to a youth ministry outreach service together. It led to them handing out gently used clothing to Katrina survivors, and Poppy had found her calling. She'd never let go of how good it'd felt and credited that one service day to the idea for the new business she started over the past few weeks in NOLA. A consignment shop for women who'd survived domestic violence and needed professional clothing for their job interviews.

"You'll get through this, Sonja."

Her stomach sank. "Thanks, boo. I never wanted to do this."

"Do what? Protect yourself?"

"You're right. Henry and I talked about this over the weekend, about how things might have worked out differently if we'd done the real, honest talking from the get-go."

"So you didn't—that's life. Focus on what's in front of you now. It sounds like you're getting along better."

"Kind of. I thought we were—but we're not really talking again, except at work." She scrolled through the photos Deidre had posted on social media. "Damn it, boo, he should have told me about her sooner. If he had, we might actually be married right now instead of tiptoeing around one another in this clamshell of a house."

"And you would have never run from me?"

She looked up from the screen into Henry's eyes, blazing with blue hot anger, his hands clenched at his sides.

"I got to go, Poppy."

"You sure do." Poppy had heard Henry's voice. "Love you, honey."

"Bye." She disconnected and looked at Henry. "Poppy heard you, you know."

"Do I look like I give a fuck?"

"She called to warn me about what Deidre's done."

Henry wasn't ready to talk about Deidre, that much was clear. "Fuck Deidre, fuck her charges against you, Sonja. Do have any idea how much it slays me that you're still blaming me for our wedding not going through? I know I'm just as much to blame, but you did make the choice to take off."

"You weren't meant to hear that."

"But I did. And I didn't have to overhear it to know how you feel. You wear it like a badge, stalking around like I'm the bad guy who didn't reveal everything to you, and knocked you up in the process. How do you think that makes me feel, Sonja?" His emphasis on feel sent a shiver of remorse through her. And made her straighten her spine. Was this what it took to have a "real" relationship? Peeling back all the layers until the fumes hit you like an onion's?

"It's not always about you, Henry. Don't you think I blame myself enough for deciding to bolt on the spur of the moment? You're not alone in self-recrimination." Tears threatened, which wasn't surprising, as she frequently got weepy when she was very, very angry. Except she wasn't experiencing anger as much as a basic need to defend herself.

Henry watched her, and she saw the fight leave him. He took the two steps to the porch and placed his hands on the railing, their gazes even due to her position on the porch. "No, it's not, but it sure as hell was about me when you decided not to say those vows, Sonja." He looked at her phone as if too tired to discuss it any further. "What now? With Deidre?"

"Deidre went to the press. It looks like she, or they, got the craft store's security footage and the part where she falls to the ground is being replayed over and over again. I know the entire footage will show that I did nothing to hurt her, but it looks awful the way it's edited."

"That wasn't supposed to happen, not before you file the motion to dismiss."

"Tell me about it." She handed him her phone. "See for yourself. It's all over social media. I particularly like the 'runaway bride has runaway temper' meme. Except that's not the best shot of my ass, is it?"

He didn't react to her attempt at humor, merely grew increasingly silent as he tapped through the links. His hair was splayed across his forehead, as if he'd been running his hand over it while driving home. Tiny lines fanned out from his eyes, lines that hadn't been there a few weeks ago. Had the wedding aged Henry? Or rather, lack of the wedding? The pulse at his temple was visible, and the tautness of his cheek indicated he was clenching his jaw. Something he did at night when stressed about work. And she'd added to his stress by jilting him, by not ever giving him the benefit of the doubt. He'd deserved that much from her.

She reached out and put a hand on his forearm. "Henry, let it go for now. We can't change it. Once Judge Perkins takes a look at all of it, she'll dismiss it, and it'll die down."

He handed her the phone, and his brilliant blue gaze raked her face, her figure. Her body immediately reacted, her enlarged nipples begging for his touch as they strained against the friction of her bra, and her face felt as though she'd been standing next to a bonfire. Hot. Uncontrollably so.

"Some things don't ever go away." He kept staring at her, knowing what made her react with unerring accuracy.

She swallowed, silently urging him to move on. To go inside and get changed before she jumped over the railing and into his arms.

"Henry—"

He abruptly turned toward the river house. "I've got to go check on today's progress." He threw the last over his shoulder, and she watched him stride away, his shoulders straining against his crisp light blue dress shirt. He stripped off his tie as he walked and shoved it into his front pants pocket.

She imagined he readjusted himself, too, before going in front of the contractors. Because he had to be hard. God damn it, the air between them still crackled with awareness.

Sonja held the half-empty glass of tea to her forehead, her throat. It offered little respite from the raging heat that she had to accept would never die. She'd never *not* been hot for Henry.

* * * *

"Sonja, you awake?"

She snuggled deeper under the light comforter, relishing the first Saturday she'd had to sleep in and not need to run to the bathroom because she was morning sick. "Barely."

"Can I come in?"

She opened her eyes and looked at the wall opposite the queen bed. Her back was to the entryway. "Sure."

When she lifted her head and sat back against the headboard, Henry walked in, carrying a tray with hot tea and breakfast. "You went to the house to get the dishes."

"I did. Don't worry, I washed them all with hot water. They're clean." He set the tray next to her on the mattress. He stood up so quickly she wanted to ease his mind that she wasn't going to bite.

Which immediately made her face hot. Morning sex had been some of their best.

"I thought we'd go do something today."

She took a sip of the tea. He'd made it with a little bit of honey, just like she did. "Together?"

"Yes." His eyes were a troubled dark sea-blue, and she felt another door in her heart creak open.

"What were you thinking of?" She stretched her calves by pointing and flexing her feet, started to nibble on the toast that he'd smeared peanut butter over. Her favorite. There was no sense asking him to relax and sit down, as there was no chair in the room, and she couldn't, wouldn't have him sitting on her bed. A silly, fragile line, but a boundary she couldn't cross. Not now.

"I think we should go for a long walk or bike ride, your choice, and then maybe end up at the botanical gardens or zoo."

She started to laugh and then coughed as the toast caught. "What? You mean like a date?"

"No, no. I mean like spending time together to start to figure out how we're going to co-parent the baby." He placed both hands on his hips, and she saw where his jeans sagged at his waist, revealing the darker hair that led to the lush growth around his cock. Who needed a botanical garden?

Stop. Sexy. Thoughts.

"Well?" He was staring at her, frustration in his gaze.

"I don't think we can all of a sudden become best friends again after... after everything."

"Again? Do you really think what we had, up until a month ago, was a best friend deal? Because I don't."

Ouch. She put down her toast and picked up the warm tea, needing some kind of comfort after that arctic slam. "Wow. You know, your friendship conversation skills could use a little polishing, counselor."

"Don't do that, Sonja. Don't go back to the legal flirting stuff. That's against the ground rules, remember?"

"Flirting has nothing to do with it. Replay what you just said to me." She watched his face as he did; Henry always had had total memory recall. His smug frustration morphed into stony remorse.

"Okay, maybe that was a bit harsh, but besides the typical friendship where I tell you about my day and you tell me about your time talking to Poppy on the phone, where was the deep part of it?"

At the word "deep" all she saw, all she felt, was how Henry's weight blanketed her whenever he thrust deep inside, filling her more completely than any other man.

"You're thinking about sex, Sonja."

"And you're not?"

"This is my point. While we obviously share some kind of cosmic physical connection, we don't have as much to show for our almost three years together as we should. You were right, getting married wasn't the smartest thing we ever decided to do."

"Whoa—wait, where's my phone." She overacted looking for it, cupped her ear with her hand. "Say that again, for the record."

"Funny." He smirked, and she remembered how much she hated this expression on him. "That doesn't mean I agree with how you decided to put a stop to it."

"But you agree it may have been for the best."

He nodded, his eyes on the floor. "Yes."

At any other time, in any other disagreement with Henry, she'd crowed when he had to admit he messed up. It was rare to ever hear him admit fault, and she knew a lot of that had to come from how he'd been brought up. When your parents shower you with conditional love that requires you're the perfect obedient son, it's pretty damned impossible to learn how to graciously admit defeat, no matter how small.

But to hear him say he agreed their wedding, their marriage, was a mistake. It still hurt.

A little wave of nausea hit her, and she laid her head back against the headboard, needing the firm grounding.

"The baby hormones?" He saw she felt sick.

"Yeah." Not really. This was the fucking sad hormones, the hormones that were sobbing as they realized their best sexy dancing with Henry's hormones were over.

"When do you want to leave? For our walk?"

"Whenever. Take your time getting up. I'll be at the house." He left the room, and she heard him puttering in the next room and at the kitchen sink before the soft slap of the screen door reached her ears. He'd locked the main door behind him, as he always did.

Henry was a perfectionist when it came to taking care of her lately. It was the baby, his child. Her child too. No longer their child, though, not when his or her mom and dad didn't have a future together. Her brain knew Henry was right, that this was the right thing to do. To build a foundation they'd use to rear this child in the best way possible. To shower it with the love they no longer gave to one another. Had they ever, though? Had she been so strung out on the constant, inimitable sex with Henry that she'd been blind to the fact that the time between the sheets was about all they shared?

Henry was only a few hundred yards away, at the main house. Her family was local, and her best friend had just decided to stay in NOLA permanently. And yet, she'd never faced loneliness like this before.

Chapter 13

They picked her favorite park, at least that's what she told him. He drove and let her chill out in the passenger seat of his pickup. He'd had it since his first successful case when he'd started out with his dad's firm.

"I can't believe you still have this thing." She'd rolled down her window, and the air was making her earrings sway, the freshwater pearls he'd bought her for her birthday last year. At least she hadn't tossed everything he'd ever given her into the trash.

"It works better than anything else out there. And you have to admit, it's paid for itself ten times over since we built the house."

"And now we're rebuilding it." She wore a peach top and black workout pants.

"Yup. You know, I didn't ask you, but are you up for this?"

"The walk or the talk?"

He grunted a laugh. "Touché. The walk. It's not too hot, and I have a case of water in the back. But if you think it could hurt the baby, just say so." Damn it, he should have thought about it before dragging her out of bed so early. She'd looked pretty beat last night, and it had been hard to let her go to sleep without following her into the room and lying next to her. He'd had to fight to stay on the foldout.

"The baby's fine. I'm fine."

"I want to go to the next appointment. Shouldn't you have had it by now?" He needed to know all he could about Sonja's and the baby's health.

"I told you, I had the initial one, to make sure I was pregnant, while we were, um, right after the wedding. I've scheduled the next one, where he'll do the first ultrasound, for the beginning of next month. My doc prescribed prenatal vitamins, which I've already picked up and take. I've always taken vitamins and I love orange juice, so the folic acid part is cool."

"Spina bifida." He could list a lot of other birth defects he'd read about in her baby books, but didn't want to freak her out, in case she hadn't read that far.

"Yes, among other things. Have you been researching pregnancy, Henry?"

"A little." He signaled and pulled into the main entry of the park, gave the teller his credit card. "Where to first?"

She told him where to drive after he got his receipt and the ticket to let them out of the parking area later. "Over there, that's a great place to hike, but I don't want to be near the water right now. Too many mosquitos."

"Right." He didn't say a word about the Zika virus. It terrified him. Pulling into the nearest empty spot, he parked as far from the water as possible.

"Henry, I've sprayed myself down with pregnancy-safe anti-bug stuff. I'm wearing longer pants, and it's still early in the season. The baby's safe."

"You can't promise me that." The words flew out of his mouth before he felt the punch of his fear.

"I can't promise you anything, Henry." Her eyes were large and luminous as the sun hit them through the truck's sunroof.

"I'm not asking you to."

They got out of the truck without speaking. Henry wondered if he needed a damn muzzle for his mouth. Since he'd found out she was pregnant, it was as if a cork had popped on the genie lamp of his emotions. Feelings he had zero control over.

If he were brutally honest, it'd been like this since she'd left him at the altar. *You had a part to play, too.*

"You're quiet." She spoke as she walked, her head high and shoulders back. Eyes ahead, anywhere but on him.

"Just absorbing the natural beauty." The green Spanish moss-draped trees towered over them, and the soft mossy ground they trod on hushed their steps.

"See this?" Sonja waved her hand in front of him, laughing. The bullshit flag—she loved doing this.

"I get it. And I'm not BSing. This place is incredible."

She looked around and breathed in deep. Her breasts had gotten larger, the nipples more pronounced, and he was in awe at how they pushed through her workout bra and her T-shirt as if it was the middle of winter and not a warm spring morning.

"Stop looking at my boobs, Henry. We're forging a friendship, I thought."

"You're right. It's just—"

"I know, they're bigger than you ever imagined. That's going to have to be your problem. What do you want to talk about?"

He wanted to keep talking about her breasts, her body, how the pregnancy only made her all the more beautiful. Not because he was some kind of misogynist dick, either. Sonja was the most beautiful woman he'd ever known, and he knew with a visceral certainty that if they lived two lifetimes he'd never meet anyone like her again. But if he shared his thoughts with her, she'd tell him to fuck off.

"How are your folks doing?" Safe topic, her family.

"Good. My parents are loving the Caribbean, and my sisters are busy with their lives, still hoping they'll find Mr. Right sooner or later. My older brother, Tyson, is hanging in there—he's determined to keep playing the field. I know it's none of my business." He saw the concern in her eyes. "My little brother is still my baby brother."

"He's never going to settle down as long as he has his looks and money." Sonja's youngest brother was a professional football player who'd been lucky enough to get recruited by the Saints and was enjoying his local celebrity to the max.

"No, probably not." She adjusted her pink baseball cap. "Daddy's upset with him, of course. Says he's got to stay grounded."

"He's not off the rails that bad, is he?"

"No, but you know Daddy. He doesn't want his kids to make the mistakes he made." She got quieter, harder to hear.

"You've never told me anything about your childhood except that it was fun and loud. Didn't you ever have a rough time? Being a minister's kid had to be rough on all of you at times, right? I mean, they say preachers' kids suffer the most and often are wild childs."

"Gee, Henry, I don't know if you could have shoved more stereotypes into one sentence if you'd planned it."

"Sorry."

"No, you're not that far off. I played the role of the eldest daughter for a long time. Taking care of my sisters was never a problem. My older brother was always busy with school, and my baby brother was off playing sports or hanging with his friends most of the time."

"And you spent lots of time at your grandmother's." He liked Edwina; she was how he pictured Sonja would look in five decades. Beautiful and strong.

"Yes, but not as much as you think, not when we were really young. Grandma was working full time still, and she was still raising her younger kids on the weekends. We saw her mostly during the school breaks. It wasn't until high school that she started to stop in a lot."

"When your mother and father went through their hard times."

"Yes."

"What was it, exactly?" She'd never said. He'd assumed that either one of them had stepped out of the relationship, or that financial troubles had affected them.

"My father got involved with one of the church members. She was a married woman whose husband traveled for his business. My mom was working long shifts at the hospital, heading for tenure at the university." Sonja wiped perspiration off her forehead, her breath even with her steps. He loved seeing her with the backdrop of the bayou forest, the way the sunbeams that struck through the canopy hit her skin and set it aflame.

"You're staring again, Henry." She met his gaze, and one side of her mouth tugged down, mirroring her raised eyebrow.

"Friends are allowed to appreciate beauty, Sonja." His voice was huskier than he intended. He looked away, at the peeling bark on the tree trunks, the birds flitting overhead, the worn path. Anywhere but at her. Because he had to play this cool, easy. No sex. No mention of sex. No sign of arousal. Fuck, he was certain she'd noticed his erection, his cock straining against his cargo shorts.

"So your dad had an affair. What did your mother do?"

Sonja shot him a sideways glance. "What do you think she did? She screamed and ranted and threatened to cut his balls off with her scalpel." Sonja paused, hands on her hips, her face tilted up at the treetops. "That was tough. You know that screaming cry, the wail that can come out of someone at a funeral?"

"Um, yes." He'd seen his best friend in college's mother cling to his casket at his funeral. He'd died of alcohol poisoning.

"You have? Where?" She tilted her head, then held out her hand in the universal "stop" signal. "No, hold that thought. Sounds like you've got something to tell me, then, too. So back to Momma. She took about a month to not growl whenever Daddy was around. It seems funny now, and when you see her as the cool-as-a-cucumber surgeon she is with her patients, you'd never believe the shit she put him through. Not that he didn't deserve it." She pierced him with her stare. "He deserved it sure as shit."

"I believe you—I don't disagree."

"Well, he immediately felt terrible, once the truth was out. I think he'd convinced himself it was all okay because he and Momma weren't getting along, Momma was always busy with work, never anything closely resembling a traditional preacher's wife."

"How did they meet?"

"College, but I don't know a lot of details there. They never talk about it, but for the record, my birthday is only seven months after their wedding date." She grinned, a flash of white wrapping him in the healing power of her humor. "So my God-fearing father and science-brained mother found themselves knocked up and in need of a preacher." She giggled.

"They didn't have to get married. It was in the eighties, for God's sake."

"They loved each other. Momma did say that she knew she'd met her future husband the day he walked into the campus bookstore with a V-neck pullover that had the football team's insignia on it."

"She didn't follow the school team?" Henry was in awe of Sonja's family's athletic genes. Her father had played football in college, as had her brother, the professional running back.

"Hell no. You can barely get her to watch my brother play in the NFL. All she sees is how much damage could happen to him. She's petrified of concussions, of course."

"That's what a mother does, sees all the risks." Too late, he heard what he'd said. "I meant, physical harm not—"

"Chill. I know what you meant. Although it's apropos, isn't it?" Her eyes were steady, the loving peace she carried with her enveloping them both. God, he'd missed this. "Your mother is looking out for her son." So they were going there—his parents. "I get that part. But that's about it."

"My mother doesn't see you as an inherently bad person. It's all about the threat she thinks you bring to all she's imagined for me. The fact that my folks pretty much disowned Brandon for not becoming a lawyer and for, God forbid, deciding to be a boat builder was the first clue they'd gone off the rails. Looking back I see how they've cocooned themselves into their little social bubble."

"Your mother sees me as the woman who'd end her hopes of a long line of perfectly white Boudreauxs."

"I have no defense of her behavior, Sonja. Both of my parents are assholes, and I'm sorry for the pain it's caused you." And would continue to, as she was now forever linked with them due to the baby in her belly. Their baby.

"Trust me, they're not causing me any pain. Not now. They think they've gotten their way—the wedding is off. But when the baby comes..."

"We'll deal as it happens. And unless they're willing to accept you as the mother of their grandchild, and their grandchild as a full-fledged family member, then I'm done."

"You're done?" This woman knew him better than anyone. She knew the loyalty he couldn't shake, the sense of responsibility he had toward his parents.

"Yes. No kid of mine is going to ever have to put up with their racist views or their rigid view of how things 'should be.'" He stopped, not sure if he should tell her the more important part. "And, for the record? I was marrying you regardless of their opinions, or whether they showed up for the wedding. I stopped caring about their feelings a long time ago."

"I know." Her acceptance made him stand up straighter. She'd noticed. Nothing else mattered. "So it stops with you, huh?"

"Yes." As his chest swelled with the strength of an emotion he'd never experienced, he was certain. Nothing was more important to him than the future of his child. And Sonja, though he couldn't, wouldn't, tell her that now. He'd done enough talking over the last three years. It was time to show Sonja he was here for the long haul. "Remember when I went and talked to my folks last week?"

"Yes."

"It was the first time I'd stopped in since the wedding. I had to clear the air with them. But they ended up doing most of the clearing, so to speak." He relayed the conversation as briefly as possible. He didn't want his parents intruding on his time with Sonja.

"And you believe them? You don't think it's just because the wedding didn't happen that they're appearing to have seen the light about their prejudice?"

"They weren't pretending. Look, I'm not going to ever change them completely. But to be honest? I never thought they'd hit bottom over their behavior like they're demonstrating. They think they've lost the only child who still speaks to them, and it was a bit of a wake-up call."

They kept walking in an easy silence, and after another mile Sonja pointed at a covered picnic area about a half mile away. "Let's stop there and eat our snacks."

"Sure thing."

He never thought he'd be enthusiastic about talking to a woman about such deep subjects all day long. Not about the Saints, or Mardi Gras, or the best place to eat a po' boy. He could talk chick talk, before-we-have-sex talk, all day long. Digging deep and pulling out thorns that had been stuck in between the paws of his life? Nope. Never.

Until now, with Sonja.

* * * *

Sonja liked the simplicity of sitting on a picnic bench under a park gazebo with Henry. No work, no ruined wedding reminders, no ex-girlfriend stalking either of them. She relished being able to eat the sliced apple with almond butter and devoured her entire portion without speaking. As for his parents, she'd seen people figure out how their own ugly racism was hurting them and make a choice to change it. So the Boudreauxs were another couple who realized how wrong they'd been. She was happy for Henry's sake, but it didn't make a difference to her. Not anymore. What mattered was that she was talking to Henry about real things, and he was doing the same.

"You're hungry. Maybe you need a meal?"

She looked up into his gaze, at once familiar and new. This was the new Henry, the one who wanted to talk about their lives, their histories. The man she'd seen in him when she'd fallen in love with him.

"No, it's just that I think I'm constantly hungry underneath the morning sickness. So when I don't feel like I'm going to be sick, all I can think about is eating. It's like my body is possessed and all it can focus on is getting more food in my belly." Until she got sick again, but that wasn't happening right now, and she'd take it.

Henry sipped from his sport bottle. "I'm impressed with how much you're changing and you're barely pregnant."

"No such thing as barely when it comes to being pregnant."

"True. But you know what I meant. The hunger swings, the mood, ah, challenges."

They both laughed.

He set his water bottle down, splayed his hands on the worn composite-material table. "We've never done this before."

She looked around as he did, noting the other hikers and park goers enjoying their picnics. Several families occupied the other tables, as well as single, and pairs of, hikers. It was a mix of what she thought of as Louisiana, her home state. Americana at its best.

"No, we've always had linen covering the tables, haven't we? Or we've been at a friend's house, or eating our fancy delivered meals." She shifted her weight on the hard bench. "In a lot of ways we were too successful, too soon."

"I don't agree. We earn what we're worth." His jaw set in classic Henry defense mode.

"Yes, we do earn what we're worth. That's not what I'm arguing. I'm not saying we didn't work for our degrees, for the ability to pull in a good paycheck." She fiddled with the plastic bag she'd packed her apple in. "I can't help but think that if we'd had to wait a little longer to build a house, wait longer to afford my car"—she couldn't point out his pickup, as it was the most frugal part of Henry—"that maybe we would have done more of this kind of thing. There wouldn't have been so many distractions from getting to know the real 'us.'"

He was quiet, his expression open.

"You don't agree."

He shook his head slowly. "I'm ambivalent on that one. I agree that we never slowed down enough to spend a day together like this. The closest we came was probably the movies, or streaming shows on TV. We've already figured out we didn't share enough of ourselves."

"Yeah." She'd spilled about her family on the first part of their walk, now it was his turn. "How is the rest of your family doing—your brother and sister?"

He stretched his neck backward, his hands on his back, before he answered. "You know Brandon's business is kaput, right?"

"Yes." Poppy had told her as much—that the famous shipbuilder's business had to shut down because Brandon and Henry's childhood friend Jeb had flown the coop along with fifteen million dollars. Jeb had been the company's CFO. All of the funds that had been wrapped up in Boats by Gus were gone. Brandon's business produced flat-bottomed riverboats by the dozens and custom sailing yachts that netted upwards of a million dollars each. "I still can't believe it's all over, all gone. Or that Brandon didn't have better safeguards around his company money."

"Brandon says he wouldn't change a thing at this point." Henry looked troubled. "Poppy told you?"

"We talk about it, sure. She's in love with Brandon, you know."

"As he is with her. Maybe that's why all this happened, to get them together." He said it with the note of a death knell.

"Maybe." She'd never heard Henry speak about fate this sincerely. "Is Brandon doing okay, though? Besides the good news about him and Poppy?"

"He's fine financially—he got hired by one of the big guys downtown." Henry named the area's largest shipbuilder. "He's fitting in well, save for having to ask permission to move forward on projects." He laughed. "If there's one thing my brother hates, it's being told how to do anything."

Sonja didn't have to imagine. She was looking at a man who shared much of the same DNA. "And you like it when someone tells you how to do your job?" They worked very well together at the firm but had butted heads on various legal points, and Henry never went down without a decent struggle. Neither did she.

"Sure, I get grouchy when my father thinks the New Orleans office needs to be run a certain way, and I want to go the other." She knew he referred to the pro bono work they wanted to accomplish together, in hopes of going nonprofit at some point. "But that's to be expected. I do what I'm told, at least, I used to." His gaze softened, and she had the feeling he wasn't thinking about the firm.

"Did your father offer to let you make the firm pro bono out of guilt, do you think?"

"No idea. Partly. But I also think he's tired of it. He and Mom seemed to be working through their own stuff. I think they want to retire, maybe start a new life for themselves."

"I know you love pro bono as much as I do. You should go for it, even if we don't decide to do it together."

"I don't want to talk about the office right now. And isn't it telling that you never asked me what made my parents tick before?" He had a look of dissatisfaction that concerned her. Was he mad at himself about it?

"I always felt your relationship with your folks is just that. No way was I going to step in there." She'd wondered if Hudson and Gloria had had a big old family fight about her and Henry, and the un-wedding, but couldn't imagine the reserved couple doing anything but stating their twisted views on life in their usual detached manner.

"I thought you didn't want to confront them about us because you didn't want to lose your job, in the beginning." Henry rubbed her shoulders, which she welcomed.

"That's low, you know. And it's not true. But it's fair." She'd deliberately stayed away from talking to Hudson Boudreaux about anything besides work, which she rarely had to since Henry was the communications link between the offices.

"So why didn't you ever talk to at least Dad about it?"

"Because anything I said would only make it worse, at that time. I can't speak for now, with the way you say they've come around." She hoped it was true, for Henry's sake. "They never approved of me as your life partner choice." She ran her fingers along the edge of the table. The rough underside was a contrast to the smooth painted top. "People who don't 'approve' of interracial, intercultural, or interreligious marriage aren't going to change their minds because of anything I'd say. But I always hoped deep down, waaaay down deep"—she smiled at him for effect—"they'd come around at least by the time our kids came."

"The grandchild fix."

"Yes. It's ironic, right? The marriage is off, but now they'll have a grandchild from both of us."

"They'll get over it." A shutter closed over his expression. His impatience with his parents had been obvious since the un-wedding day. "Or never see their grandchild." He crushed his napkin in his hand, and she was glad it was only paper. He'd have torn his skin off if he'd been holding a bottle or can.

"What else is going on there? I mean, they showed up at the wedding. No matter their motives, that was a big step for them, right?"

He sighed. "Yeah, it was. Until Deidre showed up with them."

"You said yourself that they're clueless as to how obsessed she is. They were manipulated by her, is the way I see it." The way she wanted to see it.

"You weren't so forgiving of them before. What's changed?" His head was tilted just slightly, and she fought from smoothing his hair back.

"I guess when they showed up at the rehearsal dinner I thought it was a big move for them. Looking back now, that is. That night, and a little bit the morning of the wedding, I really thought they were going to try to convince us both to call it off. Not just what they'd said to me. And I thought they'd be elated that we didn't end up getting married, after all.

"To be fair, my grandmother thought that us getting married was asking for trouble, too."

"Edwina? Aw, she's just telling you that because she knows you're in a rough spot."

"Nope. She told me before the wedding. Before..." She waved her hand instead of saying the words again.

"Bullshit. She adores me." He spoke with such confidence, his chest puffing like a hush puppy in six inches of grease. Sonja laughed, and got him to laugh, too.

"You're right. She does like you. Always has."

"Your folks, your whole family has been so nice to me."

"Yes." She didn't want to talk about her family again, not today. They still weren't done with discussing Henry's. "How's your sister?"

He scratched his head, put his cap back on. "No clue. She's off in South America for some military exercise, but neither my folks or I, or Brandon, have heard from her." Jena's military work puzzled not only Henry, but his whole family.

"She sent the video message for the wedding." It had shown only her face, with a bland white wall backdrop, as if from a hotel or military barracks.

"Yeah, but I think that was taped a week or two before we got it." His pulse jumped on the side of his temple.

"You're worried she's not doing well."

"I don't know what to think. Brandon doesn't, either. She's supposed to be home next week, and we're waiting to hear it from her that she's all right."

Something bothered him about his sister, but she didn't want to push. Henry looked like he was really upset about Jena, and since they had enough to deal with she let it drop. The few times she'd met Jena, she'd enjoyed her sense of humor and admired her sense of strength. Henry's sister had the Boudreaux stunning blue eyes, but unlike her brothers she was completely no-nonsense, always serious. Henry erred on the side of being too comedic at times, which drove Sonja nuts when they had a case to work on, but she loved it when they were alone. Or in bed.

Shit. The damned pregnancy hormones were trying to come marching in again.

Chapter 14

"Do you need anything more from me?" Alesia stood at the doorway of the conference room, her eyes all but popping out as she ogled the pile of wedding gifts heaped upon the sturdy table. They'd agreed to pull the presents from Brandon's garage, where they'd stayed for the last several weeks. The office was the only space available to them that was large enough to handle the task, which they'd agreed to do after hours.

"We're fine." Both Henry and Sonja answered at the same time, and she looked at him, still surprised that he'd agreed to do this with her. As a team.

"Seriously, I can stay and make notes, so all you have to do is send the thank you notes when you're ready to." Alesia was so transparent Sonja almost laughed.

"We're cool. See you in the morning." Henry dismissed her.

"Bye." She left, and Sonja heard the front door close tight behind her.

"It's just us and this pile of stuff." Henry seemed almost exuberant over the monumental task they'd decided to get through tonight. They'd agreed that before the baby's first ultrasound, they wanted any last threads of their un-wedding cut and tossed. So they could start fresh as parents.

"We'll get through it. Thank God most people gave us cash or cards." She motioned to the large card collection box, bedecked with silver wedding-print paper and sparkling ribbons.

"You're sure we have to send this all back?" He held up an electric grill cleaner, some kind of contraption with a motorized brush. "I've always wanted this."

"Re-wrap, send back." She pointed at the tubes of craft paper she'd purchased, along with shipping tape and permanent markers. "I'll do the same with the gift cards and checks. Any cash, I'll split with you, and we'll write checks back to the guest."

"Yes, ma'am."

She tossed a wadded piece of paper at him, satisfaction unfurling when it hit the side of his head. Henry laughed.

"Who would have thought going through the carnage of our wedding day would be so much fun?" His eyes sparkled, and his grin, holy shit his *grin*. Henry's smile could light her up like Rockefeller Center's Christmas tree in three seconds flat.

"If you're trying to drive home the point that I jilted you and made your life a living hell, it's working." Yet, no tug of regret as she knew she would have felt only a week or two ago.

"It's kind of scary how relaxed we are about this, isn't it?"

She opened another card, read the sentiments. "I don't know if relaxed is the right word. Take this card, from my auntie. She's so sure we're meant to be together, that nothing will tear us asunder." Slowly she moved the card to the "done" pile, making note of the check that her paternal aunt had gifted them before placing it in the return envelope. She and Henry had agreed to a simple "thank you" and "we're sorry it fell apart" message on a pre-printed card.

"She could be right."

Sonja froze. "What the hell, Henry?"

"Whoa, chill. I don't mean you ever have to marry me again. But think about it. We're having a baby together, going to raise a kid. Together. That's pretty biblical. As permanent as it gets."

Warmth washed over her. Not heat, but a solid, reassuring warmth. Somehow, she and Henry would make this work.

* * * *

Henry never would have imagined that the monumental task of sending back nearly two hundred wedding gifts would be such a non-issue. But if anyone had told him he'd have fun doing it, he'd have assured them they'd lost their minds.

"Can you believe Poppy? She gave us a gift certificate to Beautiful Baby." Bemusement coated Sonja's voice.

He snuck a glance at her. Phew. No tears. The pregnancy had made her far more emotional than he'd ever seen her, even when she'd been a chocolate maniac before her periods.

"What's that?" The name meant nothing to him.

"Only the most exclusive baby store in NOLA." She laughed. "What if I'd opened this in front of you after the wedding, before I'd told you about the baby?"

"It didn't work out that way, so no point worrying about it now." He still had a twinge of regret that she'd not told him right away, the minute she'd suspected she was pregnant. It was time he couldn't get back.

"Henry." She stayed silent until he met her gaze. Her laughter had subsided to a soft smile, her mouth pouty. His cock immediately reacted, no matter how much he tried to think about boring shit.

"Yeah?"

"If I had to do it all over again, I would have told you right away." She looked away. "That night, after our time together on the deck? I had a dream we'd made a baby. And we had, we did. I am so sorry I didn't tell you then."

"I am, too." He used a razor knife to open a large shipping box and pulled out a smaller box filled with crystal cocktail glasses. "But it's done. We can't turn the clock back, and it's probably best we can't, right?"

"In a lot of ways, yes. But I still wish I'd told you about the baby sooner."

Her quiet admission caught him off guard and he stilled, needing to stop the war between his physical need for her and this new, concrete bond they were building between them. "Thank you, Sonja."

"Are those Sazerac glasses?"

He laughed. "In most other parts of the country they're highballs, right? But yes. These are from my law school classmates." The cocktail glasses had the school logo on them.

"Now that is a hard gift to send back. Am I right?"

"Naw. It's not that bad."

They worked for several hours to get to the bottom of the cards and boxes. When they finished, all that remained on the tabletop were empty takeout boxes from their dinner and a neat stack of thank you/we're sorry cards.

"That wasn't as bad as I thought it'd be." She looked at him, surprise stamped on her stunning features.

"It's kind of—" He didn't want to say it. Didn't want her to misunderstand him.

"Freeing?" She had one brow arched as she looked at him with expectation.

He nodded. "Yes." His shoulders sagged. "Holy fucking shit, Sonja."

She laughed. "Talk sweet nothings to me, babe."

"Sorry. I mean, I had no idea how much stress this all was." He glanced at the pile of boxes that would get picked up by the parcel service tomorrow, the pile of cards she'd filled out. "It was too much. You deserved so much more, the wedding you wanted. Without all of"—he motioned his hand in a circle—"this."

"Not just me, Henry. *We* deserved something...more 'us.' But we weren't ready for anything else. This was all we knew to fall back on."

"I think I'm the one to blame there. I convinced you to do the whole fancy wedding deal. You would have been happy to go to Vegas." He cringed at the thought, even now.

"I said that, I know, but honestly, I wasn't any more ready to walk down that aisle of St. Louis Cathedral than I was to find out I was pregnant."

He totally got what she was saying.

"Like you said the other day, at the restaurant. Neither of us was ready for the commitment. We hadn't done the deep digging to make sure we fit."

"Exactly!" Her triumphant grin made something bigger break loose in his chest. Which triggered the usual trepidation—was this all going to disappear, just like their plans for the huge wedding and perfect life together had?

He was tired of living in fear.

"And here we are, after all the mess."

She grinned, and pointed at her belly. "And here we are!"

She deserved to be the bride of all brides, his Sonja.

Not your Sonja anymore. The mother of his child, that was his connection to her going forward. It would have to be enough, but he'd be damned if he didn't try to make it more.

* * * *

Henry lay on the pullout sofa, counting every steel rod in the folding frame as he stared at the ceiling fan that circled above him. He tried not to tune into Sonja's murmurs and sighs, coming from the cottage's single bedroom. But his cock sensed her near, that was certain. He was positive his balls weren't just blue but frozen an arctic shade of cerulean after making good on their ground rules and not allowing himself to touch her these past several days. And the walk the other day and getting rid of their wedding gifts had only underscored how much he still wanted her. How much he missed her.

They'd talked more after they got home and agreed that each time they'd acted on their sexual needs since the ill-fated un-wedding, it had been a mistake as it'd made it harder for them to emotionally detach enough to have the conversations they needed to have. Apparently his dick wanted to make an even bigger mistake, because he couldn't stop thinking about making love to Sonja.

It was wrong on so many levels. He tried what had fueled him the awful first two weeks after the wedding. She'd left him at the altar. In front of everyone. Where was his pride, his self-esteem?

In his dick. Which was still hard, insistent that Sonja was the answer.

He hadn't been much of a charmer himself in the months leading up to the wedding. Hadn't he kept some very important details about his past from her? She didn't trust him because he hadn't trusted her with his secrets. Just as a relationship took two to tango, theirs had taken both of them to mess it all up. He no longer completely blamed her for running.

The soft pads of her footfalls as she got up to go to the bathroom reminded him of how she loved it when he massaged her feet after a long day in court. Since being back in the cottage together, he'd counted her bathroom trips two or three times each night, common during pregnancy. He'd been reading in her pregnancy and childbirth preparation books when she wasn't around. He never wanted her to think he was trying to please her or woo her by learning about the baby and how it would arrive here. So he'd kept his baby research private. Besides, he couldn't be concerned about winning her back, not if he wanted his heart to survive.

"Henry?" Her whisper, right next to his ear, startled him, and he sat up quickly. Too quickly, as his head hit hers, and he heard her muffled groan.

"Sonja, are you okay?" Reaching for her in the dark, grasping her shadow to feel for her, was natural. Friendly concern.

"I'm fine but I might have a fat lip." She sat on the edge of the bed, allowed him to hold her back against his chest as he half-sat behind her. "I thought you were awake."

"Because I wasn't snoring?"

"No, not that. Well, okay, yes. You weren't snoring. And, and I felt it." Quiet, uncertain.

They'd always been able to feel when the other was near. Knew when the other was hurting. He realized it was probably why the three weeks apart had hurt so fucking much. The invisible threads that bound their hearts, no matter how fucked up their decisions and actions, were still there. Still... connected.

He kissed her shoulder, her throat, her nape. She sighed against him. "This is what you came out here for, isn't it?"

"Against my best judgment, yes." Another feathered sigh as he sucked softly on her skin. Enough to make her wet, the way he knew this kind of caress did, but not enough to leave a mark. He never wanted her to have to cover any of her beautiful skin because he'd left a love bite.

"What's keeping us from drawing up a new contract between us?" He held her back against his chest, not willing to listen to the common sense he'd just gone over with himself. Besides, her skin tasted sweeter than fresh cherries and was softer than the petals of the honeysuckle that grew alongside the cottage.

"We've never had a contract." Her voice was raspy.

He loved her like this, when he knew making her come was within reach but still far enough away to give them so many options for deeper pleasure.

He moved his fingers over her head, combing her tight Afro curls, loving the feel of her hair and scalp under his hands as he gently pressed her head forward so that he had more access to her nape. It was Sonja's sensual weak spot. She complied, and she reached behind her, her hands looking for his cock, but he scraped her skin with his teeth, softly. "No, not yet, babe. About that contract. We could agree to help one another with our physical needs, for sanity's sake. No strings. I won't try to make it more than it is."

She stilled, and fear threatened his erection. This was when she'd turn and tell him nothing was worth the risk of that hurt again. He felt her shift, turn to face him. But she didn't stand up or walk away. She found his cock with scary accuracy in the dark and grasped it through the thin cotton of his briefs, made him groan with the sheer pleasure of her touch. "Jesus, Sonja."

"Okay. What you said—we don't have to make it anything more than what it is. This"—she squeezed him, just enough to take it to the edge of good and painful—"is what we'll always share. This connection. For tonight, it's enough for me."

She leaned over and kissed him, and he fought to not get off right there, in her hand, before he had a chance to show her that he concurred with her summation.

* * * *

Sonja needed the weight of Henry in her hand, the scent of him filling her as their tongues pushed and twisted. The soft sucking noise of their kisses was sweeter than any symphony, sexier than her favorite blues. When he reached around and grasped her ass she moved her legs to splay around his hips, her legs over his, their pelvises touching in the most erotic of foreplay positions. She never wore panties to bed, so her entire femininity was pressed up against his hard length.

"We need to get your underwear off. Now." She nipped at his shoulder as she released him and scooted back so that he could free his legs. Her very center throbbed for him and felt bereft as the cool night air hit it. Henry's mouth, tongue, and dick were the only things she wanted touching her.

"We do this, it's with no regrets. No ties to who we were before, or where we're going." His voice vibrated next to her ear as he left a trail of kisses down her throat. Henry stopped and rested his forehead on hers, their breath intermingling in the moonlight that had escaped a cloud and spilled into the front room like praline caramel.

"Okay." Her voice came out as a strangled mess. All she could think about was satisfying the pulsing need between her legs and feeling like she was once again whole. "I agree, Henry. This is just for tonight. Just us."

He didn't ask for anything more but held her face in his hands as if she were a fragile knickknack. "Is it okay, with the baby?"

"Since the baby's the size of a lima bean, I'd say it's fine." Mentioning their unborn child did something deep inside her, past the physical desire, past the want to be connected with him again. It rocked her.

His kiss started as exploratory, his tongue seductive with long swirls as his hands worked magic over her breasts and nipples. When he tweaked one she jerked in his arms, the sensation so intense she thought she'd come right there. A rolling laugh rocked through her, and she pressed herself to him, both of them seated side by side.

"Does that tickle?" He did it again to the other nipple, his thumb and forefinger positively wicked in their motive.

"I'm going to explode if you keep doing that." She moaned as he did it again as he sucked the other nipple entirely into his hot, wet mouth. Sonja saw pinpricks of light in front of her closed eyelids; her body thrummed with how he played her.

"Do whatever you want to, babe." He continued his focused attention on her breasts until she pushed him back.

"I can't think when you do that."

He lowered her to the bed and followed, placing his hard cock at her entrance, balancing on his forearms. "No thinking is part of the agreement, too." He kissed her until she squirmed under him, her body reaching for his.

"Come on, Henry. Give it to me."

"Not yet, sugar." He did what she thought of as a Henry safari, exploring every inch of her front with his lips and tongue.

Sonja couldn't control her breathing and didn't want to. All she wanted was this—Henry making love to her in the river moonlight, their bodies communicating in the way they'd never figured out how to with words.

When he reached her pussy she ran her fingers over his head and soaked in the way his mouth moved over her, his tongue into her. It had never been this good.

* * * *

Henry licked and savored each drop of Sonja's arousal, her scent stronger than he remembered, her most intimate parts slightly swollen with her need. It was the pregnancy, too—he'd read that in the books—but he wanted to believe it was all for him, because she was as turned on by him as he was her.

He'd gladly stay here all night, but she was so primed that after only a few minutes of loving her clit, her lips, her slick walls, she came with all the feminine strength and beauty only Sonja could. He teased her again as soon as she came down from the ride, pushing two fingers inside her and stroking her G-spot. She rewarded him with a second and third climax, one after the other, and he fought to keep control of his cock. Full and stiff from knowing he'd pleased her, it was all he could do to not spill it all before he'd had a chance to complete their lovemaking.

"Henry, please, fuck me." She tugged on his hair, and he slid up the length of her. "Let me suck on you first, babe." Her breathing was deep and swift, her skin damp, her scent one hundred percent Sonja.

"No. I need to be inside you."

She answered wordlessly, opening her legs and hips to him. Henry searched for her eyes and thanked God for the bright moonlight because in this moment he had to be connected to her in every way possible. As he slid into her folds he watched the magic sparks ignite in her pupils, her lids slowly closing as she, too, savored their joining.

"Look at me. Please." He'd never begged her before, never needed to know she was with him through each sensation, like they were conducting some kind of sacred rite. "God, Sonja." Thrust. "It's so." Pump. "Fucking." Grind. "Good." He heard her groan and felt her muscles tighten around his cock, and finally allowed himself to do what he'd been raging to do since they'd been apart. Since before the wedding, since before they'd lived together. He took Sonja with a total freedom, trusting that she'd find her climax as he sought his.

Her heels dug into his buttocks, and her hands gripped at his back, her breath a pure pant again as she begged him to keep going, never stop.

Sonja cried out as she came, and he pushed into the orgasm, going to a place he'd never been before with her. Complete abandon.

Chapter 15

"Let me get this straight." Brandon stared at him with the same blue eyes their mother had. "Sonja hasn't left the firm, so you're still working together every day. You're both cash poor, which is why you're living together, but apart, in that shoebox guesthouse. All you need to say is that you're still fucking and I'm going to be really confused. I thought she jilted you at the altar?"

Henry moved his scrambled beef hash around on the tavern plate, not knowing how to explain it to his brother. "It's complicated."

"What's so complicated about you're either together or you're not?" Brandon took a gulp of coffee in between shoveling scrambled eggs into his mouth. They were in their favorite breakfast place and had made weekly breakfast into a routine since they'd reconciled at the un-wedding.

"If nothing else comes out of my failed wedding, at least you and I are talking again. It means a lot to me, Brandon."

Brandon paused mid—fork lift and met Henry's gaze with a serious one of his own. Then he winked. "It's mutual, but you're dodging my question. Answer it, Henry. What the hell are you doing with Sonja after she clawed your heart out of your chest, wrung it out, and ran it over with an ATV?"

Henry clutched his chest and grimaced. "With that description I swear I can still feel the pain."

"Answer. The. Fucking. Question."

Henry sighed. "I'm not who I was a month ago. Neither is Sonja. And we're, we're getting closer than we ever were. I know, it's cliché, but since the wedding, almost-wedding, whatever you want to call it—"

"A great party nonetheless." Brandon grinned. He'd made sure every guest enjoyed the custom gourmet New Orleans spread, from the appetizers to the salted caramel cake.

"Yeah, well, since we've had to see each other at work, and then deal with the house reconstruction, it's as if we're finally seeing one another for who we are. No fancy lawyer bullshit, if that makes sense."

"It doesn't." Brandon wasn't going to give him an inch.

"Before, we were, I was, wrapped up in getting the next case under my belt. Making bank, paying for the best house we could afford, making sure we'd have the best wedding ever. Sonja never wanted the big wedding. She'd even talked about one of those destination weddings, but I wanted to give Mom and Dad a chance to come around. More than that, I wanted to show the world how much I loved her, how important marrying Sonja was to me."

Brandon eyed him over his empty plate. He pointed at Henry's half-finished breakfast. "Eat. And let's talk about Mom and Dad." Brandon's usual affable expression turned grim, with a twinge of sorrow.

"They're changing, Gus. They're not the same people who took off and abandoned New Orleans after Katrina." He'd already told Brandon about his conversation with Hudson and Gloria.

Brandon looked pained. "Do you really think they're telling the truth?"

"They were flat-out depressed, very apologetic. Completely unlike their usual selves."

"I always thought they could have a change of heart once grandchildren come; it's been known to happen. But I wouldn't have ever bet on it."

"Are you saying that Poppy is pregnant?" Henry hadn't told anyone about his and Sonja's baby yet. He felt it was Sonja's news as long as they were apart. But then last night. Fuck.

Last night they'd been anything but apart. His blood pumped fiercely at the memory of how hard they'd come together, like two rogue waves meeting up with combined force unrivaled by any other.

Brandon shook his head. "Hell, no. Poppy and I are just getting the living together part down. And of course, she's agreed to marry me." Brandon's grin split his handsome face in two, and Henry leaned over the table and smacked his brother on the shoulder.

"That's fantastic! Congratulations. I'm happy for you, man." God, another Boudreaux wedding. "That's two of us down." He froze. "I mean, would have been."

Brandon gave him the side-eye. "You're not telling me everything about you and Sonja. That's cool. But if you think you're even remotely over her, you're smoking some fine stuff."

Henry nodded. "Point taken. And really, I'm so happy for you and Poppy."

"Thanks." Brandon's grin slipped. "Have you heard anything from Jena?"

"Nothing. She's supposed to be back from her reserve active duty this month, isn't she?"

"That's what she said before she left." Brandon's face looked troubled. "But Mom and Dad mentioned at the reception that they were concerned. You know how they are. They never come out and say they're worried."

Henry snorted. "Because only people who don't have everything completely under control worry. It would make their obsession with perfect appearances moot."

Brandon shook his head. "I'm not kidding here. They said she usually checks in more often. And she used to with me, too. I just figured she was busy with whatever exercise she's doing down there."

"She checked in with me more during her last active duty tour, too." He remembered laughing at her silly photos of her in the middle of God-knew-where. "Do we know exactly where she is in South America?" Henry listened with half attention as the other part of him was occupied with visions of last night with Sonja. How her naked skin felt against his, again. It was like he was a high school kid who'd just lost his virginity. He wanted more.

"...Asunción." Brandon looked at him. "Did you hear anything I just said?"

"Yeah—wait. Paraguay? Jena's in Paraguay?" His parents hadn't mentioned it to him, but they'd been busy making the amends of a lifetime. At least the start, anyhow.

"That's the last I heard. She sent a short text right before the wedding, let me look." As Brandon scrolled through his texts, Henry tried to find out if he was losing his mind.

"You make any more headway on getting your money back?" Brandon's CFO and former best friend, Jeb, had absconded with a cool fifteen million one month ago, leaving Jeb's shipbuilding business in the lurch. "Any leads on new contracts?"

"As a matter of fact, no and yes. No, no sign of Jeb since a private investigator I hired traced him to Asunción, where he disappeared. And as I'm sitting here, I'm wondering why I haven't put more than coincidence on Jena being in the same place Jeb took my money to."

Henry's hackles rose. His younger sister was precious to both of them, and the thought of her meeting with trouble made him sick. His breakfast sank in his stomach like a lead weight. "They, they haven't been together, ever, have they?"

"Other than when she tried to get him to take her to prom? No. Besides, Jeb's like a brother, or he was, at one point." Brandon dismissed the concept.

"Jeb was like a brother to you, but not as much to me and Jena. He was our friend because he was your friend." He thought he'd detected sparks between his sister and Jeb on more than one occasion but chalked it up to none of his business.

"So what, you're saying they ran away together or something?"

"Or something. Did you report this to the police?"

"Yes. And the FBI. People far bigger than us are on it." Brandon drummed his fingers on the table. "And if Jena was in big trouble the Navy would have reached out to Mom and Dad, right?"

"Yeah. Hopefully." Henry felt sad for his brother. "You're certain you won't ever get your money back?"

"Yes." Brandon leaned back in the booth and stuck a toothpick in his mouth. "That's gone. I'm starting over. And it's okay. I wouldn't want to with anyone else but Poppy."

"Have you been talking to Mom and Dad any?"

"More than the nothing we said to one another for the better part of ten years?" Brandon looked at him with complete incredulity. "No, not really. I suppose I'll need to think about Poppy getting to meet them for more than the brief introduction they had at your wedding." He grimaced, aware of the pain it caused Henry that the wedding hadn't happened. "Sorry, bro."

"No worries." And to his surprise, he wasn't as torn up about it as he might have been even a few days ago. He and Sonja were on a new road, one that he was curious about but not dreading. "It sounds like Mom and Dad are really worried about Jena. Maybe we should be, too."

"I'd give it another week or so. She shows up, we'll ask her the hard questions then."

"Like who does she really work for?"

"You've wondered, too, eh?" Brandon's eyes sparkled in conspiracy. "It is odd how she has a regular day job here in the States but then disappears for longer than a month at times. I thought the reserves meant you drilled on weekends and did two weeks active per year."

Henry laughed at him. "Yeah, back in the stone ages when we went to college and our friends took NROTC scholarships. I think it's all dependent upon the needs of the Navy these days, right?"

"Yup. That reminds me. No, I didn't get the San Sofia contract, but yes on the second part of your question. I landed a job that entails several contracts when I put a bid in for the San Sofia drug interdiction boats." Brandon had spiffed himself up with the help of Sonja's best friend Poppy and pitched his business to the foreign island nation's naval representatives. Something definitely out of his comfort zone.

"I never told you in person, but I'm so damned proud of you, bro. You could have curled up into a ball over Jeb's shit, and instead you pulled it together and went after a big fish."

Brandon smiled. "It's the Boudreaux way, right?"

"I won't deny there's something in our blood that keeps us forging ahead." Would it be enough to keep him going as long as it took to work things out with Sonja? Wait—was that the feeling that had been dogging him this past month?

Holy hell, he wanted to make it work with her again.

Could he win Sonja back?

"Henry?" Brandon had missed nothing. Fuck, it was like he wore his heart on his face around his brother.

"Yeah?"

"Don't let her get away again. Do whatever it takes. Maybe you're not going to ever get married, formally. Is it that important?"

"I can't even go there." It was too much to think they'd work it out to the point of being a full couple again, wasn't it?

Brandon laughed, the deep belly laugh Henry associated with their childhood shenanigans. "Henry, dude, you're already 'there.'"

Henry let his brother finish laughing before he stood up. Brandon followed. "Let me know if you hear anything more about Jena."

"Will do."

They did the bro hug, patting each other on the back.

Henry knew he'd be thinking about Brandon's observations for the rest of the day.

* * * *

Sonja looked with trepidation at the piles of papers on her desk. It was everything she'd been able to put together from talking to Henry and her own account of how she'd first met Deidre—at the wedding—and how she hadn't invited her. Neither had Henry.

But Mr. and Mrs. Boudreaux had, and Judge Perkins wasn't going to accept Sonja's reasoning that Deidre had manipulated her way into their nuptials. So far her testimony read as though she and Henry had invited the woman and her illness into their lives.

Unless...

Sonja went out to the reception area. Henry was nowhere in sight, at brunch with his brother if memory served her right. Alesia was gone, probably an early lunch since they weren't seeing any clients until later in the afternoon. Sonja knew what she had to do.

Later that afternoon she headed for Baton Rouge. Two hours from New Orleans, the Boudreauxs' home and Hudson's nearby law office was only a little more than an hour from where Sonja and Henry had built the house. So at least her drive back to the cottage wouldn't be as long. The two-hour drive to the Boudreauxs' was the perfect amount of time to clear her head and make sure her motives were correct. Plus she needed to gird her loins, literally. She wasn't showing up as only the bride who'd jilted their son. She was the mother of their future grandchild, whether or not they knew it yet.

It was almost six in the evening when she pulled up to the large contemporary home in the exclusive subdivision. She'd thought ahead and found the code for the keypad where Henry kept all of his computer passwords—taped on the bottom of his watchcase. Henry loved watches like she loved bags, and she'd enjoyed giving him one for Christmas this past year that she noted he was still wearing. As if he wanted something from her close to him, even after the awfulness of their un-wedding.

She parked her car on the circular driveway, under an oversize crepe myrtle before the main entryway. The element of surprise was all she had, and knowledge from Henry that his parents dined at precisely six thirty every evening, thirty minutes after his father arrived home. Unless they were at one of their favorite restaurants, where they'd treated her and Henry to nice, stilted meals.

Hopefully they were dining in tonight and she'd catch Henry's mother alone for the first few minutes. If she could convince Gloria to sign the affidavit that she'd been the one to send the invitation to Deidre, then it seemed likely Hudson would do the same. They did everything in step, those two.

The doorbell chimed like an antique gong deep in the house, and she held her breath. Light footsteps, the shape of his mother's head at the side beveled windows. Sonja bit her lip. Gloria recognized her because she visibly jerked, even through the distorted glass.

As the door swung open Sonja was greeted with shiny wooden floors, warm light spilling from the great family room beyond, and the stony glare of Henry's mother. Henry and his brother Brandon had inherited her brilliant blue eyes but unlike her sons', her eyes were brittle and detached.

"Sonja." Gloria peered past Sonja, looking for someone else. "Did you come alone?"

"I did. I wanted to speak to you and Hudson for a few minutes. May I come in?"

"Of course! Please." Gloria stood to the side and opened the front door wide. Maybe all that Henry had told her was true—she'd never seen Gloria appear this open, this welcoming.

Sonja walked into the grand foyer, contemporary but with decorative flairs that were in standing with the historical charm she associated with an older home. The kind of home that hadn't been able to survive Katrina. This modern edifice was stormproof not just in build but location, over two hours away from the initial strike zone of hurricanes in the Gulf of Mexico.

"Hudson is due home at any minute. We have dinner plans, and we'd love to have you join us." Gloria's smile was genuine. So Henry had gotten it right. There had been some kind of epiphany in the Boudreaux home.

"No, no, thank you. I have to get back to New Orleans as soon as we're finished."

"Is everything okay? I mean, besides the wedding." Gloria's face crumpled. "Shit. I'm making another mess of things. Sonja, I don't know if you've spoken to Henry, but Hudson and I are so very sorry for the way we've treated you. How can you ever forgive us?"

"Gloria." Where to begin? And clearly Henry hadn't told them they were sharing the cottage again. No matter. "That's past. I appreciate your seeing things the way they really are, though." There was nothing else to say. Their past bigotry wasn't hers to forgive.

"I'm not here about why I jilted Henry, Gloria." That was between her and Henry. "I'm here to ask you if you sent a wedding invitation to Deidre."

"Why, yes I did. After I ran into her and her mother at the Christmas Tea in NOLA last year, they asked me to keep in touch. Deidre was still married at the time, I even sent the invitation to both her and her husband. I didn't know until the rehearsal dinner that she's divorced. Why, is Deidre what made you run, Sonja? I can assure you that Henry never looked at any other woman the way he looks at you!"

Too much too late. Where was Gloria's support of their relationship six, twelve months ago? In the racist shit pile, was where.

"Why I'm really here is to obtain a statement from you and Hudson that you were the ones to invite Deidre to the wedding. She was never on our guest list. I never received an RSVP from her, either." As much as it was tempting to have a soul-baring conversation with Gloria, all Sonja needed was her and Hudson's signatures.

"A statement?" Gloria visibly blanched. "I need to wait to speak to my husband. Is Deidre in some kind of trouble?"

Sonja wasn't sure what to tell Gloria. Even after the bitch on wheels she'd been to Sonja when it came to Henry, the woman seemed truly repentant. And in emotional distress.

"Have you heard any more from Jena?"

Gloria's eyes welled up. "No. Not a thing. It's some kind of secret job she has, down in South America. We won't hear anything until she walks through this door again."

"What do we have here? Sonja!" The thunderous timbre of Hudson Boudreaux's voice, the same as Henry's but mellowed with age, made Sonja jump.

She turned to see him stride through the open front door. He stopped a couple of feet shy of where Sonja stood, her legs braced against what she expected to be a predictable dressing down from her boss.

"Hi, Hudson. I'm sorry to barge in. Gloria told me you've planned a nice evening out, so I'll be brief. I'm working on a motion to dismiss, and I need your signature on an affidavit I've prepared." She filled Hudson in, lawyer-to-lawyer. He remained silent, listening intently. As Sonja spoke, Hudson held his arm up, and Gloria sidled up next to him.

Hudson looked at Gloria. "You sent the invitation? You didn't mention it when we saw her. I assumed she was on Henry and Sonja's list."

Gloria fidgeted with her earring. "Henry gave us extras for that reason, Hudson. To invite anyone we felt was overlooked."

His glance remained on Gloria a minute too long, and Sonja's insides shook. Holy shit, Gloria had gone behind Hudson's back, as well. It wasn't only her and Henry who needed to have some truthful dialogue.

"This is a rough situation. Did you tell Sonja about us—about how we've been feeling?"

Gloria nodded. "I did."

Hudson looked at Sonja. "I am sorry for any pain I ever caused you and Henry, Sonja. You must know that I hold your legal expertise in the highest regard. But that's not enough. I acted in a most inappropriate way when I found out you and Henry were an item."

"Hold it, Hudson." Before Sonja could reply, Gloria stepped out from under his arm. "I was the one who sent the invitation. And my motive was wrong—I wanted Henry to see what he was giving up by marrying you." Tears overspilled and tracked down her well-kept porcelain skin. "I've made a horrible mistake."

Hudson cleared his throat. "We both have. Can I offer you a drink? I sure need one."

"I'm sorry, but I really do have to get back." And alcohol was off-limits until their grandchild arrived, but she wasn't about to share that with them. That was something for her and Henry to do, later. Or just Henry, depending on how well they worked things out.

Sonja sucked in a breath and purposely kept her hand from moving over her abdomen in the protective move she'd caught herself doing since suspecting she was pregnant. "I know that you have no reason to trust me as far as Henry goes. I ran out on the wedding, that's on me. But I'm here as your employee and someone who cares about Henry. I have every hope that this will be dismissed and not reflect poorly on the firm." Other than the awful news coverage Deidre was engaged in obtaining.

"I agree with you, Sonja. This will blow over." Hudson looked around. "Pen?"

Sonja handed him hers, and when he finished, he handed the document to Gloria, who signed next to his signature. Once Sonja had the folder back in her grasp, she let out a long sigh. "Thank you both."

"Judge Perkins has it, then." Hudson had his arm back around Gloria.

"Yes. She will, as soon as I file. Thank you for your time. And, thank you for, for your honesty. For what it's worth, the reason Henry and I didn't get married is on us. You really had nothing to do with it."

The Boudreauxs exchanged a look that she couldn't translate.

Chapter 16

"Hey, boo, thanks for meeting me." She looked at the country café's menu, remembering the last time she'd had a meal here. With Henry, only a couple of weeks ago. They'd covered a lot of ground since then.

Poppy waved her hand in the air as if fending off flies. "Stop it. I'll meet you whenever you want."

Sonja had called Poppy from the road, unable to drive straight home to Henry. She needed space between the vastly different Boudreauxs. And she was hungry.

"What'll you have?" The waitress wrote down their orders, after which Sonja looked into Poppy's amber eyes and laughed.

"We still pick the same thing."

"Yes." Poppy sipped her iced tea. "I've been here for a while now, I'm getting used to it being my home, and I still can't get enough of crawdads."

"They're delicious."

"Remember the first time we had them? Or rather, I had them, when I came down here for spring break senior year?"

Sonja smiled. "Sure do. You thought they were bugs."

"I did. But they taste like lobster."

"They're better than lobster. Especially the heads."

"Why did you come right back home, Sonja? You were never tempted to stay in New York like I did. I always wondered why."

"My family's here, my roots are here."

Poppy shook her head. "There has to be more. You've got all the makings of a city girl."

"Whoa—I loved New York when we went to school, and yeah, I could see myself getting by in just about any city. But only temporarily. I feel myself most here. And in case you haven't noticed, New Orleans is a city."

Poppy rested her chin on her hand. "You're my hero."

"Knock it off, boo." She'd used the Cajun endearment on Poppy since they'd figured out they were best friends freshman year.

"Wait. You helped me through my meltdown with my business and ex. Let me help you through yours."

"You're helping me by being here."

"So why don't you want to go home tonight? Was work too hard?"

Sonja filled her in on her visit to the Boudreauxs. "I only went there to get them to commit to a statement, to help my case. I had no idea it'd be so emotional. I mean, imagine, those two very stiff icons of Southern gentility, crying. Asking for my forgiveness."

"It's about time! Brandon has spoken to them several times since the, um, wedding day, and he says they're getting soft around the edges."

"Hmph." Sonja reflected on the vulnerability between them that she'd never seen before.

"You said that Hudson seemed to be a little sad that the wedding didn't happen."

"They both did. And Gloria crying, her mascara running—Jeeee-sus, don't get me going."

Poppy giggled. "That's a change, for sure. We've each got our work cut out with the brothers—What do you think about Jena?"

Sonja couldn't keep the wide grin off her face. "I adore her. We've only met a few times over the past couple of years, but she's all about saying what she means. She tosses verbal challenges out to Hudson and Gloria like Molotov cocktails at Sunday dinner."

"Wait—when did you go to Sunday dinner with them?"

Sonja nodded. "They've had me over for dinner a few times. More when I was first hired, before I made a play for their son." She grinned. "Hudson likes to keep his attorneys close to his vest, and I was more than welcome as a dinner guest. Until they found out about me and Henry dating, then getting engaged."

"So their racism was more Sonja-ism?"

Sonja laughed. "No, they're still bigots. Don't forget they moved away from NOLA after Katrina. Isn't that what kept Brandon away from them for so long?"

"Yeah. You know what, Sonja? From what I've seen with Brandon's family, his parents never got over their kids growing up and leaving. If they had their way all three kids would still be in the same house."

Sonja fingered her water glass. "Maybe." She sighed. "I don't want to talk about Henry's folks anymore." Henry's parents were going to find out soon enough they were about to have a black grandchild. She'd see how it went then. "Henry's been clear that he's not going to expose our child to their crap, that's for sure." From what she'd seen of them tonight, there likely wouldn't be any racist crap anymore, but she wasn't going to hold her breath.

"Hopefully they'll chill their bony asses out and become wonderful grandparents."

Sonja didn't comment. The benefit of a more than decade-old friendship was that she knew Poppy "got her," without having to talk.

"Here you go." The waitress slid the steaming platter of crawdads between them, placing an empty plate atop each of their paper placemats. "I had them cook both of your orders together, so you got a little more. We have a big run on them today."

"Thanks!" Poppy eyed the pile of spindly red crustaceans with glee.

"You have got a problem, girl." Sonja laughed and grabbed a crawdad.

"I know."

After they'd eaten in silence for a while, Poppy paused. "Do you ever wonder how Brandon and Henry came out of that family as such great men? And from what you say, Jena's just as wonderful."

"Sure I do. But I don't dwell on it, really." She dipped the fleshy meat into a plastic cup filled with melted butter. "I can't waste energy on it, seriously."

"I mean, Hudson and Gloria did something right. And they let Brandon bring Jeb around like another one of their kids. There's that."

"Jeb who's run off with a cool fifteen million?"

Poppy paused, butter dripping down her chin and tears welling in her eyes. "I know. Can you believe it? I swear I don't know if Brandon will ever get over it. It was a big reason why we almost didn't get together."

Sonja snorted. "My turn to say 'bullshit.' You two were crawling all over one another from the moment you met."

Poppy giggled. "I know it looked that way, maybe, but it's not true. Not entirely."

"Uh huh." Sonja wiped her hands on the paper towels. "Henry said that Brandon hired a private investigator. To find Jeb."

"He did. And chased Jeb down to Paraguay. Which it just so happens is where Jena is off doing her active duty for the Navy."

"That's a weird co-inkey-dink, huh?"

"You got it. I said the same thing to Brandon. He says there was no hanky-panky between his sister and Jeb, though. Plus that would be weird—Jena stealing from her brother."

"I heard they went to prom together."

"That doesn't mean anything."

"Of course not. But if Brandon's anything like Henry, they don't see what's right in front of them sometimes."

"Right?" Poppy's eyes widened. "Brandon almost needed me to hit him with a two-by-four to realize he was in love with me."

Sonja's gut hurt, and it wasn't from the excess melted butter. Henry had decided he was in love with her very early in their relationship. She was the one who'd needed more convincing.

And in the end she'd decided to not believe any of it. She'd let her fatal flaw, her mistrust of men, toss out what had been the foundation of a great relationship. She'd stopped sharing with Henry whenever it got too scary. She'd kept her deepest feelings locked tight.

Had she ever shown Henry what he meant to her—that she really did believe in him? That her trust issues were just that—*her* issues, and had nothing to do with him?

* * * *

When Sonja got home, the light in the tiny cottage beckoned to her as she walked up from the driveway. There was more light, however, around to the back, where she found Henry hard at work wiring some kind of box onto the back porch. His car headlights were his illumination.

He hadn't heard her walk up, so she stood to the side and watched him. His long, lean legs were propped to hold him steady as he used a cordless drill with his hands. God, his hands. She backed up until her bottom hit a tree and leaned against it, content to watch him in the night.

His ass was perfection in his jeans, and the loose white T-shirt was uncharacteristic of him. The Henry she'd lived with had always worn a polo shirt or nicer T-shirt when not dressed for lawyering. The more rustic, earthy Henry that had appeared over the past month was the most masculine, sexy man she'd ever known. A jerk of surprise hit her between her rib cage and went straight to between her legs. It was as if seeing Henry this simply, as if he'd peeled off a layer of himself, had revealed another layer to her soul, too.

Poppy had asked her if she still was attracted to him, if the spark was still there. And she'd helped Sonja see that it was Sonja's trust issues at play here more than anything he'd held back from her about Deidre. If she'd been seeing more clearly in the months leading up to the wedding, she'd have accepted that she needed to do some more digging about her own trust issues. And admit that if it hadn't been the Deidre history and Henry's refusal to tell her its entirety, it would have been something else. Her running had been just that—her reaction to her inability to fully trust a man.

Sonja hated examining her heart. Had ever since it'd been crushed by her father's doglike behavior more than half a lifetime ago.

Her heart was shouting loud and clear that this man in front of her was the man she needed. The man she couldn't live without.

Could she go there? Could she not only show Henry she was willing to trust him, but that she now trusted herself?

Henry was as committed to making a good life for the baby as she was, and he was going to have a fully active role in raising their child, no question. Was it too far of a leap to think, to trust, that they'd bridge all that had divided them? She didn't want to dwell on it tonight. Maybe it was dealing with his parents, or maybe she was too mentally and emotionally exhausted.

One thing that wasn't tired was her need for him. The constant thrum of sexual awareness whenever he was around. The way her body responded with its own vibrations. And she wanted the deep, multiple kind of vibrations right about now, the kind that Henry's tongue and hard cock delivered. She stared at him as he worked.

He stopped drilling, and the quiet of night immediately descended.

"You going to keep staring at me like a creeper or come and help?" He didn't look over his shoulder but had known she was there. Of course he did.

She shoved off the tree and walked toward him. The irises and phlox that bordered the cottage were almost luminescent as they reflected the car's lights. "When did you know I was here?"

"Since your car drove up on the gravel."

As she walked up next to the house, next to him, he lowered the power tool. It drew her attention to his real power tool—the erection that strained through his jeans.

"Like what you see, babe?" His eyes were shadowed by his hair and the way the bright white of the car lights hit him, but the tilt of his head, the way he stood proudly in front of her was all she needed to see. Henry was hot for her, and what turned her on the most was that he was never, ever afraid to show it.

"Now I'm wondering who's creepy. You're acting like that power drill turns you on." She placed a hand on the ladder propped next to the house.

He put the drill on a ladder step and clicked a button on the car key fob. The headlights flicked off, plunging them into total darkness. "The only thing turning me on these days is you, Sonja."

The vibration of his voice as he said her name made her knees tremble like Grandma's rice pudding. She watched as he raised his arm, closed her eyes and soaked in the pure sexual awareness between them as he stroked her cheek, pressed her bottom lip with his calloused thumb.

She grabbed his wrist, licked his thumb. "Since when do you have rough workman's hands?"

"Since I started helping the contractors after work." He hissed as she continued working on his thumb, pulled it into her mouth, and sucked. Hard.

"Christ." He reached around and grabbed her ass, fully and intentionally, bringing her up against him. Good thing, since her legs had given out. "Come here." He leaned his back against the centuries-old brick wall and pulled her to him, not speaking until she had her legs on either side of his, their most intimate parts touching through her panties and his jeans.

"What about the flowers?" She sounded like she'd run ten miles and was sweating like she had, too.

"Fuck the flowers." Henry tilted his pelvis at the precise angle only he knew got her going to sexyville.

Hell, she'd bought her one-way ticket for the ride the minute she saw him working on the side of the house. Her eyes closed, and she let go.

Sonja saw stars behind her eyelids as she could do little else but follow his lead and allow her body to do the talking. She ground herself against him, needing the feel of his hard cock against her most sensitive parts, swollen with her pregnancy. "I hate these clothes between us."

"Mmm." He moved his hands from her bottom to her back, tracing one hand up to her nape. "There's time for that, don't worry." The slow cadence of his voice wove into the kiss he placed on her mouth, his lips and tongue working their magic on hers.

Sonja wanted to scream with her need, shout it to the darkness around them that she was going to crawl out of her skin with wanting him. Instead she pressed her hands against the brick wall, clenched her thighs tight atop his, and enjoyed the longest kiss of their relationship. Not that she'd ever paid attention to it, but she'd remember if his kiss had ever gone on like this, like the floods that seemed to keep coming down the river, filling the land beyond its capacity. Henry filled her with love she hadn't been open enough to catch.

Until now.

Chapter 17

Henry never imagined installing a security system on the guesthouse would lead to the most erotically charged moments he'd shared with Sonja to date. Maybe getting jilted was the key to having tantric sex with an ex. She was anything but an ex to him, though. Right now, with her heat firmly planted against his cock, their frustration at still being clothed easily remedied, he didn't give a flying fuck. All he cared a fuck or two about was how to get closer to this woman, his woman.

"Don't stop, babe." He whispered into her mouth, their tongues stroking and lips sucking, straining to connect at every point possible. Her arms were stretched on either side of his head, supporting her against the same wall his back was up against. Even with clothes keeping him from the full pressure of her pussy as she moved herself up and down his dick, the sensation was sublime.

Satisfied she'd keep her part of the bargain, he reached between them and found her wet panties, completely soaked with her. "So wet." His fingers had to touch her lips, play with her pearl before he reached up to the sides of her thong. Her string thong. She whimpered, and he smiled against her mouth. "Patience." With a quick flick of both hands, the straps were torn, the underwear thrown into the blooms that carpeted the ground under their feet. Holy fuck, he was gone if he was thinking about flowers.

"Stay still, honey." She was his honey, as honey flowed from inside her as he again touched her. Their kiss never stopped, only escalated his raging need for her as he waited until he thought she was close, just from the stroking and reverently playing with her labia and clit.

"Henry," she begged into his mouth, and he knew what she wanted.

His fingers were inside her in a quick thrust, and he almost blew his load in his jeans at the utterly feminine moan she let out into the night. No measure of finesse was needed to bring her to her climax as she writhed once, twice on his fingers, her clit against his palm as he grasped her ass and helped her get what she wanted. Her cry pierced his remaining control, and he couldn't afford to wait for her to come down from this one.

Henry unbuttoned his fly and shoved his jeans and underwear down. As soon as he kicked off the clothes, he turned them around so that she was against the house. "You okay?" Fuck, his breath was trapped between his throat and dick, and he'd suffocate if he didn't get inside her now.

A soft, quick nod. "Yes." She'd kicked off her heels and wrapped one long, lean leg around his waist. Before her heel could dig into his ass for support, he thrust into her, her harsh gasps conveying the need, the sheer lust he had for her.

But it wasn't just lust. Each time he buried himself in her, each time her muscles held him tighter then began to pulse in the way only Sonja did, he was aware of being surrounded by an intensity of emotion he'd never experienced before. Belonging. Heat, white-hot and all consuming. And after he hit the edge and flew off into complete ecstasy, wondering who the hell was yelling her name like a goddamned teenager, he was wrapped in a cocoon of total peace.

True love.

* * * *

Sonja wanted to whimper when Henry lifted himself away from her. It was visceral, something more intimate than the physicality of what they'd just shared that connected them. Always. Instead of complaining verbally, she returned to the planet slowly. The lush feel of the phlox she'd crushed under her bare soles, their scent surrounding them as the night covered them with anonymity. The moon had begun its ascent over the river, and the house cast a long shadow over them, protecting them.

"God damn it." His swearing was new; Henry had been so much more polite and self-controlled before. In the dark with the cool spring air hitting her bared private parts, still tingling from his touch, it wasn't hard to imagine he was a totally different person. Except he was still the man she'd fallen in love with, only better.

"What?" She continued to lean against the wall. Just a few more minutes to savor this, savor them. Each time they'd let the sexual attraction rule over pragmatism, she expected it to be the last time.

He picked up his jeans, grabbed the power drill. "I left you totally exposed. What if Deidre had picked now to sneak up on us?"

She sobered at his words. "What if" indeed.

"She didn't. We're okay. Henry?"

"Yeah?"

His voice was steady, the gentle vulnerability slipping away. She didn't want to lose this newfound intimacy, see it disappear as quickly as she'd run. Open, vulnerable Henry was the only chance they had to make this work. God, that had been a mind-blowing orgasm in all ways possible if she was thinking about making anything more than being parents work for them. But she needed to tell him she'd been in Baton Rouge.

"What, Sonja?" Firmer. More like Henry the attorney.

"I went to your parents. To get an affidavit signed. That's why I'm home so late." She pushed away from the wall and pulled her skirt over her bottom. It was too dark to tell, but she'd bet Henry's eyes weren't anywhere but on hers, looking for what he'd heard in her voice.

"Fuck. Why didn't you tell me? I would have gone with you. You don't have to face them alone, Sonja." He stalked away toward the front of the guesthouse, and she followed, needing to get out of her clothes and into a shower.

"I wanted to get it done, and I wanted to face them on my own."

He stared at her. Lawyer Henry was back in full stony color. "Why? All that could be done on the phone."

"I wanted their signatures on what I've drawn up." She was thrilled that Hudson had said he'd sign statements from him and Gloria, too. "And technically, it's none of your business. Deidre is pressing charges against me. Your father employs me. Other than your previous relationship with Deidre, I don't see how any of this is your business. I wanted to do something for you for a change, Henry. You've dealt with her enough. Let me do this much. I realize I should have told you before I went there, though."

His head went back a barely perceptible amount, and his nostrils flared. That emotional tic of his had always turned her on, as if his animal instincts were bubbling up, and she anticipated how they'd play out sexually.

Sex between them was always very good. This part, the being totally honest, wasn't.

"They were nice to you?"

"Very. They apologized for their behavior."

"You still didn't have to deal with them on your own." He turned toward the kitchen cupboards, grabbed a glass, and reached for the bottle of bourbon he had on top of the refrigerator. She watched the muscles under his shirt, the shirt streaked with dirt from being against the house while he held her, as he pulled an old-fashioned ice cube tray from the vintage refrigerator's inside freezer. The cubes clinked against the cocktail glass, the amber liquid making the ice crackle as he poured two fingers.

"Did you tell them about the baby?"

Her cheeks grew hot. "No. That's for you, or you and me to do. I wasn't there for that, and then they were so intent on saying they were sorry about the wedding. I did tell them that it wasn't their fault, that it was on me that I'd run. It was clear you hadn't told them."

"I've not told anyone. Who have you told?"

"Poppy."

"But she hasn't told Brandon—I would have been able to tell when I spoke to him." He took a sip of his drink. "You haven't told your mother?"

"No. My grandmother figured it out, she's like that, as you know. But my folks left too soon after the wedding day." She swallowed. Really, rehashing the wedding day at this point was a bad plan. It'd only take her down the road of regrets, make her question just what she'd been thinking to back out of the wedding before confronting Henry on her long list of grievances.

The list wasn't that long, though. Because it all went back to the same thing.

"You don't trust me, do you? You think I had some ulterior motive for going to Baton Rouge."

"Do you blame me? You ran away from our wedding, from us, with very little warning. That's not what I'd call a trust-builder." He swung back a large portion of his drink, his Adam's apple working in precise, masculine motions.

"No, it's not. But we've, we've started over a little, a lot, on the friendship part, haven't we?"

"I'd like to think so, or I did, but you just went off and talked to my folks without cutting me in. Sex isn't friendship, babe." He finished the drink and slammed the glass down before he stalked off to the bathroom.

Sonja belatedly sat on the quaint sofa, any thought that they'd somehow started over squelched by Henry's caustic words. The plumbing moaned, and she could do little but sit and listen to the water as it pulsed through the piping, imagining it as it poured over Henry, splattered on the tiles. It was like hearing the tiny bubbles of hope that had started to float around in her heart pop, one by one.

For the first time since she'd returned to this tiny cottage, she let the scalding tears fall. What had she been thinking, making love with him like that, when they were through?

The squeak of the plumbing as he turned off the shower, the sound of his bare feet on the ceramic floor, another addition when they renovated. It wasn't enough to cry. Wiping her tears with a wadded-up paper towel, she sniffled and straightened her spine.

It started right now, right here. Her life without Henry's touch.

"The shower's yours." He stood in the bedroom doorway, dressed in sweats and a T-shirt, his hair damp.

"Henry—"

"I'll lock up behind me—I'm going to spend some time in the river house, going over what the contractors accomplished today."

She didn't say anything in reply but instead went straight through to the bathroom, stripped off the clothes that less than an hour earlier had been tangled between their bodies, and placed herself under the stinging spray.

Rivulets of regret and remorse ran together with the water. She'd allowed herself to get back here, to a place that only spelled hurt. There was no going back, no pretending she'd regained his trust. No matter that as each layer of her reasons for running had peeled off, she'd discovered new insights about Henry. Gone was her vision of the perfect lover, friend, and lawyer. In its place was an honest man who'd made mistakes. Transgressions she'd been unable to consider letting go of, just a month ago.

And now, she was in a different place, had given it all to him against this timeworn home's original wall not an hour before. It didn't matter how far she'd come, how much she knew Henry was the only man for her. It was too late. Henry didn't want her forgiveness, and he certainly didn't trust her.

They were through.

Chapter 18

"You can always stay here, honey." Grandma looked at her with eyes that had been Sonja's refuge her entire life. It'd been two long weeks since she'd driven to Baton Rouge and back, two weeks since she and Henry had done more than speak to one another at the firm.

"I know, Grandma, thank you. I could live with my sisters, too." They lived in the house they grew up in, while her parents remained in the Caribbean doing medical outreach. "But I'm a big girl, and it's time I faced my life on its own terms." She dug into the plate of biscuits and gravy the waitress had brought. She and Grandma were at their favorite breakfast haunt, a family-run diner off the side of an access road. The dilapidated exterior gave nothing away to tourists of how great a feast the locals enjoyed just miles from the French Quarter, but at deep bayou prices.

"That doesn't mean you have to suffer. You have your child to consider. Emotional upset's not good for the baby." Grandma drank her tea, her bowl of grits and eggs already finished. She'd eaten while Sonja poured out her discoveries about herself, Henry, and the impossibility of a life with Henry.

"The baby's fine. At least when he or she's letting me eat instead of feeling sick to my stomach." She didn't want to go there even mentally, as these respites from nausea were like manna in the world of her first trimester.

"Have you been to the doctor's yet?"

"Just a quickie appointment to verify my at-home pregnancy test. The first ultrasound is the day after tomorrow." And she'd mentioned it to Henry, before their blowup. More like breakdown.

"Isn't your court date tomorrow?"

She'd kept Grandma up to date with the Deidre drama.

"Yes, ma'am."

"You don't seem worried about it."

"You know, I'm not. I was at first, but the evidence is so clearly on my side." And get her to stop stalking her. It had been driven home to her over the past several days. She'd seen Deidre in the Piggly Wiggly, downtown near the firm's office at lunchtime, and yesterday she'd walked by a café while she and Poppy had tea. Deidre wasn't watching Henry, she was keeping her eye on Sonja.

"What's worrying you most?" Grandma's gaze was pointedly on Sonja's hand, which had crept over her abdomen.

"How I'll handle being this baby's mother, working with Henry, without getting emotional about it. We, we only talk to one another at work." And only when absolutely necessary. She seriously needed to think about transferring to another firm, her finances be damned. She and Henry had done nothing with their nonprofit idea, and she didn't see it happening. Not now.

"Talking isn't the only way to communicate."

"Grandma." She played the aggrieved granddaughter with the too-hip matriarch. "That's over."

Edwina's eyes sparkled as she sipped her coffee, her lips in that straight line that indicated she was in her wise sage mode. "Your parents aren't you, Sonja. Have you spoken to either of them about any of this yet?"

Sonja sighed. "No. I haven't told anyone about the baby, either. Except you. And Poppy."

"How's Poppy doing? She still seeing Henry's brother?"

"Yes." Sonja didn't want to go there, either. It sucked to not be the one in love, looking forward to a life together. Tears pushed at her lids, and she blinked.

Edwina placed her hand over hers, her thin, wrinkled skin as soft as it'd ever been. "You'll have love again, honey. Give it time. And if nothing else, you have the world to look forward to with the baby."

"I know." She blew her nose. "I'm feeling sorry for myself."

"No problem with that, for a minute. But don't stay there. That spells trouble quicker than anything."

"Thanks, Grandma." The warmth of Edwina's love shot straight to her heart, and she'd like to think, to the baby's. "I'm fine."

"No you're not. But you will be. Just remember, the best is yet to come." Grandma plunked a bill down on the Formica table, the denomination enough to cover four people. "Leave the change for her tip. We're all working hard. I've got to get to the library." She gave Sonja a quick kiss on the cheek before she left for her weekly book group.

Sonja watched the elder Bosco's hips sway, wondering how Grandma must have been at her age. She'd had four kids, a full-time teaching job, and a demanding husband by now. By all accounts Edwina had enjoyed a great marriage to a fine man who, at forty-six, had left her a widow far too young. Sonja had never met him. And Edwina never remarried, but Sonja wouldn't put it past her to have a date on the side here and there. Though there were few men who'd ever be a match for her grandmother.

"You need anything else, sugar?" Sonja looked into the waitress's wizened face.

"No, I'm good."

What a load of crap.

* * * *

Henry prided himself on three things: being punctual, being the best lawyer in New Orleans, and pleasing his woman. As he ran up the courthouse steps in the warm spring morning, he knew with a sick dread that he was sucking it big time at all three.

He'd almost missed getting here entirely when his tire blew out on the Lake Pontchartrain Causeway. Fortunately Brandon wasn't far away and had been able to stay with Henry's truck to change the tire and sent Henry along with his vehicle.

The courthouse enveloped him in its antique scents of oak, lemon oil, and the sweat of thousands of accused defendants. There was only one sweeter smell in the world. He had to shove that aside for now, stay focused on the case at hand. Remembering how Sonja smelled, the way her skin seemed to waft jasmine and sexy, wasn't something his head could handle at the moment.

What about your heart, stupid?

He got through the security checkpoint only after having to pull the car keys out of his pocket and step through the metal detector again. The security guard motioned for him to step onto the square mat where he wanded Henry. His internal clock counted the dreaded seconds as the guard took his time.

"Awfully thorough today." Henry made the small talk through gritted teeth, really wanting to take off for courtroom number nine. It was actually the judge's chambers, where he, Sonja, and Deidre would face Judge Perkins. Along with the filing police officer, the craft store security guard, and Deidre's lawyer. Sonja had allowed him to represent her, officially. But they were doing this as a team, no matter what kind of bullshit she'd said about this not being his business.

He mentally paused and reminded himself that he wasn't the college kid who Deidre had stalked. That was a lifetime or two ago. He had the information and legal tools to make Deidre disappear. Not thriller movie disappear, but get the help she obviously needed. And leave Sonja alone.

He shoved open the heavy outer door and nodded at the clerk. "Sorry I'm late."

"You're not. Judge Perkins was delayed. You've got about thirty seconds."

Henry didn't bother to respond as he walked through the next open door and entered the chamber. Sonja's gaze met his, and it was the first time in two weeks she'd blessed him with a full, honest look. She was relieved to see him.

Warmth pummeled his chest and spread outward. It was only because she needed him here to back her up, of course. But it was enough.

"Judge Perkins." He nodded and slid into the seat next to Sonja. They were behind a small table, and Deidre sat at another small table with a woman Henry assumed was her lawyer. The rest of the gathered sat in the few chairs behind the defendant's.

"Counselor Boudreaux." The woman who'd gone to law school with his father gave nothing away in her professional assessment of him. Without hesitation, as soon as Henry's ass hit the hard chair, she slammed her gavel down and looked at the door. "Shut the door, clerk. We're in session."

Judge Perkins got right to the point. "I've read the motion to dismiss, and I am going to get to my decision in a moment. Ms. Deidre Jones, please stand."

"Yes, your honor." Deidre was dressed in the most demure white pin tuck suit, complete with a Peter Pan collar blouse, her blond hair up in a high ponytail. Henry's gut clenched. This was the Deidre he'd faced for over a year after he'd broken their engagement.

"I've read your complaint and looked at the police affidavit, which includes the security video feed from the craft store." Judge Perkins nodded at her clerk, who hit a few buttons on a laptop and effected the widescreen television to display the video.

"If you'll notice, Ms. Jones, you appear to be doing nothing more than dropping and rolling after you clearly moved toward Ms. Bosco and knocked her phone out of her hand. Do you have anything to say about this?"

"No, ma'am."

"Here"—Judge Perkins held up a signed document, pointing to Deidre's signature—"you confirmed that this video was of you, on the date of said incident. Do you realize that Ms. Bosco is in her right to sue you for defamation?"

"Your honor, I'm so sorry. This is only because Mr. Boudreaux and I have a prior history and I, I've never stopped loving him. I was still in shock that he was getting married when I saw his fiancée in the craft supply store."

Judge Perkins looked at Sonja. Henry wanted to speak but knew he had to bide his time and only speak when asked to. If he was. Helplessness collided with his powerlessness to help Sonja, and he gritted his teeth. "What say you, Counselor Bosco?"

"Your honor, Ms. Jones approached me in the craft store over two weeks after our wedding day. For the record, the wedding did not occur."

"Your honor, they invited me to the wedding!"

"That's not pertinent for this case, Ms. Jones. But since you brought it up, I have a statement from Hudson and Gloria Boudreaux that they were the ones to invite you, without informing Ms. Bosco nor her former fiancé, Mr. Boudreaux."

Deidre's face sank in on itself. Henry thought Judge Perkins was being uncharacteristically patient. He'd worked cases where she'd verbally sliced and diced defendants and prosecutors alike, all in a single sentence. He prayed that she saw that there was something wrong with Deidre.

Sonja sat silently next to him, and he fought to not put his hand on hers under the table or give her leg a quick squeeze. Since the night of her drive to Baton Rouge, they'd passed like strangers, never talking in the guesthouse, save for minimal courtesies. They were only roommates. He looked at her, and she turned her face from the judge's bench, where Perkins was shuffling papers, preparing to make her decision.

Sonja's large liquid brown eyes were filled with tears, and he had no idea why. Damn it all, he'd lost the ability to read her. To know her, the way a partner should.

The way her husband would. *Husband.*

Holy legal case, he wasn't miserable because Deidre was back in his life, or because she was stalking Sonja. It wasn't the trust issue anymore—of course he trusted Sonja. She'd gone to his parents without consulting him first—so what? As she'd asked him, did he think he was God? Above all else, his misery wasn't because Sonja had jilted him. They'd jilted each other. Neither of them had been willing to admit they needed more work on their relationship, and on themselves, before they made a commitment that involved vows.

He had to fix this.

"Counselor Boudreaux." Sharp and insistent, Judge Perkins's query clearly wasn't the first time she'd spoken to him.

"Yes, your honor."

"Do you have anything to add?"

"No. My client rests." He sure as hell didn't, though. He had so much to say to her, to prove to his client. The woman who was a lot more than that to him.

"Okay, let's get to the point, folks. Ms. Jones, it's clear to me that you've brought false charges against Ms. Bosco at great risk to her professional and personal reputation." The judge droned on, saying the things both Henry and Sonja had heard countless times in cases where clients had done the same. It was the bottom line that Judge Perkins circled around that Henry mentally held his breath for.

"The court dismisses this case with prejudice. And Ms. Jones, I hope you get the help you need. It's clear to me that you are unreasonably obsessed over Mr. Boudreaux and his former fiancée, Counselor Bosco. I'm going to order you to attend twelve mandatory counseling sessions and as many visits to a psychiatrist. Are there any questions?"

Whomever Deidre had for her lawyer, the woman had a magical effect on her, as Deidre only nodded, her attorney's arm around her. As usual, Deidre's parents were nowhere to be seen, and Henry felt a moment of compassion, quickly doused by the singular memory of Deidre talking to Sonja at the church on what would have been their wedding day.

* * * *

"We need to talk, Henry." She stood in his office, and he gave himself a moment to soak in her beauty. The looser-fitting, frothy kind of dress emphasized her breasts and hips, and left a lot of room for what he assumed was her burgeoning baby bump. He wouldn't know, as she hadn't let him touch her again. He hadn't let himself get close enough. Even after the dismissal, when emotions were riding high and it was too easy to think they'd ever figure out a way back to one another, he hadn't hugged her or kissed her cheek.

"About work?" They'd not spoken a word to one another since they left the courthouse.

"Related." She motioned at the seats in front of his desk.

"Sure, take a seat." He swung his legs off his desk and leaned forward. "You did great in there today."

"We both did, but thanks." She'd gotten the motion to dismiss together mostly herself; he'd only proofread it and checked that she had all the necessary documents. "It went smoothly, I'd say. Do you think Judge Perkins's recommendation for mental health treatment will happen?" Normally Sonja's eyes were clear, her words direct, to the point. The vulnerability in them melted another chunk of iceberg in his chest.

"That's the kicker, right? We don't know."

"What I don't like is that the only way we'll know she didn't get help is if she shows up around the house again."

"Or wherever you are." He saw the effect his words had on her and froze. "I'm sorry. I don't want to rile you up any more than you already are."

"Yeah, well, it doesn't take much to get me spun up these days." Her hand went to her midriff, and he stared at the bare hand that had worn the carat diamond for over a year. Her gaze followed, and she shrugged. "Are you just noticing that I don't wear it?"

"I guess." He forced his gaze back to her face. "A ring doesn't make a commitment, does it?"

"No. It's not necessary for one, either."

God, did she know what her words did to him? How easily he could read between them? Especially after that fuck against the house, the fight after be damned. Because it hadn't been a fuck. It'd been lovemaking at its best.

"You came in here to talk about Deidre's mental health?"

"And how we're going forward." She fussed with her dress material. "I moved into the cottage so that you could keep an eye on me, or rather, the baby, and to save money. I still need to save money, as do you, but we have to consider our mental health."

"I didn't know it was at stake."

"You know what I'm saying, Henry. It's not the healthiest thing, living together, but not, even when we know we're going to raise the baby together. Don't you agree?"

No, he didn't agree, but her needs came first. "I'll support whatever you want to do, Sonja. As long as it's safe and I'm involved with the baby."

"How long before the house is habitable?"

"The contractor said we could live in the upstairs by next week, provided we don't use the downstairs bathrooms yet." They'd made a lot of progress. The mold was gone, and all that remained was to put up drywall downstairs and install the new flooring. "But I don't think it's smart for you, the baby."

"I agree. You've hooked up the security systems, so they're connected. I'm safe in the guesthouse, Henry. If I at all feel threatened or someone shows up at the door I don't want to deal with, you'll see them on the monitor."

"That I will." He'd demonstrated to her how to use the app that was on both their phones and work computers. Whenever anyone so much as stepped on the front porch of either building the app opened a window on their screens. "The house won't be ready for you for another couple of weeks, not until the grout and painting is done."

"It sounds perfect for you, though." She looked at him from beneath her lashes, and he sucked in a breath against the shards of truth stabbing deep inside his rib cage.

"Right. I can check it out tonight and move in now if it's good to go."

"You don't have to move that fast. You're going to need a pair of sheets and some towels." She wouldn't look at him, and he was grateful.

"Whatever. Is there anything else?" He didn't mean to sound like such a bastard.

She shoved herself out of the chair, making her breasts just above eye level for him. His need for Sonja was primal, his connection to her a forever one. And it had nothing to do with his child that grew in her womb.

"No, that's pretty much it. I guess we'll see one another later, then?" She smiled, her tiny work smile. "And don't forget, the doctor's appointment is in the morning. You don't have to come if you don't want to. But you'd said—"

"I'd said I would be at every appointment." He couldn't look at her.

"Okay, well, see you later then."

"Yup." He picked up a file and opened it, behaving in what he hoped was a professional way. As she left, leaving behind the ghost of her warmth, he turned his chair around and faced the window. If anyone walked in they'd think he was staring out at the huge magnolia tree getting ready to bloom.

And not see the tear shredding down his cheek.

Chapter 19

Sonja willed herself to change into workout clothes and go for a walk through the city before she made the trek home. The baby was constantly growing, and it wasn't going to get easier, staying in shape. She texted Poppy to let her know she'd be showing up at her boutique, and asked if she'd be willing to give her a ride back to her car.

An hour and three miles later she walked into the air-conditioned space of the Fresh Lines boutique where Poppy worked out of.

"Hey, Sonja." Bianca, the business owner, smiled warmly at her from behind the costume jewelry counter. "Poppy's in the back."

"Thanks. How's it going?"

"Good. Really good. Poppy's bringing in a slew of clients, and we're expanding our hours."

"I'm so glad! And the new renter, are they working out?"

Bianca smiled. "Yes, that's another good thing. Like Poppy, it's someone who needed respite from things for a while."

Sonja didn't press. She understood the need for discretion. It was a good feeling to know that stepping up to what she needed to do, no matter how difficult a decision, like moving into the cottage with Henry had been, had allowed another person to find what they needed.

"Hey, girlfriend." Poppy walked out into the open sales floor and headed straight for Sonja, arms wide. "How was your walk?"

"Whoa, no hug, boo. I'm sweating like a pig. The walk was good."

"Okay, well, I'm ready to go." Poppy looked at Bianca. "See you tomorrow?"

"Yes. See you."

They walked out the front door, and Poppy was practically bouncing down the sidewalk toward her car. "Have you bought any maternity clothes yet? Because there are a bunch of new outfits on their way to the shop. There's a couple of dresses I think you'll love—they'll be perfect for work."

"No, not yet." And that brought her back to her work dilemma.

"What?" Poppy unlocked the car doors with a click on her fob, and they both slid into the small car's seats. "I can tell something's going on. I thought you were relieved now that the case was dismissed. Congratulations, by the way."

"I was. I am. I'm still not convinced Deidre won't show up again, but I'm praying she'll get help before she thinks about coming to see me."

"Go on." Poppy turned the engine over, and the air conditioning blew on Sonja, raising goose bumps on her forearms.

"I told Henry to move into the main house." It sounded so final.

"You knew this was coming. You left him at the altar, Sonja. It's not fair to jerk him around."

"I'm not jerking him around." Or was she? "It's complicated."

Poppy looked at her. "What's complicated? You have a baby on the way, a child you're going to have to raise together, somehow. I get it—the baby part of it is complicated. You lost your trust in him and left your relationship. What's complicated about that?"

"It really hurt to tell him to move into the main house. I thought for a minute he was upset about it, but he didn't fight it. He's ready to move on."

"And you're not." Poppy buckled her seatbelt and put the car into gear. The traffic was stop-and-go back to the law firm, and Sonja was grateful for the cool interior, and the security of her dearest friend.

But while Poppy remained her dearest girlfriend, she wasn't her best friend. Henry was. Or had been, before their un-wedding. And she'd thought they'd started an even better friendship, before she'd gone off to Baton Rouge on her own.

"Well?" Poppy prompted her as they inched along.

"I didn't expect it to hurt. I'm the one who left the wedding, I'm the one who told him to move out, basically."

"And?"

"I feel like everything that ever meant anything to me since law school is gone. Except for the baby, and when I think about him or her, all I can picture is how sad it will be to drop them off at Henry's, or have Henry pull up in front of the house and pick them up."

"Have you told Henry how you feel?"

"What? How do I even approach him with this? We've done a lot of heavy lifting in the sharing department. But I can't erase what I did. I tore his heart out."

"It sounds like your heart is broken, too." Poppy made the last right turn before the office. "Maybe you broke each other's, I don't know. The real question to ask yourself is if you'll regret it for the rest of your life."

"Regret what? I regretted leaving him at the altar the way I did within five minutes of doing it."

"But you still ran."

"Yeah, I ran." She watched as big drops of rain hit Poppy's windshield. The humidity that dogged her walk erupted into a huge grumble of thunder.

"I think at the very least you need to keep the conversation going with Henry."

"That's just it, Poppy. I don't know if I can. It hurts. So much." Tears clawed at her eyeballs, but she refused to give in. If she did, there was no telling where she'd end up.

Poppy pulled into one of half a dozen empty street spots. "Here's the thing. I've watched you date a lot of guys, fall in love with one or two, but I've never seen you ruminate after you've left a man. This is different, Sonja. Henry's different."

She nodded. "Maybe you're right."

"You going to be okay driving home in this? If you want, you can come home with me, and Brandon can boat you the rest of the way."

Sonja opened her mouth to say no, but reconsidered. Going back to face the empty cottage seemed too heavy. She'd be able to catch a ride back into NOLA tomorrow, with Henry, when they went to the doctor's. And time with Poppy sounded great. "Are you sure?"

"I wouldn't have offered otherwise." Poppy didn't meet her gaze, which Sonja found odd, but she didn't press it. This was the break she needed at the moment. Going straight back home to face Henry so soon after she'd told him to pack up and move out, even if it was only across the backyard, was too much. "You can shower at our place, too, if you want."

"Give me five minutes to get my things."

* * * *

Henry maneuvered the flat-bottomed boat up to Brandon's dock. As he looped the line around a cleat, Brandon walked down from his house, a huge contemporary structure on a hill, unusual for the area in many ways. Before Jeb had absconded with Brandon's funds, Brandon had made a lucrative living at his shipyard and had invested in the latest and greatest technology to build the most hurricane- and flood-proof home possible.

"That was quick." Brandon held out a cold brew, and Henry gratefully wrapped his hand around the bottle.

"Thanks. Cheers." They clinked longnecks, and Henry took a long pull. "I don't drink a lot of beer, but this is very good."

"Of course it is. I bought it at the source." Brandon named the local brewery. "Glad you like it."

"Let me guess, now you're going into the craft ale business?"

Brandon laughed. "Hardly. No, I'm an engineer, through and through. And guess what, I really like my new job."

"Pay cut has to bite. Can you still afford all of this?" He motioned around them at the land, expansive dock.

"Dude, you know me. I paid cash for it all. The energy efficient systems I put in keep the utilities low, so all I have to worry about is the taxes. They're okay for now."

"Cool." They started to walk up to the house. "How's the search for Jeb going? Or have you given up?"

"I haven't given up, so much as it's out of my hands. Since I reported it to the authorities, the last I heard was what I told you—the FBI is working on it. I don't expect to ever see my money again, if that's what you're asking."

"And yet you seem so okay with it."

"I'm not okay that my former best friend took off with the company funds. And bankrupted the company, in turn, as well as made me as close to destitute as I ever want to be. But none of that matters. I never lost the roof over my head, I'm a healthy specimen of manhood"—he slapped his abs for effect—"and I have the love of a kind, good woman."

Henry stopped walking. "Holy shit, man. You're not kidding. You're in love." With a woman he'd only known a little over a month.

"Hell no, I'm not kidding. What else matters in life, really?"

Henry tried to chug a gulp of beer around the lump in his throat and coughed. "Fuck."

"Sonja." Not a question, because Brandon obviously knew the deal. And saw his brother's hurt.

"She asked me to move out."

"Out of the guesthouse? Like, where are you going to go?"

"To the main house. Since there'll still be a lot of fumes from paint, adhesive, the like, she can't move in there yet. It makes sense that I'm the one to move."

"Uh huh." Brandon turned, looked out at the water while Henry remained facing the house. "That sucks. But you're not that far from her, if that's what's bothering you. And don't you think it might be a hell of a lot healthier, since you're not a couple anymore? None of this is a surprise, right?"

"No. It shouldn't be. Why am I bellyaching so much, then? I feel like I got sucker-punched all over again, Gus. Worse."

"You're not bellyaching. Well, maybe a little. We had this conversation. You never let yourself feel your feelings about this when the wedding fell through. I hate the touchy feely shit as much as the next guy, but it never pays to ignore it."

"I know." He thought of his parents, how maybe if they'd talked things out not only with each other but their kids that maybe their family would be more willing to spend time together. It would have given his parents opportunities to let go of their sick mores from the dark ages.

"These past few months have opened my eyes to a lot, bro." Brandon, always "Gus" to Henry, looked as if he was the older brother, the wiser one.

"Like what?" Henry found he really did care. It wasn't small talk, or a calculated effort to bridge the estranged gap with Brandon. He wanted to know.

"Like I had my part to play in my estrangement from our folks. When Mom and Dad did their best bigot routine and ran away from the scene after Katrina, I never asked if they'd planned to move out of NOLA all along, if the disaster just hastened their transition. I lumped it in with all of their ugly decisions. Face it, Dad never had to hire Sonja, or any other person of color. I think his old armor started cracking a while ago. His old ways no longer serve him, from what you told me. Thank God."

"Mom's come unglued, too. In a good way."

"Mom needed some serious ungluing."

They both shared a chuckle, and Henry liked the way their shared mirth rang out in the dusk. He slapped at his arm to kill a mosquito.

"Can we go up to your house? I'm getting eaten alive out here."

"I'd say another heavy storm's coming in."

"Yeah, the air's been sticky and still all day, that's for sure." Except now a hot breeze had whipped up, and that was always a clear sign of a storm coming in from the Gulf of Mexico.

"Is steak okay for dinner?" Brandon prided himself on his grilling abilities.

"You know it." After they reached the ultra-contemporary home, Brandon left Henry alone in the huge kitchen while he disappeared into the garage to get meat out of the spare refrigerator. Henry took in the expansive granite island, the clean lines on everything. There were splotches of color, bright blues and yellows, that he hadn't noticed before. As he looked out a window, he noticed its frame was different, too. No longer bare like a Scandinavian photo shoot but highlighted by a cheerful floral-print curtain.

It had to be Poppy. A woman's touch was all over the place. Brandon caught him staring at the fabric when he came back in and laughed. "I know, it's a little different, isn't it?"

"It's good. More homey."

"It's what a woman does, Henry. Makes life more than a routine." He set the steaks out on a plate and pulled open a drawer chock-full of spices. "You okay with anything I put on it?"

"Sure." Henry looked at four steaks, eight ears of corn. "You having more folks over?"

"Nope. Just you, me, Poppy, and Sonja."

Henry choked on his beer for the second time. "What. The. Fuck."

Brandon shrugged. "Poppy said Sonja agreed to come home with her, provided I boat her home after dinner. Since you were already on your way, I figured it's perfect. You can take her home. I'm thinking she left her car at your office."

"Jesus, man, I was hoping this would be more, more—"

"A safe haven from your woman troubles? Nope, sorry. But what it will be is a safe place for you and Sonja to talk about how you're going to work out having and raising your kid."

Guilt sideswiped him. "Shit. Poppy told you."

"That I'm going to be an uncle? Yep."

"I should have told you. I'm sorry, man." And he was.

"Yeah, you sure as hell should have. What were you thinking, bro?" Brandon's words were accusatory, but his demeanor was relaxed, easy.

"I was thinking it's Sonja's decision as to when everyone finds out."

"It's your kid, too." Brandon mixed up a sauce. "So Mom and Dad have no clue yet?"

"Nope. Unless they noticed she's getting a little bigger in the obvious places. But it's too soon." He quickly told Brandon about Sonja going to their parents' home in Baton Rouge last week.

Brandon whistled as he chopped vegetables. "Henry, if you don't try your damnedest to make things right with Sonja, you're crazy. Any woman who'll drive up there, face down Hudson and Gloria, she's a keeper."

"Tell me about it. There's this little thing called trust, though. She's always had issues. It goes back to her family stuff."

"Trust, eh?" Brandon pulled another two beers out of the fridge. "Ready for another?"

"Thanks." Henry grabbed the second beer and figured he had a couple of hours ahead of him so it wouldn't affect his ability to drive the boat back home.

Back to the river house. He had to stop thinking of it as home. It had been home for a couple of years, was all, when he and Sonja were together. They were going to sell it, cut their losses.

"Poppy and I had a lot of the same going on, you know."

"Actually, no I don't. One minute you were helping me out by checking in on her during the big flood, the next she's living here and decided to stay in NOLA permanently."

Brandon laughed. "Put like that, it does sound as if it went too quickly. But trust me, we spent almost every waking hour together while we waited for you to come back and for me to pitch to the San Sofia government representatives."

"I'm sorry you didn't land that big job, Gus."

Brandon shrugged. "I was too, at first, but it's worked out better. I'm excited about my future for the first time in a long while."

"We, Sonja and I, have been spending more time together, ah, talking." They had been, before he lost it after she told him she'd gone to see his parents.

"Never hurts." Brandon took a pull of his beer. "By the way, did I tell you I got a text from Jena?"

"What? No way. She didn't as much as..." He pulled his phone out of his back pocket and scrolled through his messages. "Fuck. I missed it. Great news." She'd texted she'd be in NOLA later tonight. "I can go get her."

"Nope, all taken care of. She insisted on getting a lift from the airport to her place."

"Typical." Jena was the most independent woman he knew, besides Sonja. "She'll have stories to tell, I'm sure."

Brandon looked at him. "I wonder. You know, I can't shake the fact that she and Jeb were in the same country, at the same time he took off with my money."

Henry laughed. "What, you think Jena's been living high off your cash?"

"No. But something about this isn't sitting right with me."

Henry regarded his brother. "Same. But I've had so much of my own shit going on. I'm glad she's on her way back."

They looked at one another, the unspeakable sibling bond palpable. Brandon grinned. "Yeah, me too."

The sound of Poppy's laughter broke the quiet moment. It reached them a few seconds before she hurled around the corner and threw herself into Brandon's arms. Their kiss was respectable but on the long side for Henry, who tried to look anywhere but at Sonja.

Impossible. She stood in the kitchen entrance, wearing some kind of black exercise pants and a bright yellow top that he didn't remember seeing. It was looser than her usual kind of workout clothing, and an immediate reminder that her shape was changing to accommodate the baby. He had a rush of anxiety that manifested as a sinking feeling in his gut. Would he be able to grow, to become the father his child deserved?

"Hey, Henry. You okay?" She walked closer to him, her voice low as Poppy and Brandon continued their lover-like talk.

"Fine." He grabbed the edge of the counter, the cool surface oddly comforting. "I'm good. What are you doing here?"

Her brow rose, and he was on the receiving end of her immobilization-capable glare. "You go first."

"I came over to have dinner with my brother."

"Uh huh. And I came here to spend some time with my dearest friend." She said it with defiance, and he felt he should earn a fucking gold star for not wincing.

"Say it like you mean it, Sonja."

"What are you two having to drink?" Poppy's high-pitched excitement was a bit much for Henry, but Sonja lit right up for her best friend. Fuck that shit. He was her best friend. Even if she didn't want to see it.

"I'm going to grab that shower now. I'll be right back." Sonja left the room, and he was faced with how tired he was of being without her, without her companionship and yes, her body, each night.

Henry had never stopped loving her.

Chapter 20

Sonja wished she could replay the last hour and have chosen to go back to the cottage instead of go home with Poppy. While Poppy seemed as surprised as she to see Henry in the kitchen, Sonja wouldn't put it past her college bestie to have finagled this. Except she never saw Brandon as the scheming type, and Poppy seemed to have put her manipulating ways on the shelf when her previous serious relationship imploded.

"What made you come here instead of going home after work?" He stood next to the massive kitchen island, his hand around a half-empty bottle of beer. His posture was what she thought of as his forced casual stance—she'd witnessed it countless times as he faced a legal opponent he didn't want to make defensive.

"I thought a change would be good." She accepted the fizzy water from Poppy. "Thanks, boo."

"Sure. Why don't you two go sit out on the screened porch? Relax a bit. We'll let you know when dinner's done."

Sonja shot her friend a what-the-hell look but took the hint and went outside with Henry. Why did it feel like she was marching to a guillotine?

She picked a padded glider, and Henry sat on the contemporary love seat kitty-corner to her. "You and your brother have the exact opposite in taste." She took in the minimalist décor, save for where Poppy had inserted herself with splashes of color. Sonja knew the color was pure Poppy because it didn't quite match the more black and white and gray palette of the furniture, walls, and flooring.

"I'm more traditional, yes." Henry looked like he'd swallowed a lizard instead of beer. "I do like how neat and clean the simple lines are."

"Our, the river house is more streamlined now, without the carpet." They'd agreed on the simplest of tiles to replace the expensive hardwoods and carpets that the floodwaters destroyed. The tiles were made to look like hardwood, which kept the aesthetic quality while providing practicality. Far more flood resistant.

"It'll never be like this, though. If we're lucky the flooding won't happen again for another couple of decades. But the river could rise again next year. Brandon built this to be flood- and hurricane-proof. We don't have that luxury."

"No, but I don't regret that." The words came out of their own volition, and she put her fizzy water down. "And I mean that. Sincerely."

"You don't regret us having to rebuild the entire house, install more sump pumps, pay into the homeowners association's fund for the dam system within our neighborhood?"

"Well, there is that. But if the flood hadn't happened, I wouldn't have appreciated just how far off my chosen path I'd gone."

"What the hell does that mean?"

"Relax. I don't mean it in a rough way." She leaned back, enjoying the hum of cicadas and twilight birdsong. "After college, I wanted to go to law school so that I had a skill, a way to give back."

"I thought the paycheck was an incentive."

"Of course it was, when I was twenty-two. But we both know how much the average lawyer earns. I could have just as easily gone with an NPO or more socially conscious firm and been making as much as any other public servant. Any paycheck would have been an improvement on college hourly wages."

"True." Henry looked out over the water, his expression indecipherable. Was he thinking, like her, that if she'd done just that, they'd have never met? More importantly, did his insides roil at the thought? She hated not being able to read him as she once had.

"I wanted to work for the greater good. Sure, I'm not the social worker your sister is, I know that much about myself. I enjoy nice things, but I don't have to have them." She hesitated. "I expected to be doing more pro bono by now."

"We've talked about this. We can push my father for more."

"We will, I'm sure. But your Dad's business—it's not my dream, Henry. I planned to do corporate law for a while, then get out of it and do family law. Community law. Even tax law, for individuals."

"And yet all you've been doing since my father hired you is corporate."

"Yep. And that's on me. Nothing was stopping me from volunteering my services at a local battered women's shelter, or for small business owners. You father wouldn't stop me."

"But he'd slow down your run for partner."

"You and I both know he'll never make me a partner. He never intended to."

"Actually, I don't know that. If he thought it'd be good for the firm..."

"It doesn't matter now, because I'll be gone as soon as we pay off whatever we owe for the house."

He looked at her, something unreadable in his eyes. "He'll hold you to the noncompete."

"Which only applies if I start my own firm. I'll work somewhere else for two years." She had to. Living so close to Henry, having to raise a baby with him—that was all she could take. The longer she saw him at work each day, the more excruciating it would be.

"You're so certain about where you want to be."

"I know where I don't want to be." Fifty with a grown child and still doing what she'd only intended to be temporary. "What about you? You'll be happy working for your father for the next twenty or thirty years?"

"I'm taking the firm nonprofit. My father is done with his law career." He spoke so quietly, with such conviction, that she thought she misheard him.

"No way. He'd never give it all up."

"He has." He rolled the beer bottle between his palms. "I'm not as certain about what kind of law to focus on, though. I was hoping you'd help me figure it out. And after seeing how many of our neighbors are still barely getting by since the flood, the ones who can't even entertain rebuilding, I can't look at myself in the mirror each morning without doing something about it."

They sat in silence as she digested his words.

"We both have good reason to see the renovation through and to get going with our lives. And working together could be challenging, especially once the baby's here. Working out the hours and caseload." Would he agree or, like her, was he questioning what they were giving up?

Henry didn't reply, and she couldn't say anything more through her tight throat. Her eyeballs felt as though she'd been looking at a computer screen all day when in fact she'd spent little time at her desk this afternoon.

"There's something else I don't know about you." Henry's voice was lighter, his obvious change of topic a welcome distraction from her sorrow. "You use Southern lingo, your family is culturally Creole, except you're Baptist."

Sonja laughed. "Really? You want my family ancestry *now*?"

"Just curious."

"You know the big points. My great-grandfather left the Catholic Church because he felt called to go to the Baptist seminary. Nothing more exciting than that." She rubbed her nose as the bubbles from her carbonated water hit her nose.

"That must have been a hard road, after generations of family following one religion."

"Oh, well, nothing as hard as what my earlier ancestors went through." What the hell was he going for?

"True." He grew silent, like he always did when he thought it might be too painful for her to talk about her African American ancestry.

"It's okay, Henry. You can ask me about slavery. Yes, my ancestors were slaves. Some got free. Most didn't."

"We never talked about it."

"Part of why I, why we were... Shit." She put her glass down. "That was the best part of us, that we took one another as we were, right at the moment we met. But it was also the worst part of us, because before we knew it, it got too hard to ask the tougher questions. Hell, I don't even know how your parents met." And she didn't really care, not after everything she and Henry had gone through. Except now she was going to have a baby who might want to know how his paternal grandparents hooked up.

He snorted. "How do you think they met? While they were in college. They met while pledging for their respective Greek houses."

"Was it love at first sight?" She had a hard time picturing either of his parents in love, but most especially his mother. It seemed everything she did was according to a hidden script that only she knew.

"According to my father, yes. My mother disagrees. She's said it took her a long time to finally agree to go on a date with him. My grandparents—her family—was dead set against her marrying him."

"You're kidding? And they've given you a hard time?"

"They gave both of us a hard time, for the record. And yeah, that's the awful way of bigots, isn't it? Instead of seeing they're doing the same exact thing their folks did, they do it again." He leaned forward, his elbows on his thighs. "My grandparents didn't approve of my father because he was Catholic."

"You are fucking with me!" She couldn't stop the giggles that started low in her belly. "So your mother converted?"

His eyes wide, he nodded. And joined her laughter. "So you know when you showed up, it was a bit of a jolt to them."

She grinned. "Not just black, but black and Baptist. I have to say it says a lot for them, for who they've presented themselves as to me, that they didn't ask me to convert."

"Why would they? They don't want to support our marriage, or didn't, and I would have kicked their asses if they even brought it up."

"I liked what we'd planned, for what it's worth now." They'd agreed to have the Catholic service, but Sonja didn't want to convert. Neither of them were regular churchgoers, but they wanted their children to grow up in one church. Denomination wasn't important to them as much as community.

"Me, too. I suppose now we'll have to reassess, depending on where we each live."

"Mmm." Trying to keep it casual, this talk of all they'd undone, was harder than ignoring her worry that Deidre was going to pop out of the bayou. She stood and stretched. "I don't want to tackle that now. We've done an awful lot of talking these past couple of weeks."

"That we have." Henry watched the water. Another first—he didn't suggest they stop talking and start kissing. That part of their relationship was over.

Her hormones needed to get the memo.

"Do you think Poppy and Brandon are trying to get us to make up?" She looked at the sky as she asked him, the last gasps of the sunlight reflecting in peaches and purples on the river's surface.

His warmth reached her skin. He stood next to her, his breath slow and even. Nothing calmed her like Henry's breathing pattern, or the way his heartbeat felt under her ear. Another tangible connection she'd severed when she'd walked away from her vows.

"Have we? Made up?" His voice teased, cajoled, stirred.

She turned and watched the way his eyes simmered in the darkness, allowed herself to feel the security his nearness enveloped her with. "We've become friends, I'd say. When we don't go down into the bitter places."

He reached for her hand and grasped it, brought it to his lips. "I'll take that for now." His lips were soft yet insistent on her fingers before he leaned in and kissed her full on the lips. No tongue, no additional caresses to fan the white-hot coals that always smoldered for him. "Let's go back in. I'm afraid they may have burned dinner."

* * * *

Dinner passed more quietly than Sonja had expected, but it was pretty obvious that Poppy and Brandon couldn't wait to be alone again. They were perfect hosts, just a little too "darling" this and "babe" that for her aching heart to put up with. Whether Henry wanted to leave for the same reasons, she didn't ask, but instead took his hint when he nodded with raised brow at his brother and Poppy, who were giggling as they cleaned up dinner at the sink. In a silent consent, she and Henry made haste out of the house, away from the painful reminder of what they'd lost. They were in the boat and pulling away from the dock within five minutes, no words spoken between them.

There was a sick kind of comfort in shared torment.

Chapter 21

Henry stood behind the wheel, looking every bit the Southern man he was, as at home on the river as he was hiking in the park or throwing down in the courtroom. Although she thought his profile had more of an edge to it than she remembered. He'd shed his layers of politeness, and the raw masculinity he exuded was what she'd only seen glimpses of when they were engaged. Pity.

"I thought you hated being on the water like this, Henry."

He maneuvered his flat-bottomed boat, a gift from his boat-building brother, through the last turns onto the tributary that ran in front of their house. The river house. Oh, who was she kidding? She'd never *not* think of it as their house.

"I didn't know what I was missing." He took his time, ran the boat around in a large circle in front of their dock, one part of the house that had survived the flooding intact. "I never slowed down enough to just take it all in."

She reveled in the feel of the river breeze on her skin, cooling the heat that a full meal and Henry's nearness had produced. "You're starting to scare me. The man I knew had bigger plans than cruising the river."

"That man was a fool." Said without self-recrimination, full of integrity. More pieces of the man she'd fallen for.

"It's okay, you know. That we were immature."

He grunted. "Let's enjoy it a bit longer." Henry cut the motor, and the sudden quiet made her aware of how alone they were out here. Floating on the same creek that had swelled enough to not only overspill the banks of their land but to pour through their house. The water that buoyed them, suspending them in this paradise of tranquility, was the same that had pushed tons of mud across their deck, patio, and into the main living area on the first floor.

Henry moved from where he'd driven the boat to sit next to her on the metal bench. "This okay?" He put his arm around her shoulders.

"Yes." She had a hard time recognizing the emotion that swamped her. Shyness seemed too juvenile, and yet, she was. She was a pregnant thirty-something woman, not an innocent high school debutante. And she knew Henry, knew the man to his core, the man he'd always been to her. And more.

"We built that, Sonja. That's all us."

From the water, the structure rose up on the slight rise of land as if it were always a part of the Louisiana scenery, with no indication of the ruination the floodwaters brought. The only sign of construction at all was the new retaining wall, dug deeper and two feet wide, meant not to stop a major flood—that was impossible—but to slow the river's progress in the event of future storms.

Because there would be more storms, more floods. More unpredictable disasters that shook the ground and forced the house to withstand another cleaning, another rehab. Even a house that didn't sit on a river had its share of ailments over the years. But the best homes survived through it all, big fixes and little. It was all in the repair.

"Will it make it another five, ten years, do you think?" She fought the sting of tears as her voice struggled through her tight throat.

"I sure hope so. We've done the best repair we possibly could afford this time around. But we have no idea about the weather patterns. Luck sure hasn't been on our side." By "our" she knew he meant everyone who lived in Louisiana, who risked losing their native land to the onslaught of hurricanes and flooding rains that marched relentlessly across the globe but seemed to have a particular yen for NOLA.

"Is it possible to build a hurricane-proof house? Really? Do you think Brandon's house could survive any storm like he says it can?" She asked him for the impossible.

"I think you can plan for the worst. Hope for the best." Like her, he responded without overexplanation. They both knew they were talking about more than the house in front of them.

"Is that enough for you, Henry?" She took her gaze from the house and looked at all she cared about, no matter where they called "home." She'd live in this damn boat with him if it was what it took to go the long haul together.

His eyes surprised her, as they appeared filled with tears, too. "As long as there's a lot of living in between the major fixes, yes." The rasp of his voice conveyed his sincerity. He kissed her then, and it was nothing like the kiss on his brother's screened-in porch. Which was wonderful, because Sonja didn't want another porch kiss. She wanted open-mouthed, gasping for breath, clinging-to-each-other kisses on Henry's bayou boat. She wanted Henry.

"I've missed this." She spoke against his lips, ran her tongue around his lips.

He pulled back, and the moonlight reflected off his eyes, making them bottomless pools of knowing. "I can't keep up this tug of war with you, Sonja. Not unless you tell me it's forever."

"I'm so sorry, Henry." Tears began to fall, and she didn't try to stop them. If she was going to make a go of it with this man, the only man for her, it had to be all in. All layers gone. "I messed up, so many times. It sounds crazy, but I still don't think our wedding was supposed to happen, and I'm kind of glad it didn't. Because now I feel closer to you than I ever did, even if all we're ever going to be is this baby's parents. And I mean this." She reached around her back to find and grasp his hands tight between them. "If you don't want to go forward, or rather, further with me, with us, I'm okay with that. I'm so sorry for any hurt I caused you when I ran, Henry."

He leaned his forehead against hers, and she felt the shudders of his breath, heard the air escape his mouth. "Babe, you don't owe me an apology. I fucked up. Hell, I'm just going to say it—we both did. But what's the one thing we've always agreed upon in the courtroom?"

"How it ends is what matters."

"Exactly." He lifted his head. The slight breeze lifted his short locks, and she wondered if their baby was going to have his long eyelashes. She hoped so.

"We really threw a lot at each other with this, though."

He nodded. "We did. And there's no reason to rush anything now. If we agree to make a go of it, of us, we don't ever have to talk about getting married again. I'll take you any way you want me to, Sonja. And I'll be glad for however you'll take me."

She laughed. "That's the best part. It always has been. We've fit together perfectly and knew it from day one."

"And yet, we did our best to make a fucking mess of it, didn't we?" He stared at her, the way that made her know how precious she was to him. They kissed, their lips and bodies pressed together in a timeless stamp of commitment.

Henry lifted his head. "The office is going to be one hundred percent nonprofit by the end of the year. I'd love to have you on board with me."

"It's almost too perfect."

His face reflected what she'd felt the past week. Need. Want. Desperation. But most of all, love. "It'll never be perfect, but it'll be more than we ever dreamed of. We belong together, Sonja. As far as I'm concerned, this is our start. Today. You, me, and this baby we're having. Are you in?"

"What's my salary look like?"

"Full benefits, low pay until the business gets off the ground." He watched her, his lips twitching. "Long hours, sleepless nights, and not all because of the baby, but because we kept each other up. The good way." Heat flared in his eyes, and her insides answered with a sharp tightening. He cupped her face with his hands. "It'll be full time, no vacations. For the rest of your life."

Tears. Copious tears that his thumbs couldn't wipe away fast enough. "Yes, Henry. I'll take it."

"I love you, Sonja."

"I love you, too."

He kissed her, his lips insistent. When the heat grew too much for the boat and the bugs started to nip, Henry smiled at her. "Want to go home?"

She smiled back and hugged him tight. "Yes." She'd never felt so cherished, and as she tightened her arms around him, she realized she'd never felt so grounded, either. Pretty amazing as they were afloat. She opened her eyes and smiled at the moonlight, knew she'd never forget this moment.

There's nowhere hotter than the South, especially with three men who know how to make the good times roll. But one of the Bayou Bachelors is about to meet his match…

New York City stylist Poppy Kaminsky knows that image is everything, which is why she's so devastated when hers is trashed on social media— after a very public meltdown over her cheating fiancé. Her best friend's New Orleans society wedding gives her the chance hide out and lick her wounds…

Brandon Boudreaux is in no mood to party. His multimillion-dollar sailboat business is in danger of sinking thanks to his partner's sudden disappearance—with the company's funds. And when he rolls up to his estranged brother's pre-wedding bash in an airboat, a cold-as-ice friend of the bride looks at him like he's so much swamp trash.

The last person Poppy should get involved with is the bad boy of the Boudreaux family. But they have more in common than she could ever imagine—and the steamy, sultry New Orleans nights are about to show her how fun letting loose can be…

About the Author

Geri Krotow is the award-winning author of more than thirteen contemporary and romantic suspense novels (with a couple of WWII subplots thrown in!). While still unpublished, Geri received the Daphne du Maurier Award for Romantic Suspense in Category Romance Fiction. Her 2007 Harlequin Everlasting debut *A Rendezvous to Remember* earned several awards, including the Yellow Rose of Texas Award for Excellence.

Prior to writing, Geri served for nine years as a Naval Intelligence Officer. Geri served as the Aviation/Anti-Submarine Warfare Intelligence officer for a P-3C squadron, during which time she deployed to South America, Europe, and Greenland. She was the first female Intel officer on the East Coast to earn Naval Aviation Observer Wings. Geri also did a tour in the war on drugs, working with several different government and law enforcement agencies. Geri is grateful to be settled in south central Pennsylvania with her husband.